The Singapore Chance

The Singapore Chance

Russell Jack Smith

Bartleby Press
Silver Spring, Maryland

The characters in this novel are fictional, sired and nurtured by imagination. They are not to be identified with any actual persons.

Printed in the United States of America

Published and Distributed by:

Bartleby Press
11141 Georgia Avenue
Silver Spring, Maryland 20902

Library of Congress Cataloging-in-Publication Data

Smith, Russell Jack.
The Singapore chance / Russell Jack Smith.
p. cm.
ISBN 0-910155-16-X
I. Title.
PS3569.M537974S56 1991
813'.54—dc20 91-25577
CIP

For my sons

Stephen – Scott – Christopher

It little profits that an idle king,
By this still hearth, among these barren crage,
Match'd with an aged wife, *I mete and dole*
Unequal laws unto a savage race,
That hoard, and sleep, and feed, and know not me.

For always seeking with a hungry heart
Much have I seen and known; cities of men
And manners, climates, councils, governments

Most blameless is he, *centred in the sphere*
Of common duties, decent not to fail
In offices of tenderness

Old Age hath yet his honour and his toil;
Death closes all; but something ere the end,
Some work of noble note, may yet be done,
Not unbecoming men that strove with Gods.

From "Ulysses" by Alfred Lord Tennyson

Much Have I Seen and Known

One

The stocky Chinese policeman was firm. "Sorry, sir. No one may pass the barricade." He stood with black-booted feet slightly apart, starched khaki shorts flaring widely from his golden-skinned thighs, the light from the green mercury street lamp gleaming softly on the silver crown and "ER" insignia resting on his shoulders.

"I'm supposed to meet some people," Hank Bladesly said, beckoning down the dark street.

The Chinese officer shook his head slowly. "There's been a disturbance down there, sir. I cannot let you go in." He tapped his metal-tipped baton against his leg for emphasis.

Hank studied the impassive face for any sign of uncertainty. None there. "All right, officer." He walked slowly away. The month old bus drivers' strike against the Singapore Transit Company had apparently turned violent. He could hear no shouting or fighting but the Singapore police were out in force. He passed a Land Rover with engine idling by the curb. Four policemen in riot gear, metal helmets, gas masks dangling on their chests, sat in the olive drab vehicle. Their white eyeballs glinted in the light as they watched him pass.

Hank kept moving. He had a meeting with DAMASK, an access agent, at the Golden Flower Cafe, a meeting he did not want to miss. He looked ahead down the street and saw at the next intersection a replica of the scene behind him, a police barricade with a Land Rover standing nearby. He paused. Beside him was a dark passage between the buildings. He stepped quickly into the shadows and moved cautiously toward a looming black wall. He was nearly ready to turn back when he saw a faint light from the right and found a right-angle turn leading into a small court. Ahead were lights, the chatter of voices, and the pungent odors of Chinese cooking. Suddenly he stepped into a cheerful brightly-lighted scene: Chinese men, women, and children sitting under gay, hanging lanterns, chopsticks flying from bowls to mouths. Several smiled and nodded at him while the small children stared with round, black-olive eyes. He gestured ahead of him. "Can I get through this way?"

One of the Chinese answered him. "Street just ahead, sir."

Hank followed a narrow passage and within a hundred yards came out onto a street that curved off to the right; this gave promise of leading him closer to the Golden Flower. He walked quickly along with the early evening smells of Singapore washing around him, the sweet-sourness of burning charcoal, the enticing fragrances of fried sea food, the dark oppressiveness of curing rubber. The street was quiet and very dark but as usual in Singapore he felt quite safe. Chinese crime tended toward greater finesse and sophistication than street robbery and mugging.

After several minutes he came to a cross street and from off to the left he heard voices shouting. At first the roar was irregular but then it became a rhythmic chant. It grew steadily louder, the rhythm more insistent. He stopped and then stepped back into the sheltering darkness. In a moment he could see a procession coming toward him, several dozen people marching and holding something aloft on their shoulders. Several men were carrying kerosene torches, the flames arching and curving in the blackness. The shouting grew louder, the young male voices straining with vehemence. Then by the light of the dancing torches he could see the burden they were carrying. It was the limp body of a young man, dangling arm swinging in erratic cadence to the marching strides. Ahead of the column was a single figure, a slender Chinese who swung a club over his head in vicious arcs synchonized with the rhythmic chant.

Suddenly Hank saw a single man walking down the street toward the procession, a European, short and square. He moved steadily toward the marchers and then stopped and put a camera to his face. There was the brilliant flash of the strobe, freezing the marching legs and the dangling arm with a lightning stroke. The chanting stopped as though snipped with shears. A breathless pause followed and then the leader screamed, "Kill! Kill!" He moved forward in two quick strides and swung his club down on the head of the European. The camera flew to one side with a shattering crash and the man fell heavily. The club raised and fell again and again on the downed man and by the light of the torches Hank could see the blood surging from the smashed head. The marching column suddenly became a swirling mob and as the rioters closed around the man on the ground with stomping feet, the torches suddenly brought the pock-marked face of the young leader into brilliant light. Hank recognized the slender Chinese instantly as Peter Yee.

Police sirens screamed off to the right and the howling, stomping mob was faintly lighted by the headlights of the approaching jeeps. The shouting stopped and the crowd quickly dispersed, slipping away into the shadows. One man passed within six feet of Hank but seemed not to notice as he ran by. Hank waited briefly and then walked back to the thoroughfare. At a nearby corner he found a taxi and said "Three Meridian Road."

Back in his apartment, Hank reached for the bottle of Ballantine's scotch in the rattan cupboard and moved to the toy-sized refrigerator for ice and soda. Standing in front of the sink as he poured the amber liquor over the tiny cubes, he tried to think about the meaning of what he had seen on that dark street. *Peter Yee!* The night breeze off the Straits of Malacca stirred the tan drapes at the open windows and roused the musty air in the apartment with its mingled smells of damp rice grass matting and the worn foam rubber cushions on the cane chairs.

Peter Yee! Actually, Yee Hak Tho, a firebrand of the emerging left in Singapore politics. Brilliant, a double first at Cambridge, flamingly articulate, and very much an uncertain quantity in political and ideological allegiance. The earnest people in the political section of the American Embassy believed without exception that Yee was a dedicated Communist, targeted toward the overthrow of British colonial rule of Singapore. The languid-mannered British Foreign Office types out at Phoenix Park scoffed at this typical bit of American naivete and declared they understood Peter Yee and could find common ground with him.

Hank had met Peter Yee for the first time a few days earlier. He had gone to a political rally with DAMASK and had found himself sitting beside Yee. Just as he had been dressed in photographs in *The Straits Times,* Yee was wearing an open-necked white shirt, chino trousers, and white sneakers. His head seemed unusually large for a Chinese, the face pock-marked, and the lean body thrust forward, feet poised beneath his chair as though ready to spring. He gestured swiftly and impatiently with his hands as he listened with evident irritation to a very dark-skinned Indian droning away at the speaker's podium. The Indian, with a sharp-curved nose, complained querously and repetitively about the injustice of British rule in Singapore. His speech was studded with all the cliches of anti-colonialist rhetoric and he intoned them solemnly in a flat, singsong accent: "chains of colonialism," "trampling human freedom," "colonial slavery." "Like children they are treating us," he complained. "Making up arbitrary rules denying us our rights."

The young Chinese beside Hank shook his head. Looking down at his feet, he muttered *"They mete and dole unequal laws unto a savage race."*

Hank glanced sharply at the man beside him. He knew that line of poetry from Tennyson's "Ulysses", a poem that somehow had attracted him strongly in his sophomore year at college. For the hell of it, he quoted aloud the next line: *"That hoard, and sleep, and feed, and know not me."*

The pock-marked face turned swiftly, looking shocked. "What did you say?"

"I just quoted the next line of 'Ulysses'."

"My God, an educated man!" The accent was Oxbridge English.

"Not really. Just happens to be an old favorite of mine. One of the few I really know."

The slitted eyes in the broad face probed him. "What are you, an American?"

"Yes. Political officer in the Embassy."

"Is that why you are here? Spying on us?"

"No. Just trying to understand your point of view. Get a feel for local politics."

"For the British?"

"No. For ourselves. Americans have business interests here, you know." He hesitated a moment and then said. "We have some understanding of what it's like to be a British colony. We fought for our independence too."

The opaque eyes gazed back without expression but Hank thought he saw a flicker of disdain around the mouth. "Few Americans seem to realize that."

The dark-skinned man at the speaker's podium was at last bumbling to a close. "And that is why I am saying to you, my brothers in slavery, that we must be most vigilant to resist any further efforts — *any* further efforts — by our British masters to restrict our freedom." The young Chinese grunted. "Bloody waste of time!" He got to his feet. "Excuse me. I must leave."

Hank got up also and slid sideways along the narrow row to the aisle. "How about joining me in a drink?"

"I don't drink."

"A beer?"

The slender young man looked sideways at him as they reached the door of the meeting hall. "All right, a beer. Maybe you can tell me then how you happen to know 'Ulysses.' I did not realize that word of Tennyson had reached America." The Oxbridge English accent, issuing so incongruously from that pock-marked Chinese face, crackled with superiority.

They walked silently together for a few hundred yards to the Golden Flower Cafe. Hank ordered two bottles of Tiger beer.

"Yarmouth College," he said. "I took several courses in English literature. Thought it might be helpful somehow to be a journalist, which I planned to be."

"Yarmouth. Is that one of your midwestern universities?"

"No, it's in the East. Maine."

Their conversation had paddled about in such shallow waters for ten minutes or so until Peter Yee put down his half-empty glass and announced he had another meeting to attend. Hank had said, "Look forward to talking with you again." Peter Yee nodded and did not reply.

Back in his office in the CIA section of the Embassy later that day, Hank had made a few notes of what little he had learned: Yee Hock Tho, known familiarly as Peter Yee, Cambridge degree, unable to find work in England, had returned to his native Singapore where he got a job as a law clerk. His resentment of British attitudes of social superiority was virulent: "Fucking snobs!" Hank turned to the station's biographical file and under Peter Yee's name he found more tidbits. There were three low level reports of Communist connections, one dating back to Cambridge student days, and a half dozen quotations of anti-British statements.

But nothing in that file or in their brief conversation last week, Hank reflected as he sipped slowly and gazed unseeingly at the curtains stirring in the night breeze, had prepared him for the violence he had just witnessed in the clubbing of the photographer. Peter Yee, Yee Hock Tho, had become vastly more dangerous in Hank's view, and also far more interesting. Singapore was full of young Chinese and Indian radicals and most of them all mouth. Peter Yee had shown he would act.

The telephone suddenly rang beside Hank, filling the apartment with its distinctive British cadence: *Br-ring, br-ring,* twice in rapid succession, then a pause and *br-ring!*

Hank answered and heard Buck Jones' voice, booming and annoyed. "Need you in the office right away. Got a problem."

"Right." Fifteen minutes later Hank parked the station's 1952 Austin-50, a mousey little British car, in the lot behind the Embassy, signed the night register under the approving gaze of the Marine guard, walked up the steps to the CIA offices on the second floor, and found Buck Jones sitting behind his desk in black tie and white formal dinner jacket, his broad chest a splendor of pale blue ruffles.

"Got me at Grace Chen's dinner party," he said by way of explanation. "Ambassador called me down. Bruce Evering, the United Press guy, was murdered about an hour ago in a riot near the bus company."

"Bruce Evering?"

"New U.P. man. Came down from Tokyo a couple of weeks ago."

"Where did it happen?"

"How the hell should I know? I was minding my own

goddammed business at a party. Then the ambassador gets this wild hair up his ass." Buck leaned forward with elbows on his desk. "The old fart is scared he's going to get a lot of heat from the Department or some Congressman if he does not come up with some answers as to why this American newspaperman was not protected in a British colony. Wants us to put the squeeze on The Cousins."

Hank frowned. "Buck, I think I. . ."

"Save it, Hank. I want to get back to Grace Chen's party. What I want you to do first thing tomorrow is to check out what the Brits know about this thing. Give that gorgeous MI-5 chief, Dainty Ass Ainsley, the good old hot-foot."

"Okay." Hank hesitated. "Buck, there's something. . ."

But Buck Jones was on his feet. He cut Hank off with a wave of his beefy hand. "You got the pitch. If I hurry I can get back to Grace's in time for the coffee and brandy. Tell me tomorrow what you find out."

On his way home in the grey Austin, moving quickly up Orchard Road through the light night traffic, Hank pondered his situation. As an eyewitness to the clubbing down of the man with the camera who was obviously Bruce Evering, he probably was the only non-Asian in Singapore who knew the true circumstances of the murder. In fact, he alone could name the murderer. In Buck Jones' office he had come close to sharing his information with his station chief but had been pushed away. But now, with time to consider more carefully, perhaps he ought to think about not telling Buck Jones, or anyone else, what he knew. At least for the present.

Yee was a potential prize of very great value. He was now extremely vulnerable, and this combination of value and vulnerability made him a superb target for CIA recruitment. Hank had not made an agent recruitment in over a year. He was hungry for one. But there were several obstacles to be overcome before Hank could make that potential a reality.

First and foremost was Buck Jones. Buck was a big,

bluff outgoing man, no great admirer of the British about whom he nursed dark suspicions of double-dealing, but he had held his job as Singapore station chief for eight years and he wanted to keep it. He had become the prototypical American in Singapore, slapping rich old Chinese ladies on their silken backs, serving as master of ceremonies for their charity bazaars, his hearty laugh booming over the public address system, and in general acting like an unofficial Chamber of Commerce president. He lived well in a long, low house the Agency had built for him, entertained like a Chinese tycoon, and hoped never to be stationed elsewhere. His caution was slit-eyed whenever one of the Station's officers proposed an operation which contained any element of risk. In establishing a relationship with Peter Yee there would be plenty of risk.

The risk began with the de facto understanding between CIA and the British that there would be no unilateral operations in the other's bailiwick. To get caught breaching it would probably mean expulsion for the Station Chief and the case officer responsible. An unthinkable risk for Buck Jones to take unless. . .*Unless* Buck could be convinced that the risk of being caught was tiny when compared to the great acclaim that would come with success. Acclaim that might guarantee his remaining in Singapore until retirement.

Hank turned into Wellington Drive and drove the several hundred yards to his apartment house. Inside he found his glass on the kitchen counter, resting in a small puddle of condensation from the dwindling ice cubes. He emptied it and refilled it with a dollop of Ballantines. In the living room he took a Count Basie record from the stack and dropped it onto the turntable. To the joyous strains of Buck Clayton's "Love Jumps Out", he sat in his chair and pondered what to do about Peter Yee.

Two

Ian Ainsley, "Dainty Ass" to Buck Jones, rose gracefully from his desk as his dun-haired secretary ushered Hank into his office and extended his hand in greeting, palm down. "Hullo, Bladesly. Good to see you." His grasp, British style, was limp. "How about a spot of tea?" "Yes. Sure. I'd like it." Hank lowered himself into one of the wicker-bottomed office chairs Ainsley gestured toward. "Bad business about your newspaper chap, what?"

"Yes. Bound to cause trouble."

"But you know, Bladesly, these Asiatic mobs are absolutely unpredictable. Become violent at a flick of an eyelash. But then your man did put himself in a bad spot, didn't he? Ignoring the police barricade and walking straight up to the mob with a camera in his hand. Not the wisest thing to do. What?"

"Maybe not. But he was a newspaper man trying to carry out his assignment."

"But my dear Bladesly, to rush right up to. . ."

"Who do you think did it?"

"Haven't a clue. Not a clue." Ainsley looked up as his broad-beamed secretary entered carrying two cups of tea.

"Milk or sugar, Mr. Bladesly?"

"Neither, thanks." Hank took a sip of the acrid liquid and glanced around the small, Phoenix Park office of the Singapore chief of MI-5. A badly worn Persian rug covered the floor but the white walls were unadorned except for a limp, loosely-taped map of the Malay Peninsula and the island of Singapore.

"Have you seen a police report yet?" Hank asked.

"Special Branch has put one up. It just arrived on my desk. Care to look at it?"

"Please." Hank took the proffered report and scanned it quickly. It established name, place, time of death "from massive head injuries inflicted by clubbing at the hands of person or persons unknown." No speculation as to identity. Hank looked up at Ainsley who gazed across his desk with languid attention.

"My ambassador takes this very seriously, Ian."

"Quite understandable. Quite."

"To him, the main issue is the protection of American citizens. He is afraid there will be a strong reaction from Washington, perhaps a diplomatic protest, and he feels that we may be able to head this off if we can establish who killed Evering and make an arrest."

"I feel quite certain that the Singapore Police and Special Branch will do everything they. . ."

"Isn't this also an MI-5 problem, given the political aspects and the security implications? Haven't you been called in on it?"

Ainsley grew markedly more languid. "Not as — well, not directly. You see, this really is Special Branch ground."

Hank measured him with his eyes, having glimpsed a slight opening. "You must have files on the people who are whipping up this bus strike. Don't some of them look like possibilities?"

"The labor chappies? Not very likely. They're mostly

textbook Socialists. They'll harangue you to death with boring speeches but they will never raise a hand in anger. No, I'm afraid not much help there."

"What about the independence movement? Haven't they been trying to use this bus strike for leverage?"

Ainsley's manner again became enervated. "Well, yes, they have a bit. There has been some nipping about the edges by some of the independence movement leadership."

Hank decided for a direct hit. "Peter Yee?"

Ainsley's eyes flared briefly and he leaned forward and picked a pencil off his desk. "*Pee-tah?* What about him?"

"Hasn't he been trying to exploit this bus strike to embarrass the Government? Couldn't he have been behind this killing?"

Ian Ainsley shook his head and vented a small chuckle. He leaned back in his chair, pencil held between opposing fingertips, and smiled gently at Hank. "Really, Bladesly, you chaps down at your Embassy have such bloodthirsty, alarming thoughts about this little independence movement. You seem to see it all in terms of Bunker Hill, 1776, and the British Redcoats. You see, you don't understand Peter Yee. You mistake him for Paul Revere or one of those chaps. Peter Yee is one of us. He's a Cambridge man. We understand Peter. Just give us a little time and we'll satisfy his ambitions without too much fuss. Offer him membership in the Tanglin Club or something like that."

Hank stared evenly at the aristocratic figure across from him. "That's not good enough, Ian. We've got the murder of an American newspaper man on our hands, and you're just blowing smoke. I need something solid to take back to my Ambassador, not just fluff."

Ainsley frowned and sat up straighter in his chair. "Sorry, Bladesly, if you think I'm fobbing you off. But I really don't think — " He checked himself and frowned directly at his pencil. "Here, I have it. This is what I can do. Our research chap is doing some work on our name files, sort of suggestion from Special Branch, and I'll let you have whatever emerges from that. How will that do you?"

"When?"

"Later today or sometime tomorrow."

"Fine. That will help." Hank offered a brief smile and left. Outside the door which opened directly onto a roofed walkway, the noonday sun cast violent black shadows and its heat fell on Hank's shoulders like a heavy hand. He took off his jacket as he climbed into the meek little Austin and drove off down the hill. At the gates marking the entrance to Phoenix Park stood a white-gloved Malay policeman, standing on a small round pedestal and executing a graceful ballet as he directed the lunch hour traffic. As Hank approached his right hand rose regally to signal a stop. Then he stamped his foot and made a spectacular right-face as he dramatically waved on the cross traffic with his left hand. Hank sat patiently and admired the flame-of-the-forest tree across the road, a gorgeous tower of red and gold, rising 60 feet into the brilliant blue sky. He mused as he stared at the magnificent bespangled tree. Pretty clear there was some kind of connection between Peter Yee and the British, or maybe only something there between Peter Yee and MI-5. Something to be cautious about in approaching Yee. The brown-skinned figure in white shorts and glistening black boots stamped again, did an elegant pirouette, and waved Hank on. He smiled at the grinning Malay as he drove by and headed for his office.

Hank found Buck Jones at his desk frowning at a CIA Headquarters cable in front of him. "Dumb asses," he muttered. He looked up at Hank. "Back from a bit of a chat with the Limeys, hey, Blades? How's Old Dainty Ass?"

"About the same."

"Did he tell you about the jollies he's having with that little Chinese girl he's got stashed away in an apartment on Lavender Street?"

"Not a word."

"Or about the other one he keeps in one of their Bangkok safe-houses? Or still another one he keeps bedded down in Hong Kong?"

"Afraid not."

Buck grinned a small-boyish grin at Hank. "He sure bangs the hell out of those little Chinese girls. At least, I *think* that's what he does." He shook his head. "I could never see that yellow stuff myself. All legs and no tits." He grinned again. "Well, okay, what did our dainty *cousin* tell you?"

"Not an awful lot. He did offer to let us have the results of some research Five is doing on their name files of possible suspects. Expects to have it by tomorrow."

"A fat lot that will tell us!" Buck laughed a hollow laugh. "But at least that's something to report back to Headquarters." He picked up the cable in front of him and shook it. "They've just come through with the brilliant suggestion that we check with the British about the Evering murder. God! I don't know what we'd do without their guidance. Flip out a couple of paragraphs on your talk with Ainsley, will you, Hank? And I'll grind it into the cable I'll be sending back to Headquarters today."

"Okay." Hank started to turn to leave but hesitated. He was beginning to feel slightly uneasy about the charade he was performing, pretending to be searching for information about the killer of Bruce Evering.

The bluff red-headed man looked up at him questioningly. "Something else, Hank?"

Hank paused. "No, I guess not. I'm just rolling some ideas around in my mind."

"Well, save them. I need those paragraphs for my cable."

Having had nearly a decade to recover from Japanese occupation during World War II, Singapore by the mid-1950s had regained its soul, an astonishing mixture of British colonialism—expressed in broad avenues, green open spaces, and aristocratic buildings of white stone—and Chinese social and commercial culture as exhibited in narrow shop-lined streets and a pervading atmosphere of industrious energy. Appropriately, the American Embassy had placed itself in a part of the city where these opposing aspects of Singapore met. Late in the afternoon Hank left the Embassy and walked the two short blocks to the Adelphi Hotel. The traffic was heavy on North Bridge Road, and he waited at the curb with its grated cover over the deep gutter, a tall, broad-shouldered American in his striped seersucker suit standing amidst the kaleidoscopic Singapore street crowd: dark gentle people variously dressed in Cantonese white tops and black silk pants, Pakistani gray fur headpieces and checked sarongs, Malay *batik* saris, and naked-backed young men wearing only striped underwear shorts and thonged sandals. He crossed the street to the marquee-fronted hotel and got in a small yellow and black taxi.

"Golden Flower Cafe." He leaned back in the worn leather seat with its assertive springs as the driver merged into the complex traffic, studded with myriads of bicycles, three-wheeled motorcycle trucks, and haunch-spavined buses spouting plumes of black exhaust. He was confident that DAMASK, the access agent, would be there. Their MO called for appearances on two consecutive days in the event of a missed meeting.

The taxi threaded its way down the back streets of Singapore, narrow and clogged with bicycles, push-carts, and pedestrians. About two streets away from the big warehouses lining the odoriferous Singapore River, the water a dark soup of raw sewage, rotting vegetables, and succotashed garbage, huddled an area of small restaurants and gin shops. At the Golden Flower Hank got out and dismissed the cab. Inside the fluorescent lighted room, filled with the clatter of pinball machines and clipped Chinese voices, he found his man sitting at one of the back tables, a glass of beer before him on the porcelain top.

Hank sat down opposite and looked DAMASK over. A senior student at the University of Malaya, he was a dark-skinned Indian who did various little chores, such as obtaining lists of overseas students at the University, in return for the small monthly retainer Hank provided. To Hank's eye, his manner seemed more than usually ingratiating. Probably wanted money.

With little preamble Hank said, "Do you think you could get a message to Peter Yee that I would like to talk with him?"

Smiling the eager smile of an Indian jewelry salesman, DAMASK nodded his head. "Peter Yee? I just saw him down the street. Want me to go tell him now?"

"Yes." DAMASK jumped to his feet and hurried out the door. Hank ordered a Tiger beer and sipped slowly until the slender Indian returned.

"He will be coming in a few minutes. He said he wanted to talk with you too."

Masking his surprise, Hank said, "Perhaps it would be better if we talked alone. Meet me here again next Thursday."

DAMASK nodded and hesitated, a wistful smile on his face. Before the Indian could summon nerve for the request, Hank pulled twenty-five Straits dollars from his pocket and passed them under the table. "That's for your help today."

DAMASK's liquid eyes sparkled. "Thank you so very much. That will help buy books."

Hank had made serious inroads into the Tiger beer before Peter Yee appeared. As he made his way through the crowded restaurant, nodding and shaking hands to acquaintances, Hank thought that his manner was markedly different from their last meeting, more open and outgoing.

He refused Hank's offer of a beer and began to talk even before he got seated. "After the remark you made the other day about Americans gaining independence from the British I decided to read about your revolution in 1776. I looked over several histories in Raffles Library."

"Oh?"

"I've got some ideas about your revolution I would like to discuss."

"Fine."

"It is true, is it not, that not all Americans were in favor of independence?"

"Yes, I think so. There were a number of British loyalists, especially in cities like New York and Philadelphia. It was in part a class thing, I think. Wealthy, well-established people didn't want to risk losing what they had."

"Like Singapore. The big money people like things as they are. But one history I read said that middle class people — small merchants, farmers, mechanics — they wanted to cut the British tie and they were willing to fight for it."

"That's about right."

"That's *not* like Singapore. Chinese people are either merchants or coolies. Only Chinese gangsters like to fight, and they use only knives and — uh, clubs — not guns. They don't know guns. I read that your American farm boys were used to handling guns. They were ready to fight the British."

Hank looked at the pock-marked face with the keenly intelligent eyes. "Where does that lead you?"

Yee dropped his gaze and looked at the white table top. Across the room there was a sudden outburst of laughter followed by Chinese shouting and giggling. "It leads me," Yee said slowly, "to think that independence for Singapore cannot be won by fighting. It must be done through political process."

"No strikes, no riots?"

"No, no. Those also are political. No, I mean we'll have to get ourselves elected to office and build enough political muscle to throw the British out."

"What does that mean for you personally?"

Again Peter Yee hesitated, staring hard at the table before him. "I've decided to run for office in the next municipal elections. For the Singapore assembly." He lifted his head and looked intently at Hank. "And I *expect to win!*" His determined manner radiated power and assurance out of all proportion to the slender figure and the disfigured face.

"Good for you." Hank measured the face before him, hesitated briefly, and then said, "Speaking of riots and political action, that was a bad show last night. Who do you think killed the American?"

Yee shrugged. "That was a mob thing. No single man."

Hank scanned the face before him, a Chinese mask, opaque. He decided to attack frontally. "I happen to think differently."

Yee raised his eyes and gazed impassively at Hank. "What do *you* think?"

"I think it was a single man with a club who hit the victim several times. The man was dead when he fell. The mob moved in later."

Yee shrugged again and hooded his eyes. "That's an interesting theory."

"No theory, Peter. I *saw* it. I was there."

The dark eyes narrowed. "*Where* were you?"

"At the crossing on Selangor street."

A long pause hung over the table between them. At last Yee nodded and spoke so softly Hank could barely hear him above the surrounding hubub. "Yes, you were there." Another long pause followed. Then Peter Yee got to his feet and said, "Well, if you will excuse me. . ."

"Wait, Peter don't leave. I'm interested in you. I might be able to help you."

The young Chinese sat down slowly, looking speculatively at Hank. "What are you, a spy? CIA?

"I work in the U.S. Embassy political section."

"I'm not sure that's a direct answer to my question."

"Let's leave it there for now."

They sat silent for a moment or two. "I must leave now. If you really want to talk with me again, I'll meet you wherever you say. Tell me where."

Hank took a card out of his billfold and jotted down his telephone number. "That's my phone at home. Call me in the evening in the next day or two."

Peter Yee nodded and swiftly left the cafe.

Hank sat slowly sipping his beer for several more minutes and then sauntered out into the street. It was nearly five o'clock and he saw no need to go back to the Embassy. He decided to walk through the narrow, turning streets to Orchard Road where he could grab a taxi. Musing as he strolled, he was scarcely aware of the clashing melange of the Singapore street — the smell and sound that swirled about him. He barely heard the shrilling of the trumpet-shaped speaker over the doorway of the New Gramophone Shop as it shredded the high tones of a Chinese singer into even greater cacophony, and he did not see the fruit stands piled high with golden oranges, emerald gooseberries, and scarlet rambutans. He was sufficiently alert to avoid a black-topped Chinese trotting through the dense traffic bearing a shoulder pole tipped with heavy baskets which caused the pole to flex deeply with each stride.

His mind was on Peter Yee. Yee's declared intention to enter politics had done two things, both potentially useful to Hank. It had enhanced his value as an agent of influence if he were to be successful, and it had heightened his vulnerability to Hank's knowledge of his role in the murder of the American newspaperman. Everything depended, however, upon Hank's success in reaching some kind of understanding with the young Chinese.

He paused at the crosswalk as a Chinese food push-cart, the smells of Chinese noodles and fried fish wafting from it, passed slowly before him. Lee's acquiescence was not impossible. Hank's hand held some good cards. Yee was a serious man, determined to take an active role in wresting independence from the British. He was not likely to swerve from his path if he could find some reasonable accommodation with Hank. It would be delicate — any negotiation with a Chinese is labyrinthine — but it was not out of the question. One thing was certain. This was no time to break the news to Buck Jones that he hoped to recruit Peter Yee as a CIA agent. That could wait at least until after his next conversation with Yee.

At the corner of Orchard Road and Trengganu Street, Hank hailed a taxi, and in ten minutes was paying off the blue-turbanned Sikh driver before his apartment. Even before he could unlock his door he heard the *br-ring–br-ring, br-ring–br-ring* of his phone. It was Buck Jones. Angry. "Where the hell have you been all afternoon, Bladesly?"

"I had a meeting, Buck."

"Yes, well, shit. I know about these all afternoon meetings you case officers have. Right now I've got a red-hot ambassador on my hands and I want you to haul ass down here as fast as possible."

"Be right there."

When Hank arrived at the CIA office, Buck got up from his desk without a word and led him across the hall to the ambassador's suite. Ambassador Lampman greeted them grimly. He gestured to them to sit down and spoke in a tight voice. "You know, I somehow got the mistaken impression that you people were competent. I thought your liaison with the British security people was good. I thought you could give me answers to these questions that the Department — *and Congress* — is pounding me with. How in the world do you suppose I got such a notion?"

Buck Jones spoke in a soothing, mollifying tone. "Now, Mr. Ambassador — Dick, these things take a little time. And you know how slow The Cousins are, and —"

Ambassador Lampman's voice took on more bite. "You listen to me, Buck. You're not dealing with those Chinese dowagers you charm out of their under-drawers. We've got that firebrand senator from Wisconsin, Don Briscoe, on our tails. This U.P. guy, Evering, came from Milwaukee, and Briscoe's threatening to get a Senate resolution calling for the withdrawal of American diplomatic personnel from Singapore if this thing isn't cleared up damned fast. Now, just what are you doing to get results?"

Buck's voice now had the tone of a chastened little boy. "Well, sir, we've been putting the pressure on MI-5 to cough up some dope. They have prom —"

"Get back on them *now.* I want some kind of answer by 8 o'clock tomorrow morning."

"Yes, sir." The two CIA men retreated to Jones' office. No longer the penitent, Buck Jones was now a bull cop barking at the new recruit. "Bladesly, get hold of Ainsley *right now.* Run him down wherever you can find him. Face flaming red, he banged his ham-sized fist hard on the desk. "And get some poop out of him before tomorrow morning."

In his office Hank telephoned Ian Ainsley's office in Phoenix Park. His watch told him it was just after five, and he knew the call was futile, but to his surprise Ainsley himself answered.

"Oh, hullo, Bladesly. Caught me working late. Jill Beamis and I are just finishing up that report I promised you. Have it for you first thing in the morning."

"How about tonight?"

"Well, yes. If you wish to come pick it up."

Three

Jill Beamis, a blooming, pink-cheeked English girl, sat beside Hank on the little wooden bench watching the tiny, wrinkle-faced Malay fan the coals of his brazier as he cooked the small *satay* kebabs on their bamboo sticks. The spicy fragrance of the sizzling meat drifted enticingly to them. Overhead, giant casurina trees whispered in the sea breeze as it moved across the sea-wall several hundred yards behind them and eddied into the busy city streets beyond. The *satay* man had positioned his cart, as had several competitors, at the edge of the curb on the dead-end street which served as the turn-around point for city buses. One red bus slid alongside Jill, causing her to lean closer to Hank.

"I've never done this before," she said. "Those buses do get quite cozy, don't they?"

"Yes, but I've never lost a dinner companion yet. I hope you like *satay*."

"I'm sure I will. This was a nice idea of yours. And to offer to take me home, too."

"Well, don't forget I'm an American spy. Probably planning to gorge you on *satay* and Tiger beer and then pump you for all MI-5's secrets. Speaking of Tiger beer, here comes the waiter for our drink order."

A twelve year-old, plump Chinese boy came down the street and trotted up to them. "Something to drink? Soda, whiskey, beer?"

Hank glanced at Jill. "Two Tiger beer."

"Okay sir!" The boy turned and ran up the street toward Beach Road. Jill watched as he crossed the busy thoroughfare and continued to run as far as she could see. The smell of the cooking *satay* grew even more enticing.

"Speaking of 'an American spy', you are the least like a spy of any man I've met."

"Is this a professional criticism?"

"Statement of fact. I hope you don't mind. My mother always told me I was too outspoken."

"Don't mind a bit. I just wonder what you mean."

"You don't *look* like a spy. Or act like one. Take Ian Ainsley, for instance. The way he moves his eyes. Did you ever notice? He doesn't wear gum shoes but he has gum shoe eyes. Sly, clandestine, out-of-the-corners."

Hank smiled. "I must admit I don't much act like Ian Ainsley."

Jill turned toward him, her eyes taking in the broad shoulders under his seersucker jacket and his hard-jawed profile. It was an *American* face, she thought; smooth and unworn, the dark eyes asserting quiet confidence, the mouth both sensual and firm, the head erect and assured. "No, you don't."

The *satay* man lifted six bamboo sticks off his brazier, each about ten inches long and each skewing bits of marinated lamb or chicken. He placed them on a clean board before them. Then with rapid strokes he sliced a cucumber into dark green-edged, wafer-thin slices and laid them beside the *satays.* "Should a spy look like a spy?" asked Hank as he dipped one of the *satays* into a jar of hot pepper sauce.

"Mmmm, good!" said Jill after her first bite. Then her blue eyes blinked rapidly. "But that sauce is hot, isn't it?" After a pause, "No, I guess not. Most of ours seem to, though. Look like spies, I mean."

The Chinese boy approached with two brown sweating bottles. "Your Tiger beer, sir." Hank paid him and the boy trotted away up the street. Another bus came into the dead end street and turned around.

"Maybe your chaps are the true professionals while I. . ."

"Won't accept that," she interrupted. "Not for an instant."

The *satay* man placed six more bamboo skewers before them and they munched in silence for several minutes. When they had finished that batch, the *satay* man looked at Hank, his light brown face a wrinkled question mark. "Six more?" Hank asked Jill.

"Couldn't possibly."

"No more. Finish," said Hank, as he reached for his money.

They strolled slowly up the street in the equatorial night, the light breeze off Singapore Harbor stirring the feathery casurina branches and fronds about their heads. They paused for a moment to admire St. Andrew's Cathedral, its white spire rising dimly in the tropical night sky. When they reached the Austin Hank asked, "Come by my place for a drink?"

"Is that where the pumping takes place?" She stopped and looked stricken, her pink cheeks even pinker. "Oops. I didn't mean to be indelicate."

"Delicate or indelicate, the answer is no. A drink and some jazz records."

In his apartment, Hank poured drinks out of the square Ballantine's bottle and handed one to Jill. She sat on his dark blue sofa, legs crossed, a just slightly plump English girl in full bloom, and smiled at him with an open, engaging smile. 'What are you going to play?" she asked as he turned to the phonograph.

"Teddy Wilson."

"Don't know Teddy Wilson. Don't know much about jazz, for that matter. Never got much beyond Ray Noble."

"Teddy Wilson is my favorite jazz pianist."

The music started, Wilson playing "Rose Room," and opening with a feathery arpeggio first soaring to the top of the keyboard and then dropping in a skittering plunge into the deep bass. The sprightly melodic lines of "Rose Room" followed, adorned with lovely curving tendrils sketched with an impeccable touch.

"Oh, it's like spun glass, isn't it?"

They listened together for a while, sipping the robust whiskey. After a time, Jill's gaze grew abstracted and she turned to Hank. "You didn't really look at the report on the riot I did, did you?"

"No. I just put it in an envelope and left it with the Embassy security guard for Buck Jones to pick up."

Jill sipped her drink, her suspended foot moving in response to the rhythm of the music. "Doesn't settle anything really. Doesn't really identify the killer, but the Governor. . ."

Hank's phone began to ring. *Br-ring–br-ring, br-ring–br-ring.''*

He excused himself and picked up the phone, his back toward Jill. "Hello."

"Hullo, Peter Yee, here. Do you still want to talk to me?"

"Yes, of course. When?"

"Tonight?"

Hank paused. "All right. Later? Say 11 o'clock here?"

Slight hesitation. "Yes. What is the address?"

Hank gave it to him and the receiver clicked in his ear as Yee hung up. He turned around to find Jill smiling at him knowingly.

''*Now* you look like a spy," she said. "Act like one too."

"Nonsense. Just arranging a date with another pretty girl."

''*Another* — well, all right. You're forgiven for that lapse into clandestinity."

Hank found his drink and sat down beside Jill. Teddy Wilson was just wrapping up "Rose Room" with a set of block chords in the bass. "You were saying something about the Governor of Singapore when the phone rang, weren't you?"

"The Gov —? Oh yes, I was about to say that the Governor is going to announce tomorrow morning that five labor leaders have been arrested and charged with inciting a riot and murder."

"Labor leaders!" He stopped and chose his words with care. "Does your report link them directly with the riot?"

"Not directly. No."

He paused, dumbfounded. "Well, does it in general support the charge they incited the riot?"

"I shouldn't have thought so, but then I'm an intelligence analyst, not a politician."

Hank masked his surprise and sipped slowly at his scotch. The phonograph was silent. He gazed abstractedly at the beige curtains moving gently to the night breeze. He roused himself. "Another drink? Some more Teddy?"

"Thanks, no. Not this time. I haven't been home since early morning. I'd better get along to Braddell Rise. Will you call me a cab?"

"Certainly not. I'll take you home."

"You won't miss your next date?"

"She'll wait."

Driving along McGregor Road Hank stole a glance at Jill, her face lighted by the glow of the instrument panel. She was good to look at. How, he wondered, do so many English girls manage to resemble a bowl of dewy, fresh fruit? Not nectarines or mangoes or anything exotic but newly-washed red apples and ripe cherries. Wholesome and forthcoming. Jill seemed deep in thought.

"Penny for your thoughts, Miss Beamis."

"What?" She shook her head. "It's a little embarrassing."

She looked directly at him. "Well, all right. I was trying to decide what made you so different from other Americans."

"Well?"

"I think it's because you're so quiet, so reserved. You don't chatter. You don't show much emotion."

"I had a roommate in college who called me Big Chief Stone Face."

"Not bad, not bad. Besides, I like Indians." They rode in silence then until Hank stopped the Austin before her front door. She turned toward him, smiling mischievously. "Do Indian chiefs kiss ladies good night?"

"Usually rub noses, but in this case. . ." He pulled her to him, cupping her face with his hand and kissed her gently.

"Mmmm. That felt much warmer than stone." She pecked him quickly on the cheek and sat up straight. "Good night, Chief. And thank you."

There it was again, Hank mused as he drove back down Elgin Road, a broad avenue flanked by tall mercury lights. It was the response he nearly always met with new acquaintances. The words were different but the thought the same: he was reserved, quiet, unforthcoming. He himself knew no conscious intent to hold back or to mute emotions or responses. But sometimes he was aware that it felt more natural to watch and wait. Perhaps at bottom it was a kind of wariness, a residual from that haunted night when a strain-faced policeman had come to the door and told the 14-year-old boy his parents had just been killed in a traffic accident. Perhaps his inner core had decided then that if your whole world, the entire framework of your life, could be ripped apart without warning then it was better to stand back a bit. Not to isolate yourself but just to keep a watchful eye on the surrounding scene and to join in judiciously, not impulsively.

He turned into the parking area beside his apartment house. Whatever the source, this trait, this reserve, was not always perceived as Jill Beamis apparently had. Sometimes he was thought aloof, or proud. He recognized it when it happened, but somehow felt powerless to deal with it directly. If it was someone whose opinion he valued he could only hope that eventually, as the British would say, "it would come right."

Peter Yee was punctual. There was a firm knock at Hank's door and when it opened Yee was standing there, unsmiling, wearing his usual white, short-sleeved shirt and dark chino trousers. He stepped inside quickly, his movements a little jerky and seemingly uncomfortable.

Hank tried to convey relaxation and ease. "Come in, Peter, please, And sit down. Can I get you a beer?"

"No, nothing." He hesitated. "Unless you happen to have an orange squash?"

"I do, and I'll join you with a beer." He got the bottles out of the tiny refrigerator, poured the drinks into glasses, and handed the orange drink to Yee. "Let me put some music on as background."

"Not necessary for me. I'm not very musical."

"Well, I do it just on general principles. In case anyone is trying to overhear us." He placed a mixed bag of Tommy Dorsey, Doris Day, and Billy May on the changer. He sat down across from Peter Yee who was sitting very erect on the edge of his chair.

"Tell me, Peter, any further thoughts about having a go at politics?"

Yee looked at him steadily for a moment. "My thinking about politics came to a full stop after our conversation yesterday," he said quietly.

"I don't think that's necessary."

Yee measured Hank with his eyes. "On what grounds might it be unnecessary?"

Hank paused. "On the grounds that we are two intelligent men who ought to be able to reach an understanding."

Yee shook his head. "A very lop-sided understanding. You have information that could destroy my political career, or even put me in jail."

Hank grinned at the solemn-faced Chinese. "You know, Peter, I don't know very much about Chinese customs, but judging from what I have learned in dealing with merchants around town, I believe it is very un-Chinese to down-play your own assets in a negotiation."

Yee grinned, sheepishly. "I'm afraid I'm not very Chinese — really." He sat back in his chair, seemingly a little more at ease. "But having admitted that, perhaps you will tell me what my assets are."

Hank looked at him very steadily. "Through your political career you may attain a position of influence which could someday be helpful to my government. A friend, not a foe."

"At what price?" The question crackled with intensity.

Hank grinned broadly. "Now *that's* Chinese!"

Yee's face was momentarily indeterminate, uncertain whether to express umbrage, but then softened and he chuckled. "Yes, I agree."

"Before I answer your question let me tell you something you ought to know. Tomorrow morning the Governor of Singapore is going to announce the arrest of five labor leaders for inciting riot and murder."

Peter Yee's face remained impassive. "That's a surprise." He looked away from Hank, thinking. 'But I don't believe —"

Hank's phone broke in. *Br-ring–br-ring, Br-ring–br-ring!*

"Hello?"

Buck Jones' voice boomed through the receiver. "I've just read this lousy piece 'the cousins' gave us. Can't see that it helps a goddammed bit. Bunch o' crap."

"Buck, there's a related development I just learned about tonight that will help. I can't talk now. Can I call you back in an hour?"

"Oh-ho!" Hank could hear the leer through the phone. "What's the problem, Hank? Little piece of ass there you're working on?"

"No, a meeting."

"Oh, sure! Sure!" Buck's laugh vibrated the instrument. "Okay, Hank. Call me when you're through. But bang her one for me."

Hank put the phone down. "My boss at the Embassy," he explained. Yee nodded without expression.

A silence hung between them for some time. Yee seemed deep in thought. Finally, he spoke. "I don't believe those arrests make any difference to me."

"Oh? Why?"

"It's a political move by the Singapore Government. It has nothing to do with the incident. Special Branch will continue to investigate. And you still know the facts."

"Yes, but I thought it might turn the heat down a bit."

"Not a bit. Not a bit."

Hank groped for a new direction to move the talk. "How do you feel about five men being arrested for something you know they did not do?"

Yee shrugged. "It doesn't trouble me. We're all soldiers in the same battle. They got hit; I didn't. It happens in every war. 'Fortunes of war,' I believe the expression goes."

Hank could feel control of the encounter slipping away from him. He needed to jolt Yee somehow and regain ascendancy.

"Peter, there's one thing I must ask before we go any further."

"Yes?" Peter Yee looked up blandly.

"Do you have any kind of relationship with British intelligence?"

Yee's eyes flared. Then he looked down at the floor and slowly got to his feet. He turned and looked at a painting of a Maine lobster boat resting in a misty cove. The white boat with its red trim seemed almost suspended in the mist over the water.

"You seem to be saying, 'Yes'."

Yee turned back toward Hank. His face was as expressionless as ever but his eyes burned with intensity. "Yes." He hesitated. "Of course, I have been sworn to secrecy." He sat down on the chair and sipped his orange drink. "It goes back to my student days at Cambridge. I was badly in need of funds, and they wanted me to report on the Communist cells — the people, their activities."

"And the relationship has been maintained here in Singapore?"

"At a low level. I still report from time to time on Communist organizations and plans."

Hank's longtime practice in maintaining a "stone face" was thoroughly tested now. Peter Yee, this young firebrand, a rising leader of the radical left, the flaming foe of British rule, suspected as a hard-line Communist by the Americans, was admitting to an official relationship with British intelligence! Even more surprising, he was working against the Communists whom most observers regarded as his natural allies. Hank had to ask the question. "Do you regard the Communists as opponents? Or is this a two-way thing; you report to them about the British?"

Yee looked at Hank derisively. "Opponents? Certainly! Enemies? Yes! No thinking person, no one who has thoughtfully observed the Communist movement in Russia over the past 40 years can think of them in any other way. They want to capture me, they want to take over the independence movement and grab off Singapore. And I don't intend to let that happen!"

Hank nodded. "I don't want to see that happen either."

He looked thoughtfully at the young Chinese who had got to his feet, his face stern and determined. "Peter, *if* I asked you — mind you, I haven't asked you yet — but *if* I asked, could you report to me also about local Communist activities?"

"Is that the price?" Yee snapped.

"Price? Oh, no, not exactly." Hank smiled reassuringly at the other man. "Listen, Peter, let's understand one another. I don't intend to turn you in. I want to work with you. Give you some help now and then. And then sometime in the future it may be helpful if you feel well disposed toward my government, not antagonistic."

Yee sat down again, leaning forward with his hands clasped between his knees. "Then *that* is the price."

"Yes." Hank looked intently at Yee. "But remember, I am only speaking for myself at present. As yet, I cannot speak officially. Later, I hope to be able to."

Yee nodded. "I understand." He hesitated. "Then, yes. Perhaps I *could* give you occasional reports about the Communists. There our interests certainly coincide."

"Good. Then I hope to come back to you in the near future and make my request official."

"But". . .Yee held his right index finger up for emphasis. "I'm not ready to commit myself to anything else yet. I've got to think about it. After all, a known relationship with the United States could be as damaging to my future as one with the British."

"Understood. We'll get together again soon." The two men stood up then and shook hands as Hank let Peter Yee out the door. Behind him as he watched the slender Chinese stride away in the soft, equatorial night, he could hear Billy May's deep-chested sax section scooping and glissing its way through "The Breeze and I."

Four

It was a typical Singapore morning — fluffy, mountainous clouds drifting serenely across the deep blue sky, the clinging air warm against the skin as it moved steadily in the gentle breeze. Leaving his car in the parking lot behind the Embassy, Hank found himself falling in step with Bill McDonald, the Embassy political officer. "Hey, Bladesly, what do you think of this latest move by the British? Arresting all the top labor leadership. Did you ever hear anything so stupid?"

"I don't know. Why is it stupid?"

"The Chinese Communists will own Singapore in six months. I give it a year at most."

Hank had heard McDonald's apocalyptic predictions before but this seemed more bizarre than usual. "How does that follow, Bill?"

"Don't you see? With the labor movement paralyzed, this opens the door for guys like Peter Yee and the Communists. They will coalesce all the dissident movements under them and whoosh! Away go the British and Singapore."

"You think Peter Yee and the Communists are pretty tight?"

"*Tight?* I'll bet you Peter Yee has Commie connections that go all the way back to Peking."

"Hmm. Interesting, Bill."

They had reached the door of the office building and as they parted to go to their separate offices, McDonald said, "In six months or less you'll know I'm right."

Hank walked into Buck Jones' office. Jones sat, broad and rosy as though freshly scrubbed, reading *The Straits Times.* He looked up, all good cheer. "Morning, Bladesly. Appreciated the hell out of you tipping me off last night. I called the Old Man and he was real pleased. Pretty smart move by the Brits, too, eh? Takes the heat off them and off us too."

"Looks like it."

Hank paused. Now was the time to tell Jones about Peter Yee, and he was not quite sure how to get into it. Maybe plunge head first was best. "Buck, I've got something important to tell you."

"Sure thing, Hank my boy. Sit right down and tell old Daddy Buck all about it."

"Well, all right, here it is. I am within an inch of recruiting Peter Yee as an agent of influence."

There was an instant of silence just as there is before a gigantic explosion. The large round face rapidly turned from rosy pink to angry scarlet. "You *what?*" he bellowed. He got to his feet. He yelled, "Close that fucking door!" Hank closed the door and turned back to Buck who was standing behind his desk with clenched fists. "You dumb ass, Bladesly. I ought to beat the shit out of you. Don't you know you've broken every rule in the book, and you'll probably end up causing the whole goddammed station to be thrown out of Singapore. Jesus, what stupidity!"

Hank was surprised by the force of the explosion but still not intimidated. "Hold on, Buck. I said I was close. I haven't recruited him yet. I intended to check with you and then go back through channels to Headquarters."

"Check with me! Check with me! I won't touch the stupid thing with a ten-foot pole."

"Let me tell you how it came about."

"Absolutely not! The less I know the better." He plopped down in his chair, his large little-boy's face fiery red and bearing a massive scowl. "Look, Bladesly, I'll tell you what I'm going to do with you. I'm putting you on administrative leave as of right now and ordering you to report to Headquarters immediately. I won't have you in my station. You can catch the afternoon Manila–Tokyo PanAm flight out of Palam if you start now. Now, get the hell out!"

"Buck, I. . ."

"Get out!"

When Hank emerged from the customs area in Washington Dulles International Airport he found Jude Welby, chief of the Far East Division, waiting for him. Eyeglasses glinting in the overhead lights, he put a bony hand out to Hank. "Good flight?" he asked in his usual flat, expressionless tone.

"Long."

"Yes, long. I've done it without a break from Djakarta several times."

They picked their way through the crowd and began to walk up the slight incline to the departures exit. Through the glass doors ahead Hank could see a black Agency car with a uniformed driver standing beside it.

"We're going directly to Headquarters. The Director wants to see you first thing."

Hank expected questions from Welby on the way to Headquarters but none came. Instead, the Far East chief pulled a sheaf of CIA cables and reports from his briefcase and began reading them, neatly placing an initial "W" on each paper with his gold pencil as he finished. Hank gazed out the window at the passing Virginia landscape he had not seen for eighteen months. It was October, autumn in North America, he belatedly realized, in contrast to the perennial summer of Singapore. Dogwood trees at the edge of the woods lining the Dulles Access Road were dotted with red berries, and behind them the ubiquitous tulip poplars were turning a sunny gold. He felt sodden and disengaged from immediate reality after the long flight, or rather *flights:* Singapore to Manila to Hong Kong to Tokyo, Tokyo to Alaska to San Francisco, San Francisco to Washington. It was 5 in the afternoon here in Virginia but 5 in the morning at his apartment in Singapore of another day. His world was upside down in more ways than one.

The Agency car entered the tunnel into the underground garage at Langley and stopped before the small anteroom looking like a furniture store display room with its precisely placed floor lamps and scarcely used furniture. Jude Welby summoned the private elevator with his special key and shortly they were passing the security guard's office and entering the outer office. A plump-faced secretary said, "Go in, gentlemen. He is expecting you."

His first time in the Director's office, Hank was surprised by its flat simplicity. Standard Class A executive furniture, chocolate brown leather cushioned sofa and chairs and standard mahogany desk with leather swivel chair. The desk was unadorned with pictures, bearing only a brass reading lamp and a green blotter which almost matched the green carpeting on the floor.

But Pickard Grant looked just as he had been pictured on the cover of TIME magazine the month before: lean, darkly handsome with square jaw and thin-lipped smile. "Come in, Bladesly," he said getting to his feet and holding his hand across the desk. "I hope you had a decent flight back."

"Yes, thanks. I'm a little groggy but I'm here."

"Good. I apologize for bringing you straight in without a chance to rest up but I need to know what this is all about. All we have is the station chief's cable saying you have been placed on administrative leave and ordered back to Headquarters. What's the story?"

Hank smiled apologetically. "Basically it's a misunderstanding between Buck Jones and me about a potential recruitment."

"That's all? No sexual involvement or money or scandal of any kind?"

"No. It's a professional matter."

"Go on."

Hank proceeded to lay out the story of his cultivation of Peter Yee beginning with Hank's chance witnessing of the slaying of the UP newsman. Pickard Grant listened intently, his dark eyes fastened on Hank. When Hank finished, he said, "And that's where it stands? No actual pitch but the ground work all prepared?"

"Yes, sir."

The Director leaned back in his chair. He gazed out the window wall at the darkening woods below. "Well, you've brought home a sticky one, but thank God it's purely professional. I hate these messy personal scandals." He turned to Welby. "What do you think, Jude?"

"I'd say Buck Jones acted correctly. This would violate all the rules in the book, including our understanding with the British."

Pickard Grant nodded. "On the surface, you may be right. But maybe we ought to look a little deeper." He turned back to Hank, apparently musing. After a prolonged pause he said, "Bladesly, go get yourself a good night's rest. Tomorrow afternoon we'll bring together all the people who have anything to contribute to this and we'll sort it out."

It took Hank a little while to make out the identities of several members of the group assembled the next afternoon in the Director's conference room at Langley. As usual, there had been no introductions but gradually, as Pickard Grant referred to them by their first names they fell into place. The tall, dark, emaciated man with hot eyes who was called, "Christian," had to be Christian Peshman, the counter-intelligence chief. The smiling, somewhat balding man called "Doug" was clearly Douglas Brown, the Deputy Director for Reports and Estimates. The others were Jude Welby and George Haines, who ran the Singapore-Malaya desk. They had spaced themselves at random around a table large enough for 25 people.

At Pickard Grant's direction Hank recounted his presence at the killing of the U.P. newsman, his identification of Peter Yee, and his subsequent cautious cultivation of Yee up to the edge of recruitment. When he had finished, Grant asked, "Any questions?"

George Haines bustled into speech. "Some of the others may not know very much about this Yee fellow. It's well established, of course, that he's at least a crypto-Communist." He bestowed a knowing smile on the others.

Several began to talk at once. Pickard Grant held up his right hand. "One at a time. Christian?"

"George is right. The State Department has consistently referred to him as a Communist in its political reporting from Singapore. Also, I have other reports in my files that bear it out."

Grant turned to Hank. "Bladesly?"

"As far as the political reporting from Singapore is concerned, all of us in the Station regard McDonald, the Embassy political officer, as a nonentity. He's a knee-jerk anti-Communist who cries 'Wolf!' at every minor disturbance. He has scared himself to death thinking the Communists and the Mainland Chinese are going to seize Singapore."

"So you would discount the State Department reporting. What about other reports of Communist connections?"

"I'm not certain I've seen the reports Mr. Peshman referred to, but the ones I have seen are inconclusive, to say the least. I am more inclined to accept Yee's word on the matter, especially that he reports to MI-5 on Communist activities. That jibes with signs I have observed among the British that Yee has some connection."

"How do we know it's not a provocation?" asked Peshman, his thin lips twisting into a knowing smile.

"We don't," said Pickard Grant. "But let's clear this Communist thing up first. Doug, you've been quiet so far. Any views?"

"Yes. Generally speaking, my people agree with Bladesly. The Embassy's political reporting is silly. Predictable. We did a working paper, internal distribution only, on dissident groups in Singapore: labor, independence, and fundamentalist Malays. Yee Hak Tho, Peter Yee, emerges from the pack as a dedicated, anti-British, pro-independence leader. We found no good evidence of Communist ties. He is a charismatic intellectual who may someday run the place."

Grant nodded. He turned to Jude Welby. "I gather you oppose any further connection with Yee."

"I do. It would violate our understanding with the British about unilateral operations."

"Technically, I suppose you are correct. But would we actually be working against the British? In fact, we *could* in the long run be helpful to them after independence if we have a working relationship with Yee."

"Pick," said Christian Peshman, "I want to go on record as absolutely opposed to going any further with Yee. I'm positive it's a provocation. It fits the pattern. I could cite you a dozen cases almost exactly parallel. And to accept Yee's word that he's not a Communist is naive. To be as kind as possible, *extremely* naive." He looked directly at Hank with a supercilious smile. George Haines to his left nodded vigorously at Hank.

There was a pause of some length while everyone looked toward Pickard Grant. Finally, Hank cleared his throat and said, "May I ask a question?"

"Certainly."

"Assuming this is a provocation, just how would that work? Who would be directing Peter Yee and for what purpose?"

"The purpose," said Peshman condescendingly, "would be the usual one. To penetrate our organization, identify the personnel, learn our M.O., and then expose the recruitment publicly. Probably it is being directed by an underground overseas Chinese group."

"Do you have reports on such a group in Singapore? I haven't seen any."

"Not, as I remember, in Singapore. But we have indications there may be an active cell in Kuala Lumpur."

Hank stifled his reaction to what seemed to him a web of obfuscation. True, Peter Yee *could* be a Communist. But controlled by a problematic cell in remote Kuala Lumpur? Absurd.

Pickard Grant took charge again. "We seem to be forgetting that we hold a trump card in dealing with Yee, his role in killing the American newsman." When Peshman began to interrupt, Grant held up his hand. "Even assuming that this is a provocation — and that the opposition would be willing to sacrifice Yee, which is what I think you were going to suggest, Christian."

"Been done many times before."

"Yes, but for higher stakes than here. But, even if this is

an attempted provocation, it should be possible to handle Yee with minimum risk of exposure."

George Haines volunteered, "If we go that route, we might send someone besides Bladesly to handle him."

Grant gazed at him without answering. "So, if we take all possible precautions against exposure, then the central question remains whether the operation is worth the candle, whether Peter Yee has future potential as an agent of influence." He looked to his left at Doug Brown. "I gather you think he's a good bet, Doug?"

"Judging by our analysis of all the information we have."

Grant nodded. "Right. I think that's as far as we can go now. Christian, go back to your files and show me every report you can dredge up related to Peter Yee. I'll make a decision first thing tomorrow."

As they all rose, George Haines took Hank by the arm, grinning broadly. "Come by my office and read the zinger just in from Buck Jones."

Five

It had all worked out reasonably well, Hank thought as he gazed out the window of the New York to Boston train, gazed at the passing Connecticut countryside, the white-faced towns and the boat-jammed harbors and coves of its southern shore glistening in the early morning sun. He had boarded the overnight Washington to New York train the night before and was now bound for Boston. There he would take the Boston and Maine to Portland and on to Hanson and the Maine home of his uncle and aunt, his foster parents and only relatives.

Pickard Grant had called him to his office the afternoon following the meeting. "I've decided to go ahead on Peter Yee. But it's sensitive as hell and, as Christian Peshman points out, may contain some land mines. The Division thinks we ought to send someone else to handle Yee, but I want your view. How do you feel about it?"

Hank had hesitated before answering, testing his inner assurance. He looked up. "I'm confident I can handle it. I have a sound foundation with Peter, a sort of bond. It would be very difficult for anyone from the outside to reach the same level."

Grant had nodded. "How do you plan to proceed?"

"I've thought about it. I want to get him reporting to us about Communist activities in Singapore, pay him for it, and then tie him up with an agent agreement. Slow but sure."

"Sounds fine." Pickard Grant had turned his head to look out the window. A gentle October rain was falling, but large drops were forming along the eaves above the windows and pelting with a heavy cadence into a furrow created in the gravel of the broad ledge below. The yellows and soft reds of the trees along the Potomac shore were muted by the grey rain. He stood up and held out his hand. "Good luck. Jude Welby tells me you plan to take a few days to visit your family in Maine."

"Yes, sir."

"Good. That will give us time to send someone to straighten out Buck Jones. He ought to be in step when you get there."

Now he was on his way home to Maine, leaving behind the professional concerns of CIA and the labyrinthine politics of Singapore, the exotic mixture of permeating Chineseness and British colonial governance, the skin tight *cheong-sums* of the willow-slim Chinese girls and the flowered-print dresses and white linen shorts of the British rulers. Ahead lay the warm simplicity of small-town Maine and the gentle, unsophisticated care and affection of Uncle James and Aunt Sarah. He was glad the train journey gave him enough time to make the transition between two such different worlds.

Hanson and his uncle's house had been his home since he was fourteen, the year his father and mother were run down from behind by a gravel truck going 70 miles an hour on Route 1 outside Providence. Childless Uncle Jim and Aunt Sarah had taken him home after the funeral and had nurtured him through the years at Hanson High School and Yarmouth College. By contrast, he had lived in Singapore only 18 months but somehow the gravitational pull of the one was as strong now as the other. He hung suspended between extravagantly dissimilar worlds.

But the pull of home and Maine grew rapidly stronger as he came down the steps of the Pullman car at Hanson and found his two relatives standing on the platform. Uncle Jim's face looked more lined beneath the smile but Aunt Sarah's gentle face framed by white hair showed no change. They led him to the familiar green Plymouth, now 12 years old. "The old girl still starts and runs fine," said Uncle Jim.

"Good car," said Hank, assisting Aunt Sarah into the back seat. Seeing the worn, grey velour seat again brought back pungent memories of several heavy breathing encounters there, especially one with Margaret Rawlins and her silken thighs beneath her dark blue velvet dress.

Uncle Jim drove the few hundred yards to Maine Street and then turned right across the Boston and Maine tracks. Up a small rise, passing first the assertively dominant First Congregational Church and then the sturdy brick buildings and ancient trees of Yarmouth College. Just past the campus he turned into the driveway beside the white frame, green shuttered house which presented its narrow end to the street and ran long beside the driveway. "You'll find your room just the same, Henry," said Aunt Sarah. "Would you like a cup of tea now to hold you until suppertime?"

"Tea would be nice." He climbed the narrow stairs and turned right into his old room, tucked under the slanting eaves at the back of the house. His college textbooks still stood on the shelves of the pine bookcase, his maroon radio adorned with the Yarmouth College seal sat beside his bed. On the wall was the watercolor of three virginal young birches standing in the snow beside an icy Maine cove, his first art purchase. As Aunt Sarah had said, "just the same." But only outwardly. Inwardly he saw it differently and that changed it.

When he came downstairs into the kitchen, the center and

heart of the house, Uncle Jim said, "After our tea would you like to stroll down to *The Courier* with me?"

"Sure."

"Sit down, Henry," said Aunt Sarah, "and tell me about Singapore. What's it like?"

Seated in the snug kitchen with its plain pine table, the cream-painted cupboards, and the blue and red gingham curtains, Hank became even more acutely aware of the vast, almost cosmological distance that lay between Singapore and Maine. Outside the window a black-capped chickadee chittered and scolded at a tufted titmouse perched on the bird feeder hanging from the maple tree. Behind him, the tea kettle on the stove began to purr.

"I hardly know where to start, Aunt Sarah. It's so different from here. For one thing, it's predominantly Chinese. It's really a Chinese city."

"But isn't it terribly hot, being on the Equator and all?"

"Not really. It's an island and the breeze off the sea keeps the temperature down around 85 most days. It's humid but pleasant."

"I don't think I'd like it. Eighty-five seems pretty hot to me." She turned to the stove. "Tea's ready to pour."

Later, walking down the sidewalk toward the center of the town, Hank felt again an enormous sense of distance between the small Maine town where he had spent his boyhood and college days and his present place of work. The prim traffic moving quietly down the street, the soft subdued colors of the grass and the buildings, the sky, and the store fronts, and the pervading sense of muted sound, near silence — all in violent contrast to the teeming disorder of Singapore's streets. The jumble of pedicabs, hooting taxis, black smoke-belching red buses, the hot scarlets, yellows, and turgid greens of store fronts, and the turbulent cacophony of blaring loudspeakers, the rumble and chug of traffic and the staccato treble of Chinese voices. But the greatest difference was the smell, or the near lack of it in Hanson. Aside from an occasional whiff of automobile exhaust mingled with the nostril-tingling Maine air slightly redolent — but only *very* slightly — of red spruce trees and the sea, the place had virtually no smell. Singapore was a riotous melange of odors too exotic to identify but pungent and penetrating unforgettably.

"How's the paper going?" Hank asked his uncle.

"Pretty good. Be a lot better with a young man running it, or helping to run it." Uncle Jim cast a sidelong glance in Hank's direction. Hank caught the unspoken meaning. Uncle Jim's remark carried the freight of long years of fond expectation. *The Hanson Courier* was a family enterprise, a semi-weekly newspaper owned and run by three generations of Bladesleys. When young Hank became James Bladesly's ward he was introduced immediately into the world of linotypes, make-up jigs, and battered Underwood typewriters. He began by delivering the paper up and down the streets of Hanson. Soon he was clipping filler items from *The Boston Globe* and *The Portland Herald.* In high school and college he wrote school sports stories, and always during the summer months he worked with Uncle Jim, covering stories about commercial real estate transactions or new business enterprises. Those years of close association had established a bond of implicit understanding between uncle and ward about the future leadership of *The Courier.*

But when April came to Maine in Hank's senior year at Yarmouth and the snow began to melt into rivulets across the sidewalk, he found he had developed a strong desire to break away from the sedate certainties of Hanson. The prospect of a lifetime spent in walking each morning into *The Courier* office and chronicling the mundane activities of a quiet college town of 20,000 looked unbearably narrow and confining. The feeling became even stronger when his roommate, Bob Pintel, proudly showed him a letter from

The New York Herald Tribune offering him a job beginning July 1st. Lacking Pintel's family connection to the *Tribune* management and seeing no other avenue in sight, he had signed up for an appointment with a recruiter from the Central Intelligence Agency. The visions he formed in his mind while talking with the personable recruiter from Washington were stimulating and enticing: involvement in the arcane world of international espionage, participation in the molding of national strategy, living abroad in some place whose name at present he scarcely knew. He accepted an appointment contingent upon his security clearance.

The disappointment on Uncle Jim's face when Hank told him at supper in the homey kitchen that evening was obvious and painful. "It will give me great experience, Uncle Jim. It will complete my education."

The older man rallied quickly, and said with a gentle smile on his face, "International spy, eh? Sounds pretty glamorous." He shook his head and rubbed his long nose with a finger. "I suppose some people would feel pretty hopeless about trying to talk a young man out of becoming a spy and traveling to far places. But I guess I'm a little like Henry Thoreau. Hanson is my Concord and I've scarcely been outside it, but I'm convinced the world is real everywhere. If you're willing to accept things for what they are, you don't need to travel to distant lands to find reality and challenge. It's all right here just as surely as it is in Copenhagen, Istanbul, or Peking."

Hank looked at the earnest kind face. I'm sure you're right Uncle Jim," he said quietly. "Quite right." He paused. "The only justification I can give is that I think I need to establish that for myself."

His uncle's face slowly took on a smile of gentle resignation. "Fair enough," he said in a low voice. "Nothing else you might have said would have stopped me."

"It need not be forever," Hank had said helpfully. "We can think of it as a post-graduate course."

That conversation and the implicit promise it expressed were strong in Hank's mind as he followed his uncle into the front office of *The Courier.* At the small desk on the side of the room where Hank used to work sat a dark-haired slender woman, whom Uncle Jim introduced as Pat Long. He turned as he walked to the back of the office. "Before we do anything else, Henry, let me show you some new equipment back here."

They passed through the office door and entered the print shop. "Our biggest addition is the new Goss press. It's quite a gadget." Walking past the banks of type files, the smell of ink and grease and molten linotype metal were strong in Hank's nose. Uncle Jim stopped before the Goss, all grey painted metal frame and stainless steel.

"How fast is it, Uncle Jim?"

"Well, when George has her all greased up and everything clicking to perfection, she'll turn out 500 an hour. Pretty good for a small town newspaper."

"Darn good. How does she hold her register?"

"Perfect. Not like that old contraption. Remember how page 2 was always slipping to one side?"

"Sure do." Hank looked around. "Oh, you've added another linotype."

"One of the new 4000 series. Can you still handle one of these things?"

"Not sure. It's been quite a while since I tried." Hank walked over to the machine and slid his fingers over the keys. "I'm sure I could still set type but I might have trouble with the mechanical fixes."

Jim Bladesly looked around the shop. "Same old type saw. I guess you've seen all the new stuff. Let me check something with Pat and then we can stroll on home."

While his uncle conferred with the young assistant, Hank

stood at the window and watched the passing traffic. It was beginning to thicken in the gathering dusk as shoppers finished their rounds and turned for home and supper. On the street, cars and occasional trucks moved sedately and quietly. Hank looked in vain for a familiar face or figure among the people passing on the sidewalk. He found himself comparing the bulky-shaped women, large in hip and upper body, with the fine-boned Chinese and Malay women on the streets of Singapore. The faces, too, except for an occasional strikingly pretty one, looked lumpy and coarse-grained compared with the smooth-skinned, small-featured Asians.

"All set, Hank. Let's go home."

After they had passed the red brick Hanson National Bank and had threaded through the crowded sidewalks before the downtown stores, Uncle Jim asked, "Now, tell me, Henry, how happy are you with what you're doing?"

"On the whole, I'd say quite happy."

"Not prying into what you do, but what is it you like about it?"

Hank paused while a chubby, dark-haired girl in front of him who was carrying a fat-cheeked baby put down her shopping bag and switched the baby from one arm to the other. He took a couple of quick steps to catch up and said, "I guess mainly the *foreign-ness* of it. Both Singapore and the work. They're unlike anything I've ever known before. Absolutely, totally unlike."

Uncle Jim walked on for several moments, head down as though deep in thought. Finally he asked quietly, "How long do you think that appeal can last?"

"I don't know, Uncle Jim. But there's more than that. I feel I am a part of something important, that I'm contributing to a significant national effort."

His uncle's head came up and he said with firm emphasis, "Henry, I'm as convinced as I can be that *that* is entirely a matter of perspective." A passing car honked and a man in a red-checked wool shirt yelled, "Ho, Jim!" James Bladesly waved back and said, without pause, "You know, I count myself a modest man but let me point out to you some of the things I have accomplished right here in Hanson with our little semi-weekly newspaper. I'm not talking about the professional prizes we've won or the national attention I have received from time to time. They're not nearly as important as the services we have performed for this town." They came to the railroad crossing and stepped carefully over the shiny rails.

"You remember that ruckus a few years ago about that concrete bridge that failed on Route 93? Nobody killed but the truck driver lost his right arm, crushed just below the shoulder. Well, that bridge contractor is now in prison largely because of the pressure I kept on until they indicted him and brought him to trial. It's not a matter of vengeance in this case but I get satisfaction out of knowing other builders are going to be damned careful about not short-changing jobs in this area.

"Another thing I'm proud of is the bookmobile service I got extended into three counties around here. It took about a year of editorials but we finally got the state to allocate $150,000 for that program. Now the bookmobile goes up and down every little back road, and you know some of those farms are pretty isolated and get snowbound sometimes in the winter.

"I won't even mention the free lost-and-found ads I run for kids whose pets have strayed, but I will brag about the campaign I put on for college scholarships. I finally got the local businessmen to establish a fund, and we've got two kids in college right now. One is the Peters kid; his dad has the rural mail delivery route over Kingston way. The other is Sam Woodson's boy, the yard foreman at White's lumber yard." He smiled and said apologetically, "Quite a sermon, Henry."

"All good stuff, Uncle Jim." By this time they had nearly reached the end of the Yarmouth campus and the Bladesly house lay only a few hundred yards ahead. James Bladesly stopped and took Hank by the arm.

"There's something I want to say to you I don't want your Aunt Sarah to know. I've been getting a few irregular blips in my heart from time to time, so I went last week and had Doc Hanley examine me. He says it's nothing serious now but it may be progressive and I may have to slow down. If it turns out that way, Henry, I'm going to turn to you." The lined face was intensely earnest. "And I just hope and pray you will respond."

They walked on in silence and turned in the walkway beside the large white birch tree. It was nearly dark and the lights within the house shone a warm, inviting yellow. As they walked in the door, Aunt Sarah was just turning away from the telephone. "Oh, Henry! That was Margaret Rawlins. She just heard you were home and hopes you will call her back."

Hank, his mind still lingering over his uncle's remarks, answered, "Yes, I plan to." Planned to, that is, without great enthusiasm. More as a duty, more a matter of conscience than heart. Margaret Rawlins was unfinished business. After his conversation with Uncle Jim it began to seem that his home town was chock full of unfinished business.

Six

The sun was still low in the east over Singapore but already flexing its muscles with shafts of hot light as Hank parked behind the Embassy. He sat for a moment after turning off the engine, tasting his mouth and moving his tongue from side to side. Jet lag had laid a thick layer of gauze over his eyes and muffled his ears. His hands seemed to have a quarter inch of felt between them and the steering wheel and his body felt as though a low fever were waiting in the wings.

He hoisted himself out of his seat and walked on limp legs into the building, past the Marine guard, a new one who nodded noncommittally, and up the stairway to the CIA offices. Buck Jones' secretary, her pursed mouth registering its customary degree of discontent, muttered unenthusiastically, "Welcome back. Go on in. He's free."

Buck Jones glanced up from reading, gold-rimmed glasses incongruously giving him a scholarly look. "Well, look who's here! The boy wonder!" He laid his glasses on his desk. "Close the door. Bladesly."

Hank closed the door and took a seat on a wooden chair beside the desk. "So you sold your hare-brained idea to the top brass. I suppose I ought to congratulate you." He looked grimly down at his desk and then again at Hank. "I'm not going to pretend I'm happy about this op. It's loaded with T.N.T. and I don't think the potential comes within a country mile of justifying the risk. But I've had my orders and I'm a good soldier. Just let me tell you, Bladesly, where we stand. One slip, just one little bobble that might blow the operation, and you are on your way out of here within the hour!"

"Understood. I know the risks, but let me tell you how I plan to proceed."

"Absolutely not! I don't want to hear a word. You and the geniuses in Headquarters have got it all doped out. I'm staying way the hell clear. But I warn you, one boo-boo and. . ." He jerked his thumb up over his shoulder like a baseball umpire.

"All right, I understand. Anything else?"

"No. I'll call you if I need you."

Hank got to his feet and walked down the hall to his office. A stack of cables and dispatches stood high in his In-box. He raised the white venetian blind at his window, gazed abstractedly for several moments at the swarming marine traffic of freighters, junks, launches, tugs, and lighters in Singapore Harbor, and then sat down at the desk and pulled the top cable off the pile. His eyes ran across the jerky cable-ese littered with pseudonyms and capitalized code-names. He had covered half a page before he realized that his mind had taken in not a word. It was hopeless. Freed from the command to read and understand, his mind then wandered aimlessly off and ransacked recollections of his recent stay in Maine. It lingered, in a bemused state over the evening with Margaret Rawlins, and what it found there mostly was surprise. Away from Margaret, half a world away in Singapore, he could place her neatly in a pigeon-hole labeled "high school and college sweetheart," a cherished memory but essentially an unfinished part of his past. Up close, in her home and in his uncle's car, she was something different. He seemed to have forgotten how handsome she was: her wide-set gray eyes beneath her ash blonde hair, her generous mouth with its even, white teeth, her broad shoulders and decorous high breasts and her splendidly long lovely legs.

She greeted him without reserve. "Oh, Hank," she breathed in his ear as he held her close, "I've missed you so much."

"Missed you too." The sweet-grass smell of her hair and the discreetly feminine fragrance of her Tweed perfume stirred ripples of forgotten memories: dancing at the Phi Delta Theta house; picnicking on Heron Island in Harpswell Sound while his sailboat, *Blue Teal,* tugged and yawed restlessly at her anchor over the sandy shallows; walking together in a fresh May night down Hanson's leafy streets; kissing her good-night at her parent's front door with the fur of her coat collar brushing his cheek.

They had spent the evening driving without plan from one old haunt to another while Margaret chattered about old friends and local mishaps. "You remember, Dotty Springhallen? She married Bruce Biddle, and they just had twin boys last month. *So* cute! Funny. The babies came the day after a Boston and Maine freight train derailed while going through town about midnight and almost knocked the Union Street Bridge down. They live just a block away and Dotty said the noise made her sit right up in bed. The babies started to come about an hour later and Dotty says they just wanted to find out what was going on. She's a *scream!*"

Hank responded from time to time but gradually his mind and his attention drifted away from the young woman beside him and he found himself sorting over various approaches he might take with Peter Yee. Somehow, despite the presence of this creature whose femininity was close to his touch, the challenges and the dissonant charms of

Singapore seemed more immediate. The domestic happenings of old friends and the daily concerns of Hanson had become painfully confining to his mind. Not even this young woman who represented a cherished part of his life could give them vital significance.

But still the evening passed pleasantly enough. Toward its end they parked in a little opening in the birch trees overlooking Mulberry Cove, and he took Margaret in his arms and kissed her fondly and gently and then more searchingly. But when his hands began to move and caress her beneath her dress she pulled away from him gently and said, "No, Hank. Not tonight, dear. Not tonight." He kissed her softly once or twice after that and drove her home. They made their farewells in her parent's living room with all the poignance of dear friends but little more. As Hank drove his uncle's Plymouth home he realized that Margaret Rawlins still belonged in the realm of unfinished business.

Hank was roused from his reverie by a sudden change in traffic noise outside the window. A freighter in the harbor suddenly gave a sharp warning with four short hoots. Hank moved quickly to the window. He saw a lighter towed by a Chinese launch crossing close by the freighter's bow. It was dangerously close but not a collision, just another incident in the milling crowded harbor. He stood at the window gazing at the astounding variety of traffic, from junks to Peninsula and Orient liners, all moving with steady purpose toward disparate destinations. He gazed until his eyes slipped out of focus and none of the myriad detail registered on his brain. After several minutes he shook his head and told himself to snap out of it. Got to do something useful with this day. He decided to go to the Golden Flower and try to make contact with DAMASK. He needed to set up a meeting with Peter Yee.

Two days later Peter Yee sat opposite Hank at a small table toward the rear of the Golden Flower. Within the first few minutes, Hank realized that this was a different Peter Yee from the forthcoming young Chinese who had left his apartment two weeks earlier. He was reserved and unresponsive almost to the point of sullen silence.

"You seem troubled, Peter. Something wrong?"

He nodded. "I've given careful thought to our last conversation. I can't go through with it. What we discussed."

"Oh?" A long silence ran between them. "Why not?"

Peter Yee shook his head. "The reasons are many." He looked away. Around them the bustle and stridency of a Chinese cafe resounded. He shook his head again. "There's no need to discuss them."

"But I *want* to discuss them."

The Chinese set his mouth firmly. "No need. I've decided not to deal on the matter. You may use the information you have about me as you choose. I'll make decisions about my future in the light of what follows." He moved as if to leave.

Hank laid his hand on his arm. "Wait, Peter. You and I are two intelligent people. You owe it to me to let me understand what's in your mind."

Peter Yee looked at him thoughtfully, clearly given pause by this appeal. He looked around at the crowded room. "I really don't want to discuss it. But in any case, not here."

"My apartment?"

He shook his head. "No, too obvious. It's dangerous for me to be seen in your company or at your place."

"Name a place."

He looked down at the table silently for a moment. Then he looked directly at Hank. "A friend of mine is lending me his little villa on the shore just over the Causeway in Johore

Bahru. I'll be there with my ... with someone you ought to meet."

"Fine. How do I find it?"

"I'll write out directions. It's easy. Come after dark on Saturday."

The headlights of the little grey Austin picked out the sandy track winding through the palm grove and then flared on the siding of a white bungalow standing on low pilings. Hank cut the lights and found his way around the side of the house to the porch in front by the glow from the window. Peter Yee met him at the door. Behind him, in the center of the square room with its rattan furniture stood a slender Chinese woman in a delicately figured *cheong-sum.* "Come in. This is my sister, Mai Tin."

Hank nodded. "How do you do," and started to put out his hand in greeting but stopped when he realized she had no intention of so doing.

Mai Tin bowed her head while her eyes remained fixed on Hank. "It is my very great pleasure to meet you. Peetah has told me about you. You honor us by your visit." The words were courtly in politeness but the tone of voice was icy and edged with disdain. The accent was purest Cambridge English.

Hank recognized the time-honored Chinese ploy of extravagant courtesy to insult a person felt to be one's inferior. "Thank you." He smiled at the elegant figure, her *cheong-sum* displaying every subtle curve of her slender body. Her beauty was classic Chinese: fine-spun black hair, almond-shaped eyes, small narrow nose, and tiny mouth. Her golden skin glowed on her arms below the short sleeves and through the revealing slits of the dress along her thighs. Her legs were shaped with the grace that seemingly only Arabian horses and Chinese women possess.

Peter Yee said, "Please sit down. May I get you a beer or whisky-soda?"

"Please. A short whiskey."

As her brother left the room she gestured languidly toward a cushioned chair with cane arms and said, "Yes, do please sit down, Mr. Bladesly. As she moved her closely fitted dress hugged her small waist and rippled over her supple hips. The combination of her loveliness and her cold disdain was ensnaring and challenging to Hank. She sat opposite him and crossed her slender legs. "Have you lived in Singapore long, Mr. Bladesly?"

"Slightly over eighteen months."

"Oh? Then, not long." Her tone seemed to imply that eighteen months was a disgracefully negligible period of time.

Peter Yee returned with glasses on a pewter tray and passed them about. He held his glass before him, his eyes looking at Hank over the rim, and nodded before he sipped his drink. A silence ensued during which Mai Tin looked at the floor and then up expectantly at Peter.

Yee put his glass down. "Mr. Bladesly —"

"Hank."

Peter smiled deprecatingly. "Both my Chinese upbringing and my British education make that difficult."

"You must know, Peetah," said Mai Tin, "that Ameddicans call everyone by the first name."

Hank turned and said with elaborate politeness. "Not quite everyone, Miss Yee." Her dark eyes flared briefly at Hank and then returned to chilly contempt.

Peter smiled thinly. "I'll try again. Mr. Hank Bladesly, my sister and I have discussed our conversations quite thoroughly, and we conclude that the relationship you suggest would be most dangerous and not helpful to me."

"Dangerous? How dangerous?"

"Clearly if it became known I had a relationship with the Americans it would absolutely destroy my career."

"Our first priority would be to keep it secret."

Mai Tin gave a short laugh. "My sister," said Peter," pointed last week to three news items concerning national security secrets revealed by your Congress."

"I can assure you that my organization has an excellent record for keeping our relationship secure. I will resign immediately if it is breached."

Peter Yee looked at him thoughtfully and then gazed at his sister. After an extended silence and a sip of his scotch, Hank said quietly. "You speak of the destruction of your career. Let me ask in all friendliness, would not your career be destroyed even more certainly if the event I witnessed were made public? And isn't a jail sentence also likely?"

Mai Tin laughed again, this time bitterly. "It is just as I said, Peetah."

Peter spoke quietly, without rancor. "I believe that that is commonly called blackmail."

"Yes, it can be called that. An ugly word." He paused. "You know, I have always understood that the Chinese have a long tradition of trade and negotiation. Let's look at it in that light. I have information you wish to suppress. I offer you secure control of that information in exchange for information you have now and can hope to have in the future.

Peter's face became very thoughtful, and he nodded slightly as though in agreement. "I see that but it deals only with the negative side. Protection as of now but what are the positive benefits for me? What can you offer me now or in the future that would help me?"

"Money."

"Money? Why would I need American money?"

"You have a political campaign to mount. That takes money."

"We have friends with money," said Mai Tin.

"Yes," said Hank. "Friends who will come around later asking for favors that you, Peter, may find embarrassing to grant."

"But I don't think that much money will be needed."

"Have you looked into it? Do you know the costs of political advertising, handbills, or hiring halls?"

"Actually not. But I don't think it will amount to more than I can raise without your help." He shook his head. "No that's not enough in itself to justify the risk to me."

Hank looked first at Mai Tin who was smiling grimly and then at Peter Yee. "You know, you speak of *your* risk. My office is under great pressure to identify the killer of that American newsman. Have you thought of the risk I am taking by protecting you? It would be a great coup for me personally to provide that information. A great coup. But I have a greater goal in mind. I am confident, Peter, that if you can get yourself launched into a political career you can be a force in the future of Singapore after independence. The United States has a stake in maintaining stability in Southeast Asia. With a Communist regime in Mainland China, the Viet Minh in Vietnam, and the Khmer Rouge in Cambodia, the day may come when Americans will need a friend in Singapore."

Peter Yee seemed shaken. He nodded solemnly and looked questioningly at Mai Tin.

"Peetah," she said languidly, "this changes nothing. The things we discussed remain the same. Rather than tying yourself to a risky relationship it would be better to let Mr. Bladesly tell the world his secret and then pick up the pieces."

"After a long term in jail?" asked Hank.

Her lustrous eyes flared again but she made no reply. Peter's face remained impassive but his eyes were troubled. After a long pause he spoke softly. "I would like to think about it again, Mai Tin. Maybe we were not thorough enough."

She shrugged her shoulders but said nothing.

Hank took the last swallow of his drink and stood up. "Good. Please let me know when we can talk again. And Peter, do look into potential campaign costs. You may be surprised." He turned toward Mai Tin, sitting with her lovely legs curled under her in the chair, and made a half bow. "Miss Yee, it has been a pleasure."

She nodded without smiling. "Mr. Bladesly."

Several days passed after his meeting with the Yees without word from Peter. One evening as he left his office, Hank walked down North Bridge Road to the Gramophone Shop to look for new records. Behind a pillar toward the rear of the shop stood Mai Tin, dressed in a royal blue *cheong-sum*. She was leafing with slender fingers through one of the albums in a bin marked "Duke Ellington." Hank stopped several feet away and said, "Hello, Miss Yee."

She looked up, startled, her eyebrows arching high on her forehead. Then her face softened into something short of a smile. "Hello, Mr. Bladesly."

"You are interested in music, unlike Peter?"

"Some."

"American jazz?"

"Some." She continued to leaf through the stack and then looked up. "I had a friend at Cambridge, an Englishman, who admired Duke Ellington. He said 'The Mooche' was one of the great musical compositions of the 20th Century." Her speech, the clipped English accent enunciated with the unique voice quality of Chinese women, sounded piquantly on Hank's ear. A beguiling mixture.

"Defensible view." He watched her picking aimlessly through the albums. "Are you looking for anything special?"

"I saw a review of a new Duke Ellington release in *The Straits Times*, the *Come Sunday Suite*."

"It was released last year in the States and I have it." He moved beside her and leafed quickly through the LP albums and pulled it out. "This is it. Fine Ellington with a gorgeous Johnny Hodges solo."

"You seem knowledgeable."

"I love jazz, and I guess it's fair to say I revere Ellington." He leafed further through the bin. "Do you have many of his records?"

"No, just a couple."

He pulled out another album. "Here's a great one to own. It's a collection of Ellington compositions played by the magnificent 1940's band. Things like "Warm Valley," "Blue Goose," "Cottontail," "Rocks In My Bed," "Across the Track Blues." And all the great Ellington bandsmen: Harry Carney, Ben Webster, Johnny Hodges, Barney Bigard, Rex Stewart, Cootie Williams, Ray Nance, Lawrence Brown, Tricky Sam Nanton, Jimmy Blan—"

She looked at him wonderingly. "Perhaps I misspoke. Not knowledgeable but *expert.*"

"Sorry. I got carried away."

"Don't be sorry. You are being helpful." She permitted him a very small smile. She collected the two albums, paid the cashier and walked out the door. Hank decided to forego record shopping for the time being and followed her. In the street she stopped and looked up at him questioningly. Around them the extraordinary street traffic of Singapore swirled: Indian men in longhis; Malays in sarongs; Chinese alternately in Cantonese pajamas, European business suits and underwear shorts; Englishmen in white linen shorts, white knee socks and linen blouses. No less exotic but far more lovely to the eye stood Mai Tin, her closely-fitted royal blue *cheong-sum* asserting her elegance.

Hank decided to risk it. "Can you by any chance have dinner with me?"

She responded quickly. "No, I must —" Then she paused. "No, you've been very helpful but —. Maybe some other time."

"We could make it quick if you have an appointment later. We could have *satay* down on the street."

She wrinkled her small nose at him. "Peasant food." She hesitated, looking up at him and then at passersby. Again she bestowed on him a half smile and said, "You've been very helpful. Let me respond by introducing you to a good Chinese restaurant. It's just three streets away."

The restaurant she chose was on the second floor of a nondescript building overlooking Beach Road. Overhead fluorescent lights filled the room with white glare and bounced off the white porcelain-topped tables. The unique noise of dozens of chattering Chinese richocheted off the tile floor along with the steady clatter of stacking dishes, the banging of aluminum trays, and the scrape of wooden chairs. But in the midst of this disharmony of decor and sound the food was magnificent, much the best Hank had ever had. He said so to Mai Tin.

"I'm so glad it pleases you." She deftly picked an almond from her bowl with chopsticks and put it to her small mouth. "When I was in England this is what I missed most. Good Chinese food."

"How long were you there?"

"Three years, studying international economics. I had an opportunity to work for a Chinese bank in London but I. . . I decided to come back to Singapore."

"Your home? Family?"

"Yes, partly that. But —" She hesitated and then looked at him directly, her eyes flat. "My English friend, the man who admired Duke Ellington — I found out was married. I had to get away."

"Oh. I understand."

They ate silently for some time amidst the surrounding clatter. She looked up suddenly from her bowl, again with that half smile. "Strange I should tell you that. Something about your manner. Sympathetic. Unusual for an Ameddican."

He shook his head. "I didn't mean to pry."

She took her delicately poised chopsticks from her small mouth, her eyes thoughtful. "Let me do some prying. Why do you know so much about jazz? Are you a musician?"

He shook his head. "No, I just listen." Her eyes still looked questioningly so he continued. "My uncle gave me a radio when I was fifteen, and I listened to all the record programs. I liked all the popular bands, like Guy Lombardo and Sammy Kaye and Kay Kyser. I heard some records so many times I began to notice little things, like Lombardo using a trumpet and clarinet together so it sounded like two trumpets. Things like that."

"But Guy Lombardo isn't Duke Ellington!"

"No, hardly. But I *did* learn how to listen. Then in college I had a fraternity brother who was a *real* musician. He thought Lombardo was garbage. He got me to listen to Basie and Ellington and Teddy Wilson and the *real* jazzmen."

"But you know so many names. Did you study jazz seriously?"

"No, they just soaked in through osmosis. In college, I sweated blood learning historical dates and the reigns of kings but I could name the clarinet player in Isham Jones' band just offhand. I have no idea how I learned it." He could also have said to this exotic creature across the table from him that jazz had come to be an essential element in his life, a source of expression and release for moods and emotions that were outwardly muted. Frustration, anger, moody longing, springing joy, lyric affection, melting passion — all were embodied in the music flowing from the horns and strings of the great jazzmen. And all spoke for him with consummate skill.

They finished the superb meal. Hank paid the cashier and they walked down the dark stairs to the street. "My car," he said, "is parked behind the American Embassy. We can walk there and I can drive you home. Or I can get you a cab."

"Let's walk." They crossed Beach Road and walked down

through the Cathedral grounds, the white steeple looming in the dim light reflected from the street.

As they passed the cathedral portico, Hank said, "I could also drive you first to my apartment where we could play your new records on my machine."

She looked up at him, her eyes uncertain; then they grew more assured. "That is tempting because my machine is down at the villa in Johore, and I won't be there until the weekend."

"Then we will do it."

In his apartment with a *stengah* in Mai Tin's hand and a dollop of Ballantine's in Hank's, they sat on the sofa with the plangent melody of Ellington's *Come Sunday* washing around them. Mai Tin was a good listener, attentive to the entrance and departure of instruments. As Johnny Hodges reverently stated the theme while a choir of muted trombones crooned behind him, Mai Tin asked, "What is that lovely solo instrument?"

"Alto saxophone. Johnny Hodges."

"He's so gentle, almost prayerful. And that lovely, warm tone!"

"Yes."

The center section of *Come Sunday* resembled gospel music as Hodges rose high in soaring lines while the reed section sang in full voice. Then the theme returned, again meditative, and the entire ensemble closed with a quiet "Amen."

"That was beautiful," she said with that Chinese intoned British accent. "I'm so glad you found it for me."

"Shall we try the other album?"

"Yes, let's do."

Hank put on the 1940's Ellington which led off with the gentle bounce of "In a Mellotone" with Harry Carney's barrel-chested baritone sax leading the way. Cootie Williams' saucy trumpet toyed with the bridge section and then

Hodges entered suavely and led the band home with agile grace.

"There's so much going on," said Mai Tin. "I can't take it all in at once."

Duke led Johnny Hodges into "Warm Valley" with several Ravel-like chords and Hodges' clinging, sensuous saxophone carried the warm melody on from there. The phrasing was languorous and amorous almost to the edge of lascivious. In the middle section a quiet muted trumpet lowered the temperature briefly but then Hodges took it back and caressed it again. The full-bodied reed section commented in broad, opulent, and open lines and Hodges followed with a tender, lingering close.

"That's enough!" said Mai Tin, her voice a tone or two higher than its usual treble. "Let's not play any more."

Hank sprang to the record player and turned it off. He put the record back in Mai Tin's album and turned toward her with it in his hands.

"You didn't like it?"

She shook her head. "Quite the contrary. I liked it too much." Hank picked up his glass and sat down again on the sofa. "It's so sensuous, voluptuous." She shook her head again, pensively. "I thought I had left all that behind me in England."

"Duke titled it "Warm Valley" but I doubt he had landscape in mind. I think he's describing a woman, a lovely woman's body."

"That saxophone reaches right inside me." She turned and smiled softly at him. "I want to play it again but not tonight. I think I must go home."

Mai Tin directed him where to turn as they drove down Orchard Road and soon they stopped before a doorway in a block of row houses. "This is it. Please don't get out. I'd prefer you didn't." She offered him her hand, slender and cool and almost clinging. "Let me thank you for an instructive and — well, moving evening."

"I enjoyed it too." She opened the door and just as she was moving to get out Hank spoke.

"Please ask Peter to get in touch soon."

She turned back, her face in the most open smile he had yet seen. "I admire that. All evening long I was fearful you would try to pressure me about Peter but you did not. Now at the end you make this simple request. Yes, I will tell Peter. Thank you again, and good night."

Back in his apartment Hank looked at his day's mail: a letter from Bob Pintel in New York and one from his uncle's address in Maine. He opened Bob's letter first and instantly he was in the high tension hyperthyroid Pintel world. The man wrote as he spoke, always in italics with exclamation points. "Blades, I found the *girl!* Name is Anne Sawyer, from San Francisco. She is *super!* I am *absolutely* convinced this is *IT!* We haven't settled anything yet but I'M GOING TO MARRY HER! Obviously can't do it without my old roomie as Best Man. When can you get away from your grubby bureaucratic duties and give me a hand?"

Hank put the letter down and gazed at the tan and green curtains stirring gently in the evening breeze. Bob Pintel, his roommate at Yarmouth College, had found The Girl at least five times to Hank's certain knowledge. This probably was another of those spasms but then it might not be. In any event, to leave Singapore for either San Francisco or New York, wherever a wedding might take place, was clearly out of the question with the Peter Yee operation hanging in limbo, as it seemed to be.

Aunt Sarah's letter was much quieter, almost somber. "I am very worried about Uncle James, Henry. Dr. Hanley says he *must* slow down or his heart will give out. But *he* says there is no one here who can really help him with the paper. How I wish you were here, Henry! We *both* do."

This gave Hank greater pause. Immediately, his old recognition of an unpaid obligation to his aunt and uncle flared up. *Someday,* he knew, someday he would have to repay it unless there were an intervention of circumstance he could not begin to foresee. But not now. Now the business at hand was too pressing.

He walked back to his bedroom and put Aunt Sarah's letter on his night table. He quickly undressed, put on a dark blue pajama top, brushed his teeth, and got into bed. He moved toward sleep quickly as usual but on the way the lustrous eyes and elegant figure of Mai Tin drifted through his mind.

Next evening, as Hank was trying to decide whether to go to a Bob Hope movie or pick up where he had left off in the biography of Singapore's founder, Sir Stamford Raffles, the phone sounded, *Br-ring–br-ring.* Mai Tin's lilting voice said, "Peter wishes you to come to the villa in Johore Saturday evening. Can you come?"

"Yes, certainly." He paused. "Will you be there?"

"Perhaps," she said, drawing the word out slowly.

On Saturday night, about 7:30, Hank made his way around the side of the white bungalow. As he climbed the steps he could hear the gentle ripple and wash of the shallow waters of the Straits of Johore behind him. Peter Yee met him as before, a very restrained Peter. Behind him stood Mai Tin in still another *cheong-sum,* this one a pale willow-green. She gave him her hand, fine-boned as a quail's wing and slightly clinging. About her wafted a mysterious complex fragrance, both musky and spicy, as unlike the forthright smell of Margaret's "Tweed" as Singapore was alien to Maine. Peter soon got down to business. "Mr. Blade— uh, excuse me. May I call you 'Henry' instead of 'Hank'? I think I can manage that."

"Certainly."

"Well, then, uh, Henry. The one really troublesome thing for me is to maintain secrecy about our relationship. It concerns me."

"I am certain we can deal with it." A thought struck him. "What about your connection with British intelligence. You've kept that secret from the world."

"But that is easier."

"Aren't you fighting the British for independence? Aren't you opponents?"

"In a way, yes." He smiled quietly. "But I have many connections because of my years at Cambridge."

"I'm not going to ask you how you manage your contacts, but I know we can work out a secure arrangement."

Peter Yee gazed across the room at his sister, curled in cat-like grace in her chair, and hesitated before speaking. "Mai Tin has made a suggestion. Perhaps she could be our connection. Would that be satisfactory?"

Hank stifled an exclamation of surprise just before it reached the surface. "Why, yes. I think that would do."

"She works in the City not far from your offices."

"We could meet at the Gramophone Shop," offered Mai Tin in almost a giggle.

"That would work."

"It would reduce the chances of our being seen together. But what about security within your organization? Won't a number of people know?"

"No. I'm holding it very closely. As I told you before, I will stake my job on it. I can't go further than that!"

"No." Peter Yee nodded slowly while the lines across his forehead slowly relaxed.

A silence fell in the room with only a faint rustle of palm trees and the gentle wash of the seashore outside the house. Hank looked at Mai Tin who sat gazing down at the floor, her black hair gleaming in the light of the nearby lamp. He turned to Peter. "What about campaign expense money, Peter?"

"Oh. I *have* looked into it as you suggested. I believe I will need about five hundred dollars, U.S. dollars not Singapore dollars, beyond what I can raise. Is that too much?"

"I was planning on a thousand."

"That would certainly make everything easier." He looked steadily at Hank for a moment. "You understand I would have preferred not to have made such an agreement with you, but circumstances —" He held his hands before him, palms up.

"I understand."

"But Mai Tin and I believe you are sincere, that you have integrity. We trust you, and we are hopeful everything will work out well for all of us."

"I'm certain it will."

Peter sighed and looked at Mai Tin who smiled reassurance. He stood up. "Would you like a drink?"

"Yes, indeed. Whiskey, please."

As Peter went to the kitchen, Mai Tin smiled sweetly across the room at Hank and was just about to speak when the telephone rang. She moved gracefully from her chair and answered, "Hallo?" After a pause she spoke a rapid sentence in Chinese and turned toward the kitchen doorway. "Peetah. For you."

Peter's end of the conversation consisted of several "yes's" and a sharp "when?" He put the phone down. "I'm sorry. A serious disagreement has come up in my group, and I'm needed down there just now. I must leave at once. Mai Tin, you finish making drinks."

He shook hands briskly with Hank and soon the whirring sound of an ancient Morris starting came through the window, followed by the spasmodic coughing of the engine as the car moved off down the sandy track leading to the main roadway.

Shortly later Mai Tin handed Hank his glass and resumed her place in the cane-armed easy chair. Hank raised his glass in salute to her and said, "I'm grateful for your help with Peter."

She shook her head. "Don't misunderstand. I have very little influence over Peetah. He is an independent man. A proud man. I only ask questions. I help him to see all sides."

"In any case, you must have helped in some way. I'm very pleased it has been worked out."

She gazed at him thoughtfully. "I believe I am too. Or, at least I will be if your relationship helps him and does not hurt him." She sipped her drink and frowned. "I only wish you had not resorted to — well, blackmail to get him to agree."

"There was no other way I could have got him to listen to me."

"No. Perhaps not." She sat silent for a while, looking down at the floor. Then she glanced up, her eyes merry. "Would you like to hear some Duke Ellington on my player?"

"Love it."

Mai Tin started the record and walked slowly back to sit down beside Hank on the sofa as the ebony-wooded sound of Barney Bigard's clarinet led the way into "Across the Track Blues." They sat side by side, sipping occasionally from the glasses, as the rich and complex music, now raucous and driving, now seductive and luxurious, filled the room. Slowly, as the Ellington band moved from one compelling interlude to another, Mai Tin seemed to be moving subtly closer to Hank, and when the languorous, sensuous sound of "Warm Valley" came forth her shoulder was touching his and her hip beneath the willow-green *cheong-sum* was warm against his thigh. Again, Johnny Hodges molded the curves of the voluptuous melody into seductive song and the reed section seemed to speak of a broad, sunny upland.

When Hodges tongued the last note lingeringly, Mai Tin pulled away from Hank and turned to look at him with beguiling eyes. "That music!" she said and swiftly left the room.

In a moment she was back wearing a pale yellow silk robe. "*Cheong-sums* are not very comfortable for lounging," she said by way of explanation. "Too tight."

She sat down on the sofa and asked, "Would you play that music again? 'Warm Valley.' "

When Hank came back to the sofa Mai Tin snuggled close beside him. Before Hodges had finished the first chorus he had her in his arms and his mouth on hers, her fragrance overwhelming his senses. He pulled away and looked down at her oval face. In her dark eyes, beneath the upswept lashes, he found acquiescence. He got to his feet, slid his hands beneath her thighs and shoulders, and lifted her into his arms. As he carried her through the bedroom doorway she murmured in his ear, "Please tell me you are not married."

"I am not."

"Good," she breathed.

As he gently put her down on the bed her robe fell away and bared her breasts. He slid his hands along the side of the robe and pulled it aside full length. She was a splendor of subtle curves and lyric symmetry. The lovely skin of her body, unblemished except for two tiny cinnamon ovals on her breasts and a glistening ebony triangle below, glowed golden in the soft light. Her breasts were smooth, gentle mounds.

"I hope you are not disappointed," she said, looking up with mischievous eyes. "Chinese women are not as — well, *bovine,* as European women."

"You are lovely." He bent down and kissed the smooth place between her breasts.

"Warm valley," she said.

"Yes," he answered and joined her on the bed.

Seven

Peter Yee's maiden political speech, Mai Tin had told Hank, would take place at a rally held in the open field at the corner of Holland Road and Bukit Sembilan Drive. "Where the Chinese opera performs on Friday nights," she said.

Several hundred yards before he had reached the intersection, Hank slowed the Austin to a crawl as he approached long lines of people walking along the verge. Ahead, the road became almost blocked by crowds crossing to the field where a brass band played music of astonishing dissonance and disharmony. Hank gingerly turned right at the intersection toward Leedon Park and found an open space for the car. People pushed past him silently as he walked slowly toward the meeting ground. Torches flared and danced over the heads of the gathering throng in the evening breeze. A steady buzzing of Chinese voices surrounded him as he looked around. Predominantly Chinese, the crowd was also sprinkled with a few Malays and several British. Hank recognized one or two English businessmen whom he had met at the Tanglin Club.

Suddenly the band stopped playing on a wildly disordered

chord, and Peter Yee appeared on a small wooden platform, his arms spread wide in a plea for quiet. As he stood in the light of the wavering torches, Hank suddenly had a flashback of the night he had seen Peter, face chalky in the torchlight, raise his club and smash it down on the newsman's naked head. Now, as then, his face was set and determined. His figure, the large head on the lean body, projected power and unquenchable ambition. For Hank, it was an astonishing transformation from the mild young man with whom he had negotiated several nights earlier in the villa by the sea.

The crowd quieted and Peter Yee spoke a few words in halting, uncertain Chinese. Then he spread his feet apart and shouted in English, "Citizens of Singapore, I come to bring you freedom!" A quick murmur ran through the crowd. "Freedom! Freedom from colonial rule, freedom from foreign exploitation. Singapore must be free from alien rule. Singapore is *Asian.* Asians must rule Singapore. We must throw the foreign master out. The people, *Asian* people, must rule Singapore." He paused and looked about as the crowd buzzed excitedly.

Peter Yee resumed in a quieter tone. "For over a century we have meekly stood by while men from islands ten thousand miles away, strangers from an alien world, have ruled us, held us captive. They have taken our land, controlled our commerce, made our laws. Is this just? Is this right? No, no! A thousand times *no!* This is colonialism. Brutal, naked colonialism. We must overthrow it. We must seize control over our land, our lives. Asians must rule Singapore. Asia for Asians!" As he talked his voice had steadily risen in volume and its cadence quickened. Now his voice rose to a shout as he cried, "Asia for Asians!" and shot his right fist into the flickering light of the flaring torches.

He paused for a moment, his head thrust forward as he swept the crowd with flashing eyes. "How can we do this?

How can we break the chains that have bound us for so long? How? I will tell you how. By joining our Asian voices together, *all* of us, Chinese, Malays, Indians. By joining our voices together into one great shout, 'Freedom!' *Freedom!''* Now the crowd was murmuring excitedly and there were a few scattered shouts of "Freedom!" Peter Yee smiled a broad smile. "Joined together we can take control of Singapore. We are many. They are few. Our friends are many and are near. Theirs are few and far away. We can prevail and we must start tonight."

Again he paused and swung his gaze around the crowd. *''Tonight!''* He thrust his arm high and then said in a loud, firm voice. "Tonight we are creating a new organization, a new grouping which men of all races may join. We are creating The People's Voice Party. Our party, with the help of all of you and thousands more, will speak with one, loud voice to the Government of Singapore. It will shout in a voice that will be heard from here to London, 'Freedom! Singapore is Asian! Asia for Asians!' "

He stopped while clapping and shouts ran swiftly through the crowd. He raised both hands high, fingers spread wide. "Join me, my friends. Join The People's Voice Party and bring us victory."

Hank turned and slipped away through the clamoring crowd, now pressing forward toward the small stand. He drove down through the curving, broad residential streets of Leedon Park until he found a street leading back to Holland Road.

Back in the apartment he barely had time to open his mail, consisting of three bills, when he heard the clicking of feminine finger nails against the door. It opened to reveal Mai Tin, radiant in her classic beauty. She stepped briskly inside and, as Hank quickly became aware, every movement and gesture of her body bespoke an icy detachment. Not the supple, sinuous woman he had held in his arms only a few nights earlier, she was now encased in reserve. She turned crisply toward him and started to speak but he interrupted by holding up his hand. He went to the phonograph and dropped several records on the changer.

She cocked her head, one eyebrow raised questioningly. "I hope you don't think —" Again he stopped her, and almost at once the pungent voice of Billie Holiday lamented, "My man don't love me, treats me awful mean." Mai Tin turned away and sat down in a nearby chair. "Peetah asked me," she said in her enchantingly exotic voice, "to get your impressions of his speech."

"Fine. Get you a drink first?"

She hesitated, the veneer of ice on the verge of cracking. Then she stiffened. "Yes, please. An orange squash, if you don't mind."

When Hank returned with a glass tinkling with ice her eyes were turned toward the phonograph, thoughtfully and questioningly. "Who is that singer?"

"Billie Holiday. A great lady. Maybe the best."

Mai Tin's eyes narrowed, as Billie said, "He wears high-draped pants, stripes are really yellow. But when he starts in to love me, he is so fine and mellow." Buster Bailey's smooth skinned clarinet took over and carried forward the blues while Teddy Wilson interlaced strings of diamonds around the melody. "Her voice is so wry, so bittersweet, so knowing."

"Yes," said Hank, his regard for Mai Tin's instinctive taste mounting another degree. "Exactly." He raised his glass toward her, "Here's to Peter's success."

"Yes. To Peter." She sipped her orange drink. "What did you think?"

"I'm no judge of political speeches in general and certainly not a judge of what appeals to voters in Singapore, but I was impressed."

"Impressed?"

"Very. I thought he conveyed tremendous conviction and power. If I were a voter I think I would believe he could do what he said he could do."

"What's your American expression? *'Can do'?*"

"Exactly."

Mai Tin nearly permitted a smile budding at the corners of her mouth to come into bloom but instead straightened her back and frowned into her drink. Billie had left off lamenting her departed "fine and mellow" lover and was now singing nostalgically of "Yesterdays," Oscar Hammerstein's ornately romantic lyrics strikingly delineated by that bittersweet voice: "Joyous, free, and flaming life then sooth was mine!"

She stood up suddenly, placing her glass on the low table before her. "I must go," she said with that beguiling lilt. "Peetah will be expecting me."

Hank walked over to her. "I have something for you to take to Peter." He pulled an envelope from his jacket pocket.

"What is it?"

"A receipt for him to sign for one thousand dollars."

She pursed her mouth. "He won't sign it."

"Why not?"

She shook her head. "On principle. Peetah is a gentleman. He keeps his word. It would be demeaning."

"It's just business."

She gave him an icy look. "Not exactly."

Hank felt stymied. He knew Headquarters would insist on a receipt. "I must have his receipt for my accounting record."

"That's between you and your organization. Doesn't concern Peetah."

Hank sighed and gazed at the elegant, indomitable little figure before him. "Well, Mai Tin. Then I'll have to take it up directly with him."

"As you like. But he won't sign it. He never signed anything for the British." She turned and strode quickly to the door, her back stiff. Hank moved quickly behind her and took her by the shoulders. With one swift motion he pulled her to him and kissed her. The mouth he had known before to be clinging and searching was now tight at first but then softened slightly. She broke away and looked up at him, more vexed than angry.

"Mr. Blade —Hank. You must understand something. We *both* must understand something." Her eyes with their lashes that curved up slightly at the corners were intently serious. "We are not lovers. We cannot *be* lovers. Despite the other night —"

"Do you regret the other night?"

Her eyes softened a little. "No. No regrets." She took a deep breath and looked directly into his eyes. "I will not even say it may not happen again, but not —"

"Not as an assumed right," he finished for her.

She nodded. "Yes."

He smiled warmly. "You are an extraordinary woman, Mai Tin. Unique."

She smiled thinly. "Maybe you find me different because I am neither entirely Chinese nor entirely European. Like Peetah, I am something in between."

"It's an enchanting mixture." He leaned down and kissed her forehead. "Goodnight. Tell Peter I would like to meet him at the villa when he can arrange it."

She shook her head firmly. "It will not do any good."

On the way into his office next morning, Hank was hailed by Buck Jones as he passed his office door. "Hey, Bladesly," he yelled. "Come in here. I want to check something out with you."

"Yes?" Hank stood in the doorway gazing at the big, bluff man wearing a small boy's knowing grin.

"What's this I hear about you nosing around some of that yellow stuff?"

"What?"

"Peter Risko tells me he saw you strolling down Beach Road the other night with a tight-assed little Chinese filly."

"Oh." Hank shook his head. "That was a girl I happened to meet at the record shop."

"Yeah, I know. I'll just bet!" Buck nodded knowlingly. "Are you sure that wasn't one of Ian Ainsley's left-overs?" Hank shook his head and waited for the grin to subside before moving on. "Oka-a-ay. Okay." Then the grin vanished from Buck's face as though wiped with a squeegee. "Put a note on your desk. Special staff meeting. Hizzonner, the ambassador, has got some kind of burr up his ass."

Ambassador Lampman's face was set and serious as he sat at his desk and waited for the embassy officers to find seats. "I've called you together because I believe we moved last night into an emergency situation, a *dangerous* emergency situation. I want to discuss the situation with you and then determine how we can best protect all of you and your families. Bill McDonald will outline where we are and what the future holds."

McDonald, a somewhat formless man with a doughy face, rose. "Any of you who read the front page of *The Straits Times* this morning must realize that the Chinese Communists declared war on the British and the Singapore Government last night. Yee Hak Tho, in words as plain as they can be, called for all Asians to unite in a struggle against non-Asians. And that was stated in barely disguised Communist terms: 'Asia for Asians,' 'The voice of the people,' 'Our party,' and so on. There was also an allusion to the millions of Overseas Chinese in the region: 'Our friends are near.' Having made this declaration of war, it's only a matter of time before Yee Hak Tho leads the charge. It may start out as a riot or a large demonstration, but after it starts it will spread like wildfire. The British will be no match for such massed violence. They will be overwhelmed. The only thing we Americans can do is hole up and wait for the Seventh Fleet to come to our rescue. A week ago I said it could happen in six months. Now I think it could happen tomorrow. Or today."

Ambassador Lampman nodded. "Thanks, Bill." He looked grimly around at the assembled staff. "Any questions?"

Buck Jones turned and looked with a knowing smile at Hank who refused to meet his eyes.

"All right," said the ambassador. "Nick will now outline our Emergency Plan."

Nick Proctor, the deputy chief of mission, stood up. "Our plan is to assemble all official Americans and their families in this building at the first sign of trouble. Each section chief will be responsible for making out a roster for his people and for contacting them when the ambassador gives the word. We are requisitioning cots immediately and requesting the Air Force at Clark Field in Manila to provide us with a stock of emergency rations." He paused and looked around. "Okay. That's it."

The ambassador turned to Buck Jones. "Your people getting any twinges on the grape vine about this?"

Buck threw out his chest and looked thoughtful. "Nothing very specific yet, sir, but we're working on it. I must say it doesn't come as any great surprise — to me, at least." He looked around and his gaze came to rest on Hank.

The ambassador nodded. "All right, people. Everybody keep his ears and eyes open. We've all got to stick together."

Walking back to their offices, Peter Risko muttered to

Hank. "Can you think of anything more idotic than jamming us all together so we'll be easy to find if trouble comes?" He looked at Hank who just nodded, his thoughts in turmoil. His confidence in Peter Yee was not quite unseated but it certainly had been disturbed by what he had just heard, coming on top of Peter's refusal to sign a receipt for the money he had been given. Headquarters always insisted that agents had to be tied down with a signed agreement, and the usual first step was to get a signed reciept which made the signing of an agent's agreement seem less traumatic to the agent. Peter had balked at the first jump so the whole operation was in limbo. Besides, McDonald had spoken with such assurance. To be sure, Hank had little regard for McDonald's judgement but he was after all a serious student of Communism. Was it possible he was right and Hank, who had only the word of a young, fiercely ambitious Chinese, was wholly wrong? Had he been duped by one of those elaborate charades at which the Chinese are so skilled and for which they are so justly famous? Was the whole thing a hoax to get Yee out from under the charge of murder which Hank could bring against him?

Peter Risko paused before his office door. "I don't know, Blades. The whole thing sounds bizarre to me. Uncharacteristic. Un-Chinese. Don't you agree?"

Hank shook his head. "I just don't know, Pete. Who can be sure?" He walked into his office and found on his desk a FLASH precedence cable. It was stark: "UNCLE CRITICAL. COME IMMEDIATELY." Beneath it was another message: "HEADQUARTERS AUTHORIZES IMMEDIATE COMPASSIONATE LEAVE." He stared at the two papers for a moment, stone-faced while his mind was reeling, and then carried them in his hand to Buck Jones' office.

"I know. Ethel just told me. Tough luck, fellow. Better close up your safe and start packing.

Before leaving his office for his apartment, Hank wrote

a quick cable on the back channel to Headquarters. "PROVIDING LARK WITH LETTER DROP FOR TRANSMISSION REPORTS FROM KINGBIRD." This told the people in Washington who were monitoring the Yee operation that Mai Tin was being given a means of transmitting Peter Yee's reports on Communist activities. Then he telephoned Mai Tin and insisted she meet him for lunch. After a hurried packing at home he met her in the crowded, incredibly noisy cafe on Beach Road.

Unlike their most recent meeting she was relaxed and her smile enchanting. She brought all her delicious femininity and glistening beauty to bear on Hank and said archly, in her exotic voice, "You know, we were together just last night. Does business require meeting this regularly?"

Hank was abrupt. "In this case, it does." He then told her he was leaving for the United States and explained to her the procedure for using the letter drop. She promised to set it in motion and then asked, her face thoughtful and eyes questioning, "When will you be back?"

"I don't — know."

An hour later he watched out the window as the Pan Am Boeing Stratocruiser gathered speed on the runway and lifted off over the ship-strewn harbor. His mind returned to Mai Tin's question. "Maybe never," he muttered to himself.

Centered in the Sphere of Common Duties

One

Morning had come to Hanson fresh and sweet after the storm. During the oppressive mid-July night a tremendous thunderstorm had shaken the Maine sky with great shocks of thunder and torn the clouds with lightning. The flashes glared blue-white through the curtains in Hank's bedroom. But now the air was crystalline and new washed, smelling of spruce needles and salt water, and the grass and leaves were tipped with glistening rain-drops. Hank strode vigorously along Maine Street on his way to *The Courier* office, feeling his hearty breakfast within him and savoring the crisp post-storm air.

His first task of the day would be to write an editorial for the up-coming edition. Recently he had written about the need for Hanson citizens to be patient and courteous with summer visitors, the requirement for better traffic control, and the threat of national inflation. He kept a list of potential editorial subjects in his desk but he really wanted something new.

Waiting at the curb to cross Maine Street to *The Courier* building he saw the green Portland bus coming toward him. It stopped at the bus stop half a block away for a waiting passenger. A middle-aged woman about a hundred yards farther away came running toward the bus stop, hand raised in the air. As the bus moved out into the street, Hank ran toward it, one hand held palm up and the other pointing to the running woman. Without slowing the bus driver snarled something inaudible through the windshield as he went by, leaving the woman panting at the bus stop.

"I tried my best to stop him," said Hank.

"I saw you did. They're just awful, those bus drivers. That's twice this week they've pulled out when I was less than twenty feet away. They wouldn't wait an extra second for the Queen of England. Now I'll miss the morning visiting hours for my husband at Portland Hospital. Next bus isn't till noon."

"That's a shame. Do you take the bus every day?"

"Have been for three weeks, since his heart surgery. About to go broke doing it. The fare's four fifty each way."

"Four dollars and a half to Portland? That's an outrage."

"Sure is. And the buses are dirty, rattle-trap affairs with torn seat cushions and cracked windows."

Crossing the street, filtering through the stream of passing cars bearing license plates from New York, New Jersey, Pennsylvania, and Illinois, Hank realized he had found his editorial subject. Pat Long, his assistant editor, greeted him as always with her over-eager smile. "Good morning, Chief. How does it look this morning?"

"Looks good. I've just got an idea for an editorial. Have you got enough to keep you busy this morning?"

"I've got to write up that lecture last night on Maine colonial history, and I've got to get over to the court house at 11 to get the results of that damage suit trial."

"How are we for fillers? Got enough for this issue?"

"Betty Craig is coming in to work up some more after high school this afternoon."

"Okay. I'm going to start making up the paper as soon

as I write this editorial." Hank took off his jacket and sat down before his Underwood typewriter, sliding two sheets into the roller and centering them. Before starting to write he thought of his Uncle Jim who had sat at this desk for so many years and wondered how he would handle the subject. Probably would have approved, Hank felt. In fact, he probably would have approved most, if not all, the changes Hank had made since his just-too-late arrival from Singapore three years before. He had found his Uncle Jim dead of a devastating heart attack and his Aunt Grace reduced to blubbering confusion. His uncle had left his widow a house, a mildly successful newspaper, and a few thousand dollars in insurance. She was unable to cope with her grief, let alone take command of her life. Her younger sister, who came from California to assist, took her home with her after a few weeks and Aunt Grace had remained in California ever since. Bound by his promise, Hank had taken over *The Courier,* his aunt's sole source of income. Within a year he had transformed Hanson's local newspaper from a semi-weekly to a thrice-weekly, and the rise in advertising revenues that the move had accomplished made him feel *The Courier* could become a daily in due course.

But now to the editorial. "The people of Hanson," he wrote, "are poorly served by the Hanson-Portland Bus Line. This is true on three counts: (1) the buses are old and poorly maintained; (2) the drivers are neither considerate nor courteous; (3) the fare is exorbitant. The time has come for the Hanson-Portland Bus Company to improve itself."

He flipped the line lever and spaced the next line for a new paragraph. "Simultaneous improvement in these three areas," he wrote and the telephone on his desk began to ring.

"Hank, this is Anne Pintel. I'm at the cottage down at the Point. I just got in on the morning train from New York, and I can't get some of the windows to open. I also can't figure out how to turn the water on. Do you know someone who can do it for me?"

"Anne, I'll run out there at noon-time. Is Bob with you?"

"No. No, he's not."

"Oh? Well, okay. I'll be along in about an hour." He put the phone down and turned back to the uncompleted sentence on the yellow copy paper before him. Anne Pintel. He remembered first meeting her at an engagement party Bob had given shortly after his return from Singapore. She was Anne Sawyer then. She wore a severely tailored blue suit, and she seemed to move with a strange, jerky gaucherie. Words came sharp-edged and clipped from her small mouth, and her wit was often stinging. As he took Margaret home that night in his uncle's old Plymouth, Hank had said, "Not to be crude, but I wonder whether Bob is going to find porcupine quills under his bride's nightgown on their wedding night." Later, marriage seemed to transform Anne unbelievably. She returned from their Bermuda honeymoon radiant and sunnily open. That was over three years ago and Hank had seen her only once since their return from Bob's post as *Tribune* correspondent in London. Then she had seem subdued.

He picked up the sentence where he had left off, ". . . may prove difficult but drivers can be instructed starting tomorrow to drive with greater consideration for other traffic, to treat passengers courteously, and to wait two or three seconds for those running to catch the bus."

He checked the editorial over and took it out to the print shop to George, sitting amidst the clatter and smell of molten linotype. On his way back to his desk he caught Pat as she was leaving for the court house. He described the slant of the editorial. "Take the Contax with you and see if you can get any pictures to support a story. See if you can catch him stopping out in the middle of the road with a line of cars behind him or something like that."

"Do my best, Chief." Hank stood at the window for a moment, watching her angular, nervous figure as she made her way through the passing throng of summer tourists in their shorts and halter tops, Yarmouth faculty wives in dirndl skirts and kerchiefed heads, and native, French-Canadian women, swarthy and dumpy. Momentarily, his mind strayed to the contrast of street scenes in Singapore but he shook his head and dismissed the thought. That was three years ago and in another life. He turned away and headed toward the make-up bench in the press room. Now for the part he enjoyed most in the newspaper business: make-up.

He decided to run the bus line story as a block across the bottom of the front page with whatever picture Pat got placed in the center. If she failed to connect, he could re-do the bottom of the page with something else. He went ahead laying out the rest of the issue. As usual, he found it absorbing and satisfying, and he was surprised to find it was nearly 12:00 when Pat came running in.

"Oh, boy, did I get it! I caught the inbound bus at Church Street with a line of about ten cars stopped behind him, and I got him at Coffin Street on the return, just pulling out as a middle-aged woman was trying to catch the bus. I got a separate picture of her later and an interview about the lousy bus service. She really unhooked her corset cover."

"Great! Take the camera over to Herbie and see if he can do a rush job on the prints. We'll have to get them down to the engraver this afternoon and back first thing in the morning."

After Pat had left, Hank stuck his head in the cubby-hole office of Agnes, the fifty-ish spinster who served as secretary, file clerk, bursar, proof-reader, and general assistant.

"Back in about an hour, Ag."

In the alley behind the building he started the green panel truck with "The Hanson Courier" in gold letters along its side, and elbowed his way into the traffic headed east along the road to Summer Point. He crossed the railroad tracks and passed the Yarmouth College campus, glancing at his house with its white siding and green shutters as he went by. Odd he should suddenly think of Singapore this morning. He was doing it less and less as time passed. Three years now. Someone in Singapore must have been thinking about him. Mai Tin, perhaps. He smiled, savoring the very act of thinking of Mai Tin.

At first, during those terrible months of forcing himself to accept the violent change Uncle Jim's death had bestowed on him, he had followed events in Singapore with avidity, reading every scrap to be found in *The New York Times* and on the UPI ticker. They had been exciting times in Singapore as Peter Yee, known to the formal *Times* only as Yee Hak Tho, had won his election to the Singapore assembly overwhelmingly, had assumed unquestioned leadership over the People's Voice Party, taken a leading role in negotiating Singapore's transition from British Crown Colony to an independent city-state, and had been made prime minister of the new-hatched government at the astonishingly early age of 33. Erudite correspondents in Singapore had written learned comparisons of Yee Hak Tho with William Pitt the Younger and his ascension to British prime minister at age 25.

It seemed likely he would never see Singapore again although CIA Headquarters had insisted on an arrangement that theoretically could cause it to happen. When he had got Aunt Grace bundled off to California and had faced with finality the bitter realization that his CIA career was over and he was condemned to spend his life as a small-town Maine newspaper publisher, he had gone to Washington to resign from the Agency. He quickly found himself involved in a prolonged negotiation which ended in a session with Pickard Grant, the Director. "We can't let you resign, Hank. You're the man who set this Yee Hak Tho thing in motion, and we may need you sometime if it gets off the track. I want to put you on indefinite leave of absence with an option to call on you when necessary. That way, we can hold your clearances intact and can use you at a moment's notice."

"That's very flattering, sir, but I —"

"We're agreed then," said Grant and put out his hand to shake in goodbye. That was three years ago and things seemed to be progressing splendidly for Peter Yee. Hank's judgment about Yee's future had been absolutely right. All, and even more, that he had foreseen for Peter had come to pass. He had cause for pride.

A speed bump at the entrance to Summer Point jolted the panel truck and brought Hank back to reality. He slowed as he approached Bob Pintel's house, the fifth one on the left. As he stepped down to the gravel driveway Hank paused to gaze at Fisherman's Cove, a bare fifty yards away and glittering and flashing in the noonday sun. A half mile out a white-hulled, red-cabined lobster boat was working, the lobsterman leaning over the gunwale to re-bait his wooden-slatted trap and drop it back in the green water. The chugging of his diesel engine accelerated and slowed, with blue exhaust wafting across its stern.

Ann Pintel met him at the screen door. "I'm such a nuisance, Hank. So useless. You're very good to come." She stood back for him to enter, feet slightly apart, her shoulders set stiffly back, her head cocked slightly to one side. She was as tall as Margaret, five feet six or so, and she gave the impression of being more slender than perhaps she was. Her breasts lifted her white blouse handsomely and her navy blue linen skirt smoothed over strong hips.

"Good to see you Anne. How's Bob?"

"He's, uh" — she stammered — "all right."

Hank located the breaker in the circuit box which started the pump for the water. Two of the three stuck windows responded to a strong upward shove but one required a little prying with a screw driver. He found one in a box on the floor beneath the circuit box and shortly had the window moving smoothly. "There you are. Anything else?"

"No, thank you so much. Before you go, I found a bottle of sherry in the cupboard. Will you join me?"

He hesitated. "A very quick one. I've got to stop by the house for a sandwich, and I'm in the midst of putting tomorrow's edition to bed."

"A quick one." She poured two small glasses, handed one to Hank, and raised hers in salute. "Cheers!"

He responded with a nod, noticing how her deep-set blue eyes above her high cheek bones shone beneath her dark brown hair. It was a strong face, strong bones and firm chin, but the small mouth looked hesitant and uncertain. Its smile was tight and thin. "When is Bob coming up?"

She gulped, nearly choking on her drink. Her eyes looked stricken and she averted her face toward the shimmering light glancing off the water below the house. "I don't — know." Again she gulped. She turned back. "I'm sorry, Hank. Dammit, I told myself I wouldn't cry. Well, I haven't — quite." She wiped her eyes with a tissue and produced another of her thin smiles. "Bob and I are separated at present. I think he wants a divorce. He found someone else, an English girl, in London."

"Anne, I'm sorry." He put out his hand to her and to his surprise she came into his arms, her strong body pressed hard against his. He held her for a moment and then, with pats on her shoulder, released her. "Maybe this will pass like some of Bob's other wild-eyed enthusiasms."

She shook her head, her fine hair flying out away from her head with the movement. "I doubt it. But I'll be all right."

"I'm sure you will." He smiled at her. "Sorry I can't stay. I've got to run. But I'll be back. Call me whenever you need anything."

"Thank you." She held out her slender hand and her grip

was firm and strong. Quickly she rose on her toes and kissed his cheek. "You're nice," she said.

"Bye, Anne. Call me."

He drove the panel truck quickly back to his house and hurried inside. On the pine kitchen table he found a ham sandwich wrapped in wax paper left for him by Mrs. Church who came in daily to house-keep. He took a bottle of Molson's Export Ale out of the refrigerator and ate his sandwich in quick bites, washing it down with the ale.

Back at the wheel of the truck, Hank suddenly found himself remembering the strong thrust of Anne's body against his and the playful peck on the cheek. An intriguing woman. Complex. Compelling.

The finished prints of Pat's pictures were just what he wanted. All except the close-up of the woman she interviewed were sharp — "damn, I forgot to re-focus after that distance shot" — and the picture of the woman running vainly after the bus clearly depicted her dismay.

"You did fine, Pat. Let's get these on their way to the engraver in Portland."

"Okay, Chief." She took the prints into her cubicle and shortly later he heard her chuckling to herself.

"What's so funny?"

"Do you know how we get these rush jobs down and back?"

"Special delivery mail?"

"No. It's a deal I made with the bus driver. I just hand them to him and he drops them off at the engraver's."

"Oh, no. Well, this may be the last time we can do that."

Hank went back to making up and by late afternoon the edition was set. In the morning he would drop the cuts in place in the matrix and start the run. He glanced around the office with its scraps and crumpled paper balls here and there on the worn floor. Everyone else had gone for the day, so he pulled the large white blinds on the windows across the front of the office and went out the door, locking it with the big brass key his Uncle Jim had left behind. He strolled down the street to the post office to pick up the mail. There was a letter from Bob Pintel in the box which Hank read as he walked slowly along the sidewalk.

"Dear Blades. Just a quick note to ask you to keep an eye out for Anne. As she will no doubt tell you we are separated. I'm sorry as hell but it just didn't work out. Too many problems. Meanwhile, I found The Perfect Woman for me in London. Diane Morgan. You'll love her. Write again soon. Bob."

"Perfect Woman number six," Hank muttered. Bored with the butterfly immaturity of Bob Pintel he turned his mind to the enjoyment of a late summer afternoon in small town Maine. The grass on the Common along the west side of Maine Street had just been mowed and the new-cut blades suffused the warm air with a pungent, green smell. The quintessence of summer, he said inwardly. The noble Federal-style houses across the Common shone immaculately white through the densely-leaved maple trees. Ahead, the traditional First Congregational church lifted its prim, clean-lined steeple in the afternoon sky. On the campus of Yarmouth College a half dozen summer students were playing one-o'-cat softball while a hand-holding couple smiled at him as they passed by, their young legs tanned and slender below their shorts. It was Hank's favorite time of day, the quiet calm and the slanting yellow light after the heat and the bustle.

But this time of day inside the lonely white house was another matter. Ahead of him lay a long, solitary evening unless he yielded to the easy alternative, which he did more often than he thought wise or really enjoyed, of telephoning Margaret. Margaret was still unfinished business. Their relationship was becoming more and more unbalanced: she assuming it to be permanently established; he finding doubt within him steadily growing. They had a sporadic sexual relationship which, he recognized, acted each time to cement certainty in Margaret's mind but left him with a faintly guilty and uneasy feeling. He was not ready for permanence. Not with Margaret, at least not yet, and possibly not with anybody. Ever. Just over the horizon of his mind the nascent thought was glimmering that perhaps commitment to one person was not within him. He decided not to call Margaret.

He opened the green porcelain-knobbed door of his uncle's house and walked straight to the refrigerator. He poured a dollop of scotch over ice cubes and, holding the glass in one hand, opened the oven door with the other and found the casserole and glass-covered carrots Mrs. Church had prepared for his supper. He turned the oven on to 300 and walked, drink in hand, to his phonograph and put on the top record of the stack. It was Count Basie and soon Jimmy Rushing was hollering in his lyrically sorrowful voice, "I lef' my baby, standin' in the back door cryin'." Behind him, Lester Young wove a counter-melody with his smooth-skinned, limber-jointed tenor sax while Basie's piano commented sparingly and drily. After Jimmy's solo the muscular ensemble took over the blues theme. Toward the end of the record, as the brass section hit solid block chords and the reeds climbed a rising stairway in a vain attempt to shout the brass down, Hank decided he was right not to call Margaret. He took a long swallow of whiskey while Harry Edison ended the bickering between the brass and reeds with a broad-toned trumpet flourish.

While he ate supper in the plain kitchen, Hank put the latest copy of *Newsweek* beside his plate and read while he ate his solitary meal. Nothing much of interest in Periscope. He turned the pages idly with his left hand while his right handled his fork. Suddenly he stopped, his eyes arrested by a model in a full-page Chevrolet ad. She was standing, feet wide apart and shoulders stiffly back, just as Anne Pintel had stood while greeting him at her cottage door. He paused for a moment, remembering Anne's sharp-lined comeliness and then, later, the strong thrust of her body against his and the mischievous toss of her head after she had kissed his cheek.

Next morning he was waiting at the office door as Pat entered with the package from the engraver in her hand. He took the cuts for the bus story into the press room and ran off proofs on the hand machine. They came out sharp as diamonds, the blacks deep and glossy and the edges clean. He checked the alignment of the cuts after Walt, the assistant press man, had dropped them into place and then had page proofs done for each page. After he and Pat checked off each headline, relying on the galley proofs to keep the text clean, he was satisfied he had done all he could for the issue. He waved his hand to George and the press began to roll.

Back in his office he reflected on the bus story and what its impact might be. Combined with the editorial, it represented his most aggressive stance since his uncle's departure. His position was sound he knew, but public opinion can be unpredictable. Also, some of his advertisers might find a bond of sympathy with the bus company owners. But then he shrugged. Occasional risks were inevitable in the news business, just as they had been in the spy trade. He could only wait for the reaction that was likely to come.

Two

When the sharp buzzing of the little clock at her bedside at last pierced Anne Sawyer Pintel's consciousness, she reached out her hand and pressed the little plunger. The buzzing stopped as though snipped with shears, and then she could hear the rhythmic beat of a lobster boat engine offshore from Summer Point. Through the window across the bedroom she could hear an assertive chickadee, "Chick-a-dee-dee-dee." Gradually these morning sounds dissolved and flowed into nonsensical fancies as her attention loosed its moorings and drifted into drowsing. There her mind flowed sightlessly and soundlessly through time, unaware and unaware it was unaware, until somewhere within her a bubble of sentience let go inexplicably and rose slowly to the surface. It broke soundlessly and Anne woke up.

The clock said ten past eight. Time to get up. She flipped the covers back and put her feet over the side, her nightgown rising up over her hips and then settling back to her ankles as she stood straight and stretched.

Then came the morning ceremony of brushing her teeth, the toothpaste running through her mouth like iced fire, and rinsing her face with cold water. Her mind noted without purpose the erratic splash of the water as it struck the sloping white side of the bowl and leaped away in odd-sized splinters and fragments.

She stood for a moment, irresolute and undirected. Morning decisions were always difficult, especially before coffee and orange juice. Coffee. She went down the creaking wooden stairs into the little kitchen and started the coffee. Outside the kitchen window the tiny black-capped bird was still insisting he was "chickadee-dee-dee." With a glass of orange juice, she went slowly into the living room and stood before the phonograph. Set in their racks were the albums with the magic names: Mozart, Bartok, Sibelius, Haydn, Barbour, Ravel, Corelli, Bach . . . At random she pulled out an album: Robert Casadesus playing Ravel's *Tombeau de Couperin.* Then with the intricate texture of the Prelude filling the room she went upstairs and into the bathroom. Her eye fell on a pair of stockings hanging over the back of the white wooden chair. They needed washing out.

Standing before the lavatory while the water flowed cold and then gradually warm, her eyes ran unjudgingly across her mirrored face, the deep-set blue eyes and the strong cheekbones. She ran her fingers lightly over her face and then hard along the cheekbone back to her ear. While the pool of water gathered quickly in the bowl and crept up the sides, the lilting cascades of Ravel's music washed into her mind and gently stirred it toward wakefulness and delight. She pulled her rapt attention away from the rising water and rinsed out her stockings.

In a moment Casadesus was playing the Forlane and Anne listened with expectant joy to that marvelous upward leap of the opening phrase, springing so lightly and landing so improbably at the most unexpected and exactly right place. "The most superb interval in modern music" her professor of music history at Columbia had called it. It was to her the very essence of agile grace and muscled elegance. Suddenly, unbidden,her mind presented an image of David leaping up onto a rock, his lean thighs ridged with tensed muscle, the slanting western sun glistening on his tanned back and the wash of the Pacific surf below.

David. David Link. Her first love. Her true love. His father an Army colonel at the Presidio. David now living somewhere near San Diego, married to the daughter of another Army colonel. That day at the beach had ended, like so many other days at the shore with the group around the fire eating their sandwiches and laughing at the horseplay of the boys. Later the group dissolved into the darkness, and Anne and David, with their blanket, found a soft patch of sand near an enormous boulder. Then the kisses. Happy, gay kisses; hard kisses, abrupt, more expressive of joy and youth than passion. But then David's hand, gritty with sand, had found her breast beneath her bathing suit, and suddenly they were caught up in a mounting, blinding necessity. Later, after the tumult, when awareness returned, Anne heard the gentle wash and hiss of the Pacific and the spent boy beside her whimpering.

"Oh, Anne, Anne! What have I done to you? I'm so sorry. So sorry."

Anything, she thought. Anything in the wide, wide world. But *not sorry!* "Darling," she said, "darling. It's all right." She stroked his head with languorous fingers, full of love and — infinite — *infinite* — tenderness. "It's all right."

He shook his head. "No, it's *not* all right. I don't know why I didn't stop. I'll do anything to make it up to you. Anything."

Love me, she thought to herself. Love me. But she continued to stroke his handsome head and crooned gently, "It's all right, David. All right."

He lay silently a moment and then slowly raised up. "You mean you really didn't mind? You mean. . .?"

Mind? Of course she minded. It was tragic and wrong but it was perfect and right. It was an unforeseen and heedless farewell to girlhood but it was David and the sea and darkness and young love. It nearly overpowered her, just thinking about it and it was much, *much* too much to say to David. Then or ever. "It's all right, darling," she repeated.

He lay quietly for a long time and then slowly got to his feet. "We'd better go back, Anne," he said.

She had pulled her clothing back together and followed him, still numb with love and wanting somehow to cry. They walked slowly back to the campfire and shortly later went home. And that was the end of her love affair with David.

What it was she never knew for certain. The only explanations that came to mind were too wounding to her fragile self-esteem. But it was over. They saw each other occasionally but after their graduation next year from high school he went East to college and she never saw him again. But she never forgot him. Still, even now, she had sudden starts when the sight of a distant figure tricked her mind momentarily into thinking it was David. And yet, she would never see him again.

Then along came Robert Pintel, self-assured certainty personified, and after wrestling her self-doubts to earth, willing herself to believe she could make a full-hearted commitment to him and to marriage, she had accepted him and clung to his certainty like a swimmer to a rock. And now, that too —

Enough, Anne, she told herself. Enough. Pull yourself together, old girl. The world outside is brimming with summer and inside the music of Ravel, Bach, and Mozart still lifts the spirit. With set purpose she quickly dressed herself and came down the stairway just as Casadesus was sounding the last vigorous chords of the *Tombeau.* In the kitchen she turned the coffee off, made toast, and sat down to her spartan breakfast. Afterward she took her bottle green, gold-striped Raleigh bicycle, with its wicker basket strapped to the handlebars, out of the shed and rode off down the road toward the College.

She loved bicycling, the soft morning air on her face, the tang of the red spruces, and later the quiet fragrance of sweet meadow grass and purple clover, the occasional cry of a nearby meadow lark. She had gone less than a half mile when she saw a green truck coming toward her. It slowed and stopped and the smiling face of Hank Bladesly greeted her, "Where are you bound, my pretty maid?"

She stopped, her feet wide apart straddling the low bar of the bicycle. "Good morning, Hank. I'm on my way up to the college. I want to see whether I can enroll in a summer school course."

"Sounds like a good idea. I was just coming by to see you."

"Oh?"

"I want to invite you to have dinner with me tonight at the Inn."

"Lovely. I'd love it."

"Great. I'll come by about 6:30."

With a nod of his head, Hank dropped the truck into gear and went down to a cross-road to turn around. Handsome man, thought Anne, as she slid back up on the seat and pedaled on. No, *handsome* wasn't good enough. Strong, purposeful. By comparison, she reflected as the wind of her passage blew her fine hair off her forehead and rushed softly past her ears, Bob Pintel's assurance seemed flashy, almost contrived. This man had strength. Inner strength.

At dinner that night she sipped at her daiquiri and gazed out the broad, small-paned window of the Yarmouth Inn. Outside, the lawn glowed bright green in the slanting yellow light of the early evening. The flagstone walkway leading to the Inn was edged with summer flowers: purple asters, brash red and yellow zinnias, droopy-headed peonies and demure pink and yellow roses, all basking in the glory of the setting sun. She watched without directed attention as an elderly couple, she in a flowing white dress and he in a leaf-green jacket, came slowly up the walk.

Across the table, Hank was describing the incident of the missed bus that had triggered his editorial. Anne was experiencing one of those moments, not uncommon to her, when reality seemed to slip out of focus. Here she was in this rough-beamed New England dining room, noisy with the clatter of forks and plates and the chatter of well-dressed diners, sitting across from this strong-jawed man. Her presence there at that moment — she who had been born and spent her girlhood on a seacoast the span of a continent away — was so unlikely, being the consequence of innumerable fragments of interacting incidents, as to make its reality questionable. And yet, here was Hank Bladesly talking quietly to her with a calm assurance that was comforting.

"It's hard to predict how this thing will turn out," Hank was saying. "People may be alienated, especially business friends of the bus owner, and I may lose my shirt in advertising. But I felt I had to do it."

"You will come out just fine." She sipped her daiquiri slowly, trying to stabilize the irresolution within, trying to be a good guest for this man whose presence reassured her. She looked up, smiling brightly. "Guess what I did today. I enrolled in two courses for the second half of summer school. History of art and history of music."

"Ambitious. Are they special interests of yours?"

"Yes. Music more than art. Music is my passion."

'What kind of music?"

"Everything from baroque to the moderns, Bach to Bartok."

"Only classical."

She was puzzled. "Well, the French impressionists, Debussy and Ravel, are not..."

"Not jazz."

She wrinkled her nose at him. "Not jazz. Jazz is just a lot of fast noise."

"Do you know Duke Ellington?"

"I know his name. He has a jazz orchestra."

"Right so far. But fast noise is not what he plays." He smiled across the table at her. "Tell you what I'll do. On the way to your house I'll stop by and pick up a couple of Duke's records to play for you."

When they arrived at Anne's cottage a grey fog was rolling in, softening the glow of lights from nearby houses and muting the sound of the nearby shore. The moist air smelled of the sea and stranded seaweed. In the distance a hoarse bellow sounded, paused, and sounded again. "Listen to that!" Anne whispered. "It sounds like a mournful bull separated from the herd."

"That's Halfway Rock fog horn."

"How unromantic you are. I like the mournful bull better."

He chuckled. "All right. It *is* a lonely bull, his name is Beauregard and he's calling for his missing loved one, Chloe Belle."

She giggled. "That's better. A little."

Inside she turned to him, cocking her head. "Shall we have a drink with our music lesson?"

"Do you have any scotch?"

"I believe Bob left some. Let me see." In the pantry she found a bottle of Chivas Regal and made two drinks. As she handed Hank his glass she asked, "What are you going to play me?"

"A thing called 'Dusk', and I dedicate it to the lady who defines jazz as merely 'fast noise'."

She lifted her chin and nodded. "All right."

After a series of short runs and trills by Duke's piano, the piece began with three muted horns playing wide-spaced chords, stating a slow quiet theme while Duke inserted brief trills between the phrases. Then Rex Stewart's open cornet restated the theme while the reed section lay a spacious, luxurious background behind him. After a trombone trio had treated the melody with quiet solemnity, the original voicing of muted horns returned while Duke made a final brief comment.

Anne turned her cocked head toward Hank, her eyes expressing her pleasure. "That's lovely. Lovely. But is it jazz?"

"Well, it has a regular beat, though a slow one, and it's played by a jazz orchestra."

"Who wrote it?"

"Duke Ellington. He writes most of the things his band plays."

She reflected. "It's really a kind of tone poem. Something like Sibelius." She watched Hank as he crossed the room to the record player. "All right, I'm surprised. Impressed. Have you another record?"

"This one's faster, middle tempo. It's called 'Johnny Come Lately'."

Again, Duke's piano led the way and was immediately followed by Harry Carney's brisk and robust baritone saxophone, leaping wide minor key intervals down and up again, each leap stretching improbably farther and landing unexpectedly, then climbing a long minor stairway up to the firm landing of a major key. After Carney's first several leaps, Anne straightened suddenly and raised her finger as though to speak but then shook her head and leaned back, listening intently. After Lawrence Brown's suave and immaculately-garbed trombone gave voice to the bridge, the whole ensemble returned to the leaping melody, rising and falling with the precision of a ballet company. Tricky Sam Nanton growled with his trombone, giving the melody a rough-textured variation, followed by Duke playing a series of tightly-jammed complex chords. This led the reed section to emulate him with a similar series of mellifluous dissonances, and then Harry Carney took up the melody again, his heavy-bodied baritone displaying the light-footed agility of a gazelle.

Anne sat up straight again and said excitedly, "That interval" — she sang it in her high clear voice — "dah, *dah,* dih dah dah dah dih *dah,* that same interval is in a Ravel thing I was playing this morning." She leapt to her feet. "Let me show you." She went to the record player and dropped the stylus onto the Forlane section of *Tombeau de Couperin.* She pointed with her finger as Casadesus improbably leaped upward in an interval virtually identical to Duke's. "See? See?"

"Yes, I see."

As Ravel's gleaming sophisticated melody continued to unfold she brought Hank's record over to him. "You've convinced me. This is music worth knowing. Definitely not fast noise," she said with a crooked grin.

He got to his feet. "Good. You've opened a new vista for me too. You know, we ought to continue these music lessons."

She was delighted. "I'd love that."

"But now I must go, Anne. Big day tomorrow."

"Thank you for dinner."

His face became thoughtful and serious. "Anne, is Bob in the apartment in New York? Can I call him there?"

"I believe so."

"I will then. See if I can knock a little sense into his head. Or maybe I'll go down to New York for a day and straighten him out."

She was horrified, all her pleasure in the evening shattered. "Oh no, Hank! You mustn't. Please don't! Please *don't!*

"But why, Anne?"

She was very close to him now, and as she broke into sobs she stepped into his arms. "It's — over. I want it to be — over."

He stroked her head gently and held her in a firm, close

embrace. Neither spoke for a minute or two while he continued to stroke her. Her heart was beating violently and she began to tremble. In a moment she raised her head and looked up at him questioningly. He paused and then bent and kissed her gently. She responded gently at first but then pent-up emotion surged over the top and she kissed him passionately. Her knees were fluid when at last he released her. He held her with his hands on her shoulders, his dark eyes thoughtful. "I won't call Bob," he said. "And I'll be back to see you soon."

Three

Response to Hank's bus story was brisk. The first call, appropriately, was from Mrs. Adamski who said that the picture of her running for the bus was awful but she approved of the account and hoped it would do some good. Another call came from a man who commuted to Portland daily and thought it was about time someone did something about the bus situation. More calls came in all morning. About 10:30, Roger Boudreau, the round-faced mailman who wore a perpetual frown and complained about his feet, brought in several letters from readers who said *The Courier* was doing a good thing. But the morning and the rest of the day passed without any response from the Hanson-Portland Bus Company.

Hank spent the afternoon writing stories about the sale of a local shoe factory to a big Boston company, the struggle and survival of two lobstermen whose boat was rammed in dense fog by a 90-foot cabin cruiser from Connecticut, and the fall college plans of a group of recent Hanson High graduates. With these stories in hand and three more he had assigned to Pat, he began to block out the next issue. Without any response from the bus company, he decided to keep the pot boiling by printing several of the letters and by running a brief editorial calling for some public response from the bus line management. Before closing up the office he selected the letters and blocked out the editorial.

Next morning he handed a short, moderate-toned editorial — "No one expects the Hanson Bus Company to transform itself overnight into an ultra-modern system, but a beginning can be made" — to the linotype operator and stood by to read it as it emerged. George was already running a four-page advertising insert on the big Goss press and the floor of the old building vibrated in response to the beat of the heavy bed as it slammed back and forth. He could read cast type upside down, and he stood beside the make-up bench as young Bill dropped the slugs into the space in the editorial column. The editorial was letter perfect but it ran about two lines short. Bill dropped spacers between the lines until it justified and Hank waved an okay for George to start the run.

During the course of the afternoon and the next day he continued to get calls of congratulation, but there were also two post-cards in the mail, unsigned, which called him a trouble-maker. One referred to him as a "socialist meddler."

That afternoon the phone rang and a heavy, harsh voice said, "Mr. Bladesly, this is Joe Harding."

"Yes."

"You've been writing some criticisms of my bus line."

"That's right, Mr. Harding."

"I don't see any reason why two grown men can't sit down and talk out some kind of agreement, do you?"

"It ought to be possible."

"How about getting together sometime tomorrow?"

"I'll be ready any time."

"How'll it be if I come by around 10?"

"I'll be here."

Hank put the phone down and leaned back in his chair. Well, at least the threat was past that the bus company owner would simply ignore him. But then there was another worry. Suppose Joe Harding had nothing to offer. It was entirely possible he was already running the bus company to the best of his ability. Hank realized he might have to grasp at any straw to terminate his campaign, any gesture by Harding toward improvement might have to do.

He got up, restless, feeling confined, not in control. He had a sudden thought. He went to the doorway of Agnes' cubby-hole office. "I'm going down to the marina to check on my boat, Aggie. Tell Pat when she comes back to handle things the rest of the day."

On his way through the shop he waved a hand at George. "See you tomorrow." He let himself out the back door into the alley and got into the green *Courier* truck. As he was crossing the Boston and Maine railroad tracks the impulse came to drop by Anne Pintel's house. Perhaps she would join him. He had not talked with Anne since the night he took her to dinner but more than once in the intervening days, and nights, the memory of her strong embrace had surged into his mind. Surprise still lingered over the thrust of her strong body and the sensuousness of her kiss. Astonishing from a mouth so patricianly small. A part of his mind had longed to be with her again during the past few days but a restraint he could not quite identify had kept him away. Now, needing some brightness, something refreshing, he pushed the restraint aside.

He found her reading in her living room, a notebook on the small table beside her chair. She was wearing a loose yellow blouse and tennis shorts, her thighs beneath the shorts porcelain white but surprisingly full and luxuriant.

"Hi," she said and produced a smile more restrained than he expected.

"Studying?"

"Yes. I'm doing some advance reading for my courses."

"Can I lure you away to go look at my boat?"

She hesitated, frowning. "I told myself I had to finish this chapter before supper. But. . ." She looked away and then back. "Sure," she said, "I'll go." In a moment they were together in the truck, jouncing along the Upper Bay Road. "What is your boat?"

"She's a Seagull, small cabin sloop."

"My uncle had one in San Francisco. He kept her at Sausalito."

In ten minutes they were at the Safe Harbor Marina. Hank found an available dinghy and handed Anne into it. The sea as they rowed out to the mooring was shimmering and sparkling in the late afternoon sun. It was a glorious mid-summer day, the kind seacoast Maine produces infrequently enough to lend each one the value of a precious jewel. Anne sat in the stern sheets, looking off toward the opening of the cove, eyes squinting slightly in the bright light. She said nothing and to Hank's eye she looked pensive, quite unlike the gay young woman when they were last together. "Lot of boats," she finally said. "There's a Seagull just ahead. *Blue Teal.* Is she yours?"

"That's the one." Hank eased the dinghy alongside and flipped a loop of the bowline around a stanchion. He held the boat steady as Anne climbed over the gunwale into the cockpit, white thighs flashing in the afternoon sun. Then he shipped the oars and the oarlocks, let the dinghy drift astern and tied her painter with a figure-8 on the starboard cleat. "Just a second. I'll get some cushions." He unlocked the brass lock securing the hatch to the companionway and slid it back. Inside the cabin he lifted the locker lid and pulled out two cushions. Tucking them under his arm, he paused for a moment, savoring the snugness of *Blue Teal*'s cabin, the curved sides as they rounded to her bottom and narrowed to join at her bow lending the space enclosed a kind of magic. There is something quintessentially *right* about the shape of a boat. Like the curves of a woman's body as they dip to her waist and flare out over her hips, it makes a man's heart rejoice.

A slow swell coming through the entrance of the cove, a diminished survivor of a wave which had rolled off the Atlantic Ocean and up Casco Bay, lifted and rolled *Blue Teal* gently. Anne's head was peaking into the cabin as he turned to go back to the cockpit. "How beautifully you keep her!" she said. "She's immaculate."

"Thanks, but not quite. Those splash boards up forward need a coat of varnish. Here, have a cushion while I check a few things." Hank went forward and checked the roding on the bow cleat and found it snug and secure. One tie on the sail cover had worked loose but otherwise it was sound. Aft, he tightened the tiller lashings, and then went back into the cabin where he lifted up a floorboard and checked the bilge. She was carrying a couple of inches of water but he stuck a finger into it and tasted it. Definitely unsalty, it was condensation, the interaction of the cold sea against the outside of the hull and warmer air inside the boat. Not to worry. He dropped the board back in place and moved to the hatchway. He smiled up at Anne. "How about something to drink? I have sherry, gin and tonic, and some stale water. Alas, no ice."

"All things considered, I'll take the sherry."

"Wise choice."

Anne was gazing off to port watching a motor cruiser coming in through the winding, buoy-marked channel. As he handed her a glass of sherry, she turned back and smiled perfunctorily.

He raised his glass to her and said, "Problems?"

She frowned and looked down into her glass. "Yes. Oh well, not really. They're not worth talking about."

The cruiser, blue-hulled with white superstructure and a canopied flying bridge, slid past, laying down a wake that rolled *Blue Teal* vigorously. Anne held her drink out away from her body and balanced dexterously so that not a drop spilled. She smiled wryly. "There, you see? All Bay Area girls are natural seafarers."

"Very impressive."

Her smile faded, her face serious once again. "I guess I'm still trying to adjust to the change. Not being married, I mean." She shook her head and then looked seriously at Hank. "But you've made a major change in your life too, haven't you? A violent change, from Singapore to Maine. How have you handled that?"

Now it was his turn to gaze at the passing cruiser. "Oh, for the most part it's been all right, but recently. . ." He trailed off.

She smiled and reached out to squeeze his hand. "Yes?"

"Oh, it's that bus thing I told you about. I'm just not certain I'm doing anything more than creating a stink. Maybe I'll have to back down and look foolish in the process."

"Stuff and nonsense. It's a good cause and you know it. This is no time for a faint heart. Stay with it."

He grinned a little foolishly. "In other words, steady as she goes."

"That's better. More nautical."

They both chuckled and sipped at their drinks. Off to port a lobsterman was working his traps, the engine of his boat chugging a slow steady beat while he pulled up the crate-shaped traps, emptied the contents, re-baited, and tossed them back. Over the water the soft breeze wafted mingled smells of diesel exhaust and rotting fish bait. A clutch of seagulls circled the lobster boat and mewed shrill comments. Anne wrinkled her nose and turned back, the smile of a moment ago replaced with a pensive look.

Hank gazed at her thoughtfully. "Maybe you ought to talk about it. Might help."

She looked up quickly, her deep-set eyes troubled, and then looked away. After a while she murmured, "Yes." She took a deep breath. Hank watched while she leaned back against the coaming, her lovely thighs glowing in the afternoon sun. A sudden wave of affection mingled with burgeoning desire surged within him.

"I'm not certain how I can say this." She paused, looking stricken. She took another deep breath. "You see — well, dammit — I've never had much self-assurance." She hesitated, her deep-set eyes blinking. "I guess that's what attracted me to Robert. After Daddy died, I had no mooring to fasten to. Then along came Robert and he seemed so positive, so completely self-confident. I told myself his confidence could hold us both up. That would be enough. And now. . ." She stopped, biting her lower lip, her eyes welling.

Hank longed to take her in his arms but just then the lobster boat moved closer and the lobsterman in his yellow slicker pants yelled, "How you doing, Hank?"

It was Billy Dibbs, a high school classmate. "Hey, Billy! How's the fishing?"

"Lousy."

"Too many fishermen these days, I guess."

"Nope. Too few lobstahs."

Hank chuckled and waved a hand dismissively. "Okay, Billy."

Hank turned back to Anne, his eyes thoughtful. "I can only think of dumb things to say, Anne, but if. . ."

She leaned forward and took his hand again. "Good friend," she said. She squeezed gently. "It's time for me to get back."

"All right. I'll button up the boat." He took the two glasses down the companionway and rinsed them in the stainless steel basin. He glanced up into the cockpit where Anne was standing in the slanting afternoon sunlight, her hair radiant, her light blouse pressed against her breasts by the gentle breeze. "Before we go, Anne, let me show you the cabin."

She came down the varnished wood steps, moving with that characteristic delicate awkwardness. She started to say, "It *is* snug," but before she could finish he had folded her in his arms and pressed her body close to his. He curved his hand under his chin to raise her mouth to kiss but she turned her face aside. "No, Hank. Not now. I'm not ready. Not yet."

They drove back to Summer Point in silence. As the *Courier* truck stopped before her house, Anne leaned over and kissed Hank lightly on the cheek. "You're good for me. Don't let it be too long."

Four

Joe Harding's appearance matched his rough telephone voice, dark-hued, blunt-edged, and heavy. He stuck out a broad hand, "Hullo, Bladesly. Joe Harding." He looked around the small, worn office. "I don't believe I've been here for ten years or more. Came up one time to set up an advertising campaign with your uncle."

"Hasn't changed much."

Harding looked at Hank with stern eyes. "You say nothing's changed much. Well, *something's* changed. Your uncle didn't write crap about my bus line."

Hank smiled, hoping to delay a confrontation. "Call it 'crap' if you like, Mr. Harding. But in my opinion and a lot of my readers, you're providing poor service. Fare's too high, your drivers—"

Harding was not to be deflected. "Fare's too high? How the hell do you know they're too high? What are you comparing them with? Big city bus fares? There's no connection between big city fares and short-haul country fares. What are you basing that on?"

"Common sense, mostly. That works out to a higher cost per mile than the railroad."

"Well, does that make it too high? Just how much do you know about bus line operation?"

Hank paused, stopped dead. The man was right. "Okay, okay, Mr. Harding. You've got a point. I haven't made any actual price comparisons with other bus lines in the area. But by Thursday, I'll have such a survey, and if I turn out to be wrong I'll admit it in print, but if I'm right you'll hear about it."

"Well, now look here, Bladesly. I want to find some way to cut out this publicity. This ain't doing me any good."

"Any time you say. Just give me some sign you're doing something to improve your service."

Harding shook his head in exasperation. "Bladesly, the only thing I can tell you is that I'm shopping around for new equipment. I'd like to buy four new buses."

"Good. When do you think you will get them?"

"Probably not until January."

"Not much cause for celebration right now but at least it's something. Are you pretty definite about this?"

Harding looked evasive. "Definite as I *can* be until I can work out the financing. But I'll tell you something you're not going to like. When I get these buses I'm going to have to raise the fares. No other way to swing it."

"For God's sake, that's ridiculous! You're already robbing the public blind."

"Okay, okay. You just check around and see what you find. We may be a little higher than some but not out of line."

Hank set his lips grimly. "I'll have that answer soon. Meantime, how about giving me a story about new buses? Have you got any literature I could make a cut from to run with the story?"

"Hold on, Bladesly, not so fast! You can't rush into print with something that will definitely commit me on that. What if the deal falls through?"

"Mr. Harding, you can't afford to let the deal fall through!

It's up to you to do something. I thought buying new equipment was the one concrete thing you had decided to do."

Joe Harding's dark-hued face turned a deep, angry red. "Maybe it is but I'll be goddammed if I'm going to let you run my bus line with your newspaper."

"So, what it comes down to is you have no definite plans for new equipment."

"I have plans but I don't have *definite* plans. When I get ready to buy new units I'll let you know."

"And in the meantime, what would you like me to tell the people who are paying through the nose to ride your broken-down bus line?"

Harding's face became hard and taut. "Tell 'em to shove it! Tell 'em if they don't like the service they can stay the hell off. Tell 'em we're doing the best we know how and if any smart bastard thinks he can do it better, let him try!"

"That's quite an answer, Mr. Harding. I don't know whether I can print that or not."

Harding stared at Hank in hot anger. "You know, Bladesly, I came up here honestly thinking I could work something out with you. As far as I can see, you're just a cocky newspaper guy who thinks he knows all the answers. And let me tell you this; if you want to play rough, I can play rougher."

Hank watched Harding slam out the door and walk past the window on the way to his car. He suddenly felt tired of the whole mess. Why the hell did he get into it in the first place? He sat for some time, staring out the window at the passing traffic, hearing the sounds of the print shop through the door behind him, the steady clicking of the linotypes and the occasonal screeching whine of the type saw. Finally, he stirred himself and called Pat.

"Let's do a survey of bus fares in this area. Call up a dozen or so bus companies in nearby towns in Maine, New

Hampshire, and Massachusetts. Work in such things as size of the towns, length of the run, number of runs per day, and so on. Think you can do it?"

"Sure." She looked at him speculatively, her eyes too bright and her smile too eager. "You and Mr. Harding did not reach any agreement."

"Right."

She smiled brightly at him, wriggling slightly in her nervous way. "Don't let it worry you, Chief. We'll lick him sooner or later."

He walked home slowly that evening, the warm afternoon cooling with a smell of rain in the air. In the kitchen he poured himself a scotch, turned and let himself out the screen door and sat down in one of Uncle Jim's old white-painted rattan rocking chairs. He sipped the brisk whiskey slowly, feeling the amber liquid slide over his tongue and down his throat. The late afternoon noises of the town were quieting one after another. The chittering sparrows slowed to an occasional sleepy cheep. The traffic along the street past the old white house thinned to an occasional car. Across the campus he could faintly hear a fraternity house phonograph. Snatches reached him now and then of Elvis Presley's twangy voice singing "Houn' Dog." Then that stopped and the subdued quiet of a small Maine town took over. He was alone with his thoughts.

Freed from other stimulus his mind turned back to the meeting with Joe Harding. But before it could become fully engaged he wrenched it away with an act of will. Think pleasant thoughts, he ordered himself. He took another sip of whiskey and suddenly out of nowhere the elegant image of Mai Tin appeared. Mai Tin, her enchanting speech, the Chinese intonation with its light flavor of sing-song and impeccable Cambridge consonants and broad vowels. Her perfume, a bewitching fragrance like none other. Her golden skin, the classic restraint and symmetry in the shaping of her lovely body. And her surroundings in Singapore. The cacophony of color and the clashing sounds of the teeming streets, the unparalleled mixture of races, skins, and native dress, the quiet villa in the palm grove at the verge of the Straits of Johore.

Suddenly he was blindsided by a full realization of the staggering contrast between his former life as a clandestine agent amidst the rich dissonant textures of Singapore and his present domesticity in the quietude of a small college town. His present mood of futility and defeat cast the change he had made in new perspective. Two worlds could scarcely be more unlike. The world he now occupied seemed painfully mundane and flat. He had been plucked virtually overnight from one of the most exotic metropolitan centers in the world where his energies were engaged in the official business of the United States, where he dealt personally with a political leader who now was prime minister of a modern city-state, and where he had an intimate relationship with a woman whose exotic beauty would stop traffic if she were magically to appear on Maine Street in a skin-tight *cheong-sum.* The contrast was not only extreme. It was painful. He was caught, ensnared — no, what was Tennyson's word in "Ulysses" — *centred.* That was it, *centred in the sphere of common duties.*

Never since he had responded to Aunt Grace's frantic telegram and had flown home from Singapore had he permitted himself to complain or even inwardly criticize the necessity for giving up his career in CIA and taking over the family newspaper. Now he did. Now he wondered for the first time whether he could find lasting satisfaction in a life modeled after his Uncle Jim's. Could he grow old as a small town newspaper publisher? But even while wondering he felt there was no other route to take. He could see no way out. He was yoked and pinned by intangibles.

Next morning, while reading through a recent batch of letters to the editor about the bus line problem he found an intriguing proposal. "I drive down to Portland twice each week, and I will be glad to give rides to four people each trip if they will meet at your office. I will set a departure time the day before. Anyone wanting a ride can get the information from you."

Hank found this pretty appealing. It was a positive step, something constructive he could do aside from carping and nagging at Joe Harding. He did not see how it could lead to any legal difficulty so long as no money changed hands. He decided to box the letter on the front page and run an editorial of endorsement, offering the facilities of *The Courier* office for the scheme. He shoved back the worrisome thought that this decisive step might impel Harding to retaliate in some equally harmful way.

Later in the day Pat appeared at his desk with her survey of regional bus fares. He went over it with her, and was impressed. It was thorough and precise, answered four-square the questions he had asked, and demonstrated conclusively that by the standards of the region, Joe Harding's fares ran high. One bus line at Cartwright had fares roughly the same but all the others were lower, one by almost a third. "This is great stuff, Pat. You've made an air-tight case. Look at this set of figures here for the Augusta bus line. They coincide almost exactly with Harding's as far as mileage and number of stops are concerned but the fare's a good 20 percent lower."

Pat leaned over his desk to see where his pencil was pointing. "That's right."

"Good work." He turned to look at her and found himself looking down her loose blouse, her narrow breasts hanging down in her white brassiere. Hank ordinarily found Pat as sexually attractive as a store window dress mannequin but despite himself he felt a surge of response.

"Thanks, Chief." She looked down in his eyes and straightened quickly, smiling a slightly knowing smile.

"Write several summary paragraphs on what you've found. Then we'll tabularize the numbers and run them inside somewhere."

"Right. I'll get right on in." She leaned over and picked up her report, her hip pushing firmly against his shoulder. He watched her as she walked away, her nervous almost jerky walk, her narrow hips wiggling with motion.

He spent the afternoon making up the issue and by the end of the day he was beginning to feel a degree of satisfaction. He had made the case solidly but fairly. He had found a tone in the editorial which conveyed objectivity and balance. He did not want to spoil the case by seeming petty or mean, and he felt he had avoided that. Pat's summary of the figures was compelling, and the proposal to arrange rides and riders was presented as a public-spirited solution. He locked up the *Courier*'s front door and stepped out into the late summer afternoon traffic of Maine Street with a greater feeling of accomplishment than he had known for some time.

He walked home with a fairly springy step. The morning had begun shrouded with thick fog but by noon a pale, milky sun had burned its way through. Now the air was cooling in preparation for a typical Maine summer evening, cool almost to crisp, the air moist and tangy with the mingled smells of nearby spruce woods and sea. He passed in succession Bonar's Department Store, Lavaliere's Pharmacy, the Yarmouth National Bank, and the Maine Hardware. All had been there since he was a boy, and they sat solidly on their sites with an air of permanence that promised another century of existence. Several passersby nodded and spoke to him, and one man, an unshaven, weather-lined faced fellow in his 50's reached out to shake his hand and said, "Sure as hell like what you're doin' to that bus fella!"

At home he bounded up the front steps and went directly to the telephone. "Margaret?" he said to the answering voice. "How about a pick-up supper here?"

In fifteen minutes she was coming through the door, her ash blonde hair brushed and glossy. In response to his question about a drink she accepted, looking back over her shoulder as she passed him while he held the door, her grey-blue eyes smiling at their corners. "A sherry would be nice."

He had already put Count Basie's "The Fives" on the turntable, and as he went to the kitchen to pour Margaret a sherry and himself a scotch, he heard Basie's solo piano, backed only by guitar, string bass, and drums, setting forth a blues theme in his uniquely spare style, each note as sharply struck as though cut from glass, the guitar and bass behind him, dry and lifting. Like all blues, the melody line was simple, winding through the traditional chord sequence — as implacably unchanging as eternity — and ending each twelve-bar segment with a crisp run up in the bass register. It was light, witty music, a twentieth century black gavotte, in its way worthy of standing alongside 18th century incidental chamber music.

He smiled across the room at Margaret as he came back, drinks in hand. She sat straight in her chair, her long, truly wondrous legs crossed at the ankles, her knees peeping out from beneath her blue skirt.

Supper from the casserole and vegetable dish left in the oven by Mrs. Church passed quietly. He told Margaret briefly about his fruitless talk with Joe Harding but said he thought he saw some daylight in the free rides to Portland scheme. She told him she had had a long telephone conversation with Midge Oliver who said she believed she was pregnant with her third child. "I'm the only unmarried one left in the crowd," she said. "The others are already mothers."

Conversation on the sofa after supper was desultory, and during one pause Hank put his arm around her and pulled her closer as he kissed her. Her response was mild as he caressed her shoulder, then down across her breast and her belly and her thigh. She pulled away. "You're mussing up my dress." Her voice was petulant.

Striving to control his urgency and lighten the mood, Hank said, "I have a revolutionary idea. Let's take it off!" When she made no reply, he took her hand and led her up the stairs to his bedroom. He helpfuly unzipped her in back and carefully lifted her dress over her head. She folded it neatly and hung it over a chair, turning back toward him in her white slip with an almost rueful smile. In bed he began again to caress her and the glow across his loins became an exuberant ache. Margaret lay passive, one arm lying lightly across his shoulder, until his caressing hand slid between her knees and moved slowly up the inside of her silk-smooth thigh. "Uhnh, uhnh," she said and twitched slightly away from him.

He raised his head and looked at her questioningly.

"I just don't feel like it, Hank."

His mind racing with hot-blooded desire, his body poised and ready at battle stations, he said, "No?"

"I just don't think it's right."

He lay back, staring at the ceiling, trying to subdue his surging loins. "What's not right?"

"You know what I mean. This. It's not right."

They lay silently for a moment. "Up till now it's been right."

"Not really. I've never really felt right about it. And lately —" She stopped, hesitating. "Well, lately I've begun to realize we're not getting anywhere. You and I."

He continued to stare at the ceiling. He knew precisely where this was leading. He knew exactly what he was expected to say next. And a part of him, a sympathetic, understanding part, was half inclined to say it, but it lay muffled and stifled beneath a thick layer of resistance, an armor-like guard that forbade reaching out, that barred the way to commitment and accompanying vulnerability.

After a long silence, Margaret roused. "I think I'd better go home." She got up, dry-eyed and subdued, and put on her dress.

"I'll walk you home," Hank said.

Debussy's *Dances Sacred and Profane* was nearly drawing to a close before Anne realized what effect the music was having on her. The silky, sensuous blend of strings, flute, and harp had set up deep yearnings within her of the kind she had first known during those blossoming years between 12 and 14 when her hips began to broaden and her breasts to swell. Then adolescent idealism had transmuted those yearnings into romantic fantasies of knights and chargers and castles. Now, with the knowledge and insight of a mature woman who had experienced the tumult and ecstacy of coupling, she understood the exact nature of those yearnings.

She needed physical activity to break what threatened to become a self-perpetuating cycle. She found her sneakers beneath a chair and set out for a walk. Fog was hanging low and heavy over Summer Point, and Poplar Island off to the east was a ghostly silhouette of trees. She walked down to the shore and strolled distractedly along the water's edge. It was half tide and little molluscs, their dark, round shells glistening, were clinging to the green sea grass spears, waiting for the life-sustaining sea to return and engulf them. A cormorant, lazing along the verge, took fright at her approach and took off in heavy, skittering fashion, wings beating valiantly and feet slapping at the water's surface, leaving little scalloped imprints on the calm sea.

She tried to subdue the yearnings within and to marshal her thoughts. There was an uncharted future to face. She had known that the readjustment to the life of a single woman would be difficult, the change extreme. Like it or not, and now she certainly did not, her life with Robert had been that of a planet orbiting a star. Now her sun had left the sky.

She stooped to pick up a flat stone and bent sideways to throw it as she had seen Robert do to make it sail and skip over the flat water. It left her hand and dove straight into the green surface with a hollow ka-thunk. Not surprised, she walked on. She had never been able to make a stone skip over water. But men seemed somehow to be born with the knack or else learned it easily as boys. Hank, of course, would be an expert stone skipper.

Hank. Something surged within her, the thought of the name releasing attraction like a magnet deflecting a compass. Its strength surprised her, and for the moment she was half inclined to take issue with it. A kind friend, certainly, but more than that?

She paused and watched three seagulls, mewing and screaming over a dead fish one had found along the shore. Their white wings fluttered and arched against the grey sky. Soon one gull got firm hold of the fish and flew off in triumph, the others pursuing and stridently protesting.

She turned back to her walk and her mind immediately turned back to Hank and cavalierly took a positive view. Why should she resist the attraction she felt? Why should her recent scarring experience frighten her now? At the least, she and Hank were, and could remain good friends. Why not?

She bent to pick up a fragment of glass, a glowing lapus lazuli gem fashioned by the eternally restless sea, its edges worn smooth and gentle to the touch. She put it in the pocket of her shorts.

She lifted her gaze from the verge of the sea and felt her

uncertainty and hesitancy lift at the same time. Maybe she was complicating a simple natural situation. She began to walk with strong, swift strides, dispelling irresolution with every step. Stop dithering like an old woman, she told herself. Her legs began to glow with the exercise and her thighs became rosy. She glanced at her thighs beneath her shorts and knew they were handsome. And she remembered catching with that infallible female instinct the lingering glance of Hank's eyes on her legs as she sat in the cockpit of his boat. Anne my girl, she said inwardly as she strode briskly toward home, let whatever happens happen.

Over the next several days the telephone in *The Courier* office rang again and again with calls offering to participate in the Hanson to Portland free rider arrangement. Hank set up a regular column on the editorial page listing the names and telephone numbers of drivers willing to take riders. By the end of the week the list had grown so long that anyone wishing to get transportation to Portland could do so at almost any time he chose. It seemed to Hank only a matter of time before Joe Harding signaled a willingness to compromise.

On Friday morning Hank was in the press room making the final fixes before putting the edition to bed when Aggie approached him and touched his sleeve. "Telephone. Zeke Cushing. Says it's important."

"Okay. Hold it a minute, Bill. I'll be right back."

Zeke Cushing, president of the Yarmouth National Bank, had been a college classmate of Hank's. Thin-faced, squirrel-toothed, sullenly dark, he had been a loner, never joined a fraternity, the typical college "grind". Now he was Hank's banker, and a good one with a mind as sharp as his face. Hank picked up the phone on his desk. "Morning, Zeke."

"Mornin'. Somethin's come up. I need to talk with you."

"I'm putting the paper to bed. How soon do we need to talk?"

"Soon. Later this mornin'?"

"Sure. I'll be there before 10:30."

Mid-morning Hank walked into the red brick building and across the black and white checkered marble floor to Zeke Cushing's desk at the rear of the bank. It was set off from the center aisle by an oak railing. Zeke got to his feet as he saw Hank approaching and opened the little gate which swung in. He extended a bony hand. "Mornin', Henry. Come in and take a seat." Hank sat down in a black wooden chair which bore the seal and name in gold of Yarmouth College. He was facing the large window which looked out on Marsh Lane running alongside the building.

"Afraid I've got some bad news for you, Henry."

"Oh?"

"You remember that fifty thousand loan you took out for capital improvements three years ago? Well, you remember the directors didn't think we ought to carry the whole amount ourselves, so we sold half of it, twenty-five thousand, to investors in Portland as demand notes."

"I had forgotten that."

"No special reason for you to remember. The investors assured us at the time they had no intention of calling the notes before the full term of our loan. Besides, we reckoned we could handle that amount ourselves if they ever did."

Hank gazed at Cushing thoughtfully. "I gather from this that they have called the notes."

Cushing's dark eyes squinted. "Yes, they have. Payable the first of next month."

"And I gather you don't think you can handle it."

"Right again." Cushing's face became stern and his eyes narrowed. "Looks like we put you in a bind, Henry. We made the decision last week to put up the building money for that expansion the shoe company's goin' to do. Good thing for the town, but it will soak up our liquidity."

"But, my God, Zeke, there's no way I can pony up twenty-five thousand dollars. What do you expect me to do?"

"Well, now, Henry, the bank's goin' to do everything it can to help. But I got to tell you. Money's tight right now. Real tight."

"Mmm." Hank ransacked his mind for assets he had which could be converted to cash. What about the house? "How about my house, Zeke? Can I re-finance or maybe take a second mortgage?"

Cushing shook his head. "Nope. I've already looked into it. Your uncle took out a new mortgage with us just the year before he died. There's not more than five thousand equity there."

Hank watched a passing Wonder Bread bakery truck ease by the window. There must be something he could lay his hands on. "What about mortgaging the print shop equipment?"

Cushing shook his head again. "I've talked around with two, three banks in the area. Nobody seems to have any money to lend right now." He paused. "Unless you can find some individual. They's a lot of rich widows in those Federal houses on Union Street. Maybe one of them."

A new thought suddenly struck Hank. "By the way, who are these investors in Portland? Do you know?"

Cushing nodded. "Thought you might ask that. I did a little askin' around. Best I could find out they're connected with Joe Harding. Friends, maybe, or investors in the bus company."

"I thought so." Hank gazed out the window at the blank brick wall across the lane. His prospects, he thought, were just about as blank as that wall. Then anger began to mount. "Goddammit, Zeke, this sure is a lousy deal you've let me get into."

Cushing's face became sterner still but it was the expression of a man who feels no embarrassment and does not intend to apologize. "Well, Henry, I've just done what's best for the bank." He went on in this vein, explaining the bank's need to keep loans and assets in balance, and as he talked his accent moved further and further toward the Maine Yankee intonation of his ancestors, an accent which four years at Yarmouth College had gone far to erase. "Just done what's best for the ba-ank."

Hank got up to leave. "Well, good for the bank."

Cushing remained seated. "I'll let you know if anythin' comes up, Henry."

"You just do that. Write me a letter." He stalked out. He walked back to his office without seeing anyone or having any awareness how he got there. His focus was all inward. Now it was clear what Joe Harding meant by "playing rough". And this was rough, possibly even rougher than Harding had hoped. This could mean the end of ownership of *The Hanson Courier* by a Bladesly. Collapse of the whole enterprise was staring him in the face. He walked in the door of the office in a daze. Pat Long was lying in wait.

"Oh, Chief, I wanted to find out how big you want to play that warehouse fire last night. Do you —"

"Later, Pat, later. Catch me after lunch." He walked on back into the press room where the big Goss was slamming back and forth and causing the old oak floor to shake. He moved around to the folder where the finished edition was falling into piles. The front page looked a little light. "Hey, George, ink's running a little light on page one."

George stepped to the side of the press and opened a feeder valve another notch. "That ought to catch it, Hank."

Hank nodded and continued to stand watching the falling papers until his eyes slipped out of focus. He wondered how many more times he would be standing there as owner and editor of the proud *Courier* watching an edition emerge. He turned away and went slowly back to his desk. He looked out the window at the passing people and thought that his defeat, his collapse, would soon be known to them all. Out of the best of motives, but possibly without an adequate anticipation of possible outcomes, he had taken on a man who turned out have heavier guns in his arsenal than he had. Joe Harding had warned him, rough play would be met by rougher play. Indeed, "rougher" could this time mean terminal.

He tried to concentrate on positive steps he could take. He was sure nothing could be done with Joe Harding; he could not be persuaded to call off his friends. Hank had bought Harding's angry response by cutting into his ridership, lowering his income, and now he would have to accept the reaction. The only avenue of relief he could envisage would be some private lender, as Zeke Cushing had suggested, possibly one of the wealthy widows on Union Street. Hank had known them all since he had been a boy but he doubted he knew any of them intimately enough to ask for the loan of twenty-five thousand dollars. He ran down in his mind the addresses on the west side of the street below the college President's House, 23, 49, 57, 63, 87, until he came to the railroad overpass; then back on the other side, 84, 72, 66, 48 — Bolding. Possible Mrs. Bolding? Helen Bolding was a magnificently-fronted, frosty *grande dame,* very difficult to approach, but she had been a generous donor to Uncle Jim's college fund for indigent Hanson boys. Maybe a chance, slim as a knife edge, but maybe a chance. He could see no other possibility.

His reverie was interrupted by a rattling sound against the window, and he looked up to see a young woman leaning a bottle green bicycle against the frame. Looking again, he saw it was Anne Pintel. She was wearing a white blouse and navy blue shorts, and as she came through the door into his office he saw that summer sunshine had sprinkled a few freckles across her nose and had laid a gentle tan on her thighs. He tried to rally to meet her smile as she came to his desk, head slightly cocked to one side and shoulders set stiffly back in a kind of delicate awkwardness. "Hi!" she said. "Caught you in your lair."

"Come in. Have a seat."

"Well, maybe. I was hoping I could find you without luncheon plans, and you would take a famished lady bicyclist to lunch."

He looked at her soberly. "Why not?"

"Your enthusiasm is breathtaking."

"You don't want enthusiasm. You want lunch." He got out of his chair. "Come on."

He took her across the street to the Bos'n's Chair, a small place that served the best fish in town. The tables were boards set on trestles and the chairs were benches. The waiters were mostly Yarmouth College summer school students. Anne looked around at the lamps shaped like binnacles and the fish nets hung on the walls bearing starfish and huge shells. "Do you come here often for lunch?"

"Whenever I don't go home."

"My lucky day." Anne's eyes on his face were speculative, questioning. "You're fiercely chatty today. I'm having trouble getting a word in edgewise."

"Yeah."

She looked at him intently for a moment and then smiled brightly. "You know, Bob told me once they called you 'Big Chief Stone Face' in college. Are you demonstrating your Indian stoic manner?"

He looked down at the plank table. "Something like that."

Anne pursed her small mouth into a bud. "Maybe this wasn't a good idea." She made a move to get up. "Maybe you'd rather be doing something else."

He reached out and held her wrist. "Stay. Don't go." He

managed a brittle smile. "I've just taken a real jolt. I've got a problem as big as all outdoors."

She sat down, smiling broadly and patting his hand. "Well, now, that's better. You tell Auntie Anne all about it."

After hesitating, he recounted the conversation with Zeke Cushing including the discovery that calling the demand notes was probably a counter-move by Joe Harding.

"And what does this banker intend to do to bail you out?"

"He suggested I find some wealthy old widow who might lend me twenty-five thousand."

Anne looked at him blank-faced for a moment and turned and looked out the window at Maine Street for a longer time. She turned back, smiling softly. "Would a young grass widow do as well?"

"What do you mean?"

At this moment the waiter arrived to take their order. "Anne?" She shook her head and picked up the large parchment menu. Hank said, "I'll have the mako shark platter and a Heineken's."

"Shark? Is that good?"

"Excellent."

"I'm game. The same for me." She handed the waiter the menu. After he had left she reached for Hank's hand. "My father left me several times twenty-five thousand dollars. It's all sitting out in San Francisco in bonds in the bank. I see no reason why some of it should not be brought here to help out a friend."

"Anne, I couldn't let you do that!"

"Why not? Because I'm a woman?"

"Well, yes. Partly that."

She smiled a wry smile, her mouth turned down at one corner. "Just because I'm adorable, cuddly, and sexy is no reason to spurn my money!"

They both broke out laughing. "Besides, I'm going to charge you interest. All I can get."

He shook his head and looked out the window. "I'm not sure I could feel right about it."

"Of course you could. We'll go over to your bank after lunch and set it up. Where is it? That red brick horror over there?"

"It's that fine, traditional red brick New England structure," he corrected teasingly. His gloom was lifting.

After lunch Hank took Anne over and introduced her to Zeke Cushing with the explanation, "My friend, Mrs. Pintel, has money she wishes to lend me."

Cushing allowed no semblance of surprise to cross his narrow face or permitted his professional banker's manner to be ruffled. "Please sit down, Mrs. Pintel. Henry." He folded his hands together and gazed at Anne without expression. "You say you wish to lend Henry money for his business. What form is this money in at present, Mrs. Pintel?"

"Bonds. In a bank in San Francisco."

"Bonds." He nodded approvingly. "You realize of course that investing in a business, a newspaper, involves more risk than bonds."

"Yes. But I have confidence in *The Hanson Courier.*"

"Greater risk means higher interest ordinarily.'

"I know that. Mr. Bladesly and I have discussed it in a general way."

"What's the name of the bank in San Francisco? Would you like me to prepare a letter for you to inquire about the transfer of funds?"

"It's the United Bay Bank. And I'd like you to telephone them right now. It's just 10:30 in San Francisco." She produced the telephone number from her check book. "And tell them I want twenty-five thousand as soon as possible."

Later, after the transaction had been arranged for its completion in a week's time, they walked back to Hank's office and stopped beside Anne's bicycle. Hank looked down at her, at her deep-set eyes, her nose sprinkled with tiny freckles, and her small mouth above her strong chin. "Anne dear, I don't know how to thank you."

"Tut, tut! None of that 'dear' business. This is strictly a business deal. I'm going to get rich on that interest."

"Hardly seems adequate return for so great a favor."

"Wel-l-l." She grinned at him impishly. "I'll think of something else." She walked her bicycle over to the curb and set off up Maine Street. He watched her go, the comely figure on the bottle green Raleigh.

Five minutes later he heard a sound outside his window. It was Anne parking her bicycle. She met him at the doorway. "Got a flat," she announced.

"Oh, too bad. Well, let me take you home. We'll put the bike in the truck."

"I couldn't let you do that!"

He began to say, "Why not?" before his ear registered the mocking tone and he saw the ironic smile. They passed through the shop where George and Bill were bundling the newspapers before turning them over to the three distributors in their trucks outside. Hank walked the bicycle, lifting the front wheel to avoid further damage to the tire. Anne came behind him, smiling, with a nod at the two press men.

They drove through the town, passing the white Congregational Church and out along the Summer Point road. "I'm surprised you got a flat here on Maine Street. You must have hit a nail."

"Unless someone let the air out."

He laughed, scoffing. "Who would let the air out of your tire?"

She looked at him with a quirky smile. "Me."

While Hank was unloading the bicycle and walking it around to the woodshed at the back, Anne walked through the house and met him at the back door. She was holding a split bottle of champagne in her hand. "Look what I found in the refrigerator! Let's have a toast to our new business partnership."

The cork came off with a celebratory pop. They carried their glasses into the living room and sat down side by side on the sofa. She held her glass high. "Here's success to all our endeavors!"

"Success!"

She sipped her glass and set it down on the walnut coffee table before them. "Sealed with a kiss."

"What about 'strictly business'?"

"That's all right. This kiss *means* business."

He put his glass on the table beside hers and turned to her. She met him with eager mouth, her hands moving across his shoulders to the back of his head. He started to release her after a moment but she clung to him, her mouth open and her tongue caressing. The signal was clear. He leaned her back until her head was on the cushion of the sofa and he let his hand stray down from her face over her lovely contours. He was fumbling with the zipper on the side of her shorts when she suddenly broke away.

"What nonsense! You'd think we were a couple of teen-agers making out on the couch," she said, her voice sounding slightly strangled. She took his hand, got to her feet, and led him up the stairway to her bedroom. She strode to the bed and yanked the covers down over the end. "Make yourself comfortable," she said and went into the bathroom.

Hank undressed slowly, his mind a torrent of rushing desire, and lay down on the bed. Outside, in the distance, he could hear a busy lawnmower, and from the other window came the slow chug of a lobster boat working the traps. A white-throated sparrow on a limb near the house sang his tentative piping song, the song of one who is not quite certain he has it right. Hank smiled as he always did when he heard those faltering notes and turned his attention to the sound of rushing water in the bathroom. In a few minutes, the bathroom door flew open and Anne came running toward the bed, nude from head to toe, brown-tipped breasts bobbling wildly. Four feet away she took off in a belly-smacking dive, landing with a thump across Hank's belly. She raised herself on her elbows and grinned mischievously at him, her fine hair making a delicate screen across her eyes. "Do you you play chess?" she asked.

So their affair began. It was an exuberant romp from the beginning and remained a joyous celebration throughout. Anne brought playful zest and whole-hearted intensity to her love-making. Every sinew of her body and spirit came into play. And she was constantly surprising him. Once, after knowing touches and caresses had lifted them to new planes of desire and they had entered, as Shakespeare says of Venus and Adonis, into "the very lists of love," she suddenly gave a supple seal-like flip and tossed Hank aside. "Do it again!" she said, her eyes glinting with delight.

She was eagerly inventive. One sunny afternoon when Hank had anchored *Blue Teal* in a birch-lined cove behind Duck Hawk Island, she disappeared into the little cabin and reappeared a minute later blindingly naked in the hot sun and carrying a towel. She stepped carefully along the rail to the forward deck and spread her towel. "Come lie with me," she said as she lay back on her elbows, the soft wind rustling her hair. Another time, when the first snow of autumn had mantled the countryside with nearly six inches of glistening beauty, Hank had stopped by her house to make certain she was snug and warm. She had seen him coming, and she met him at the door wearing a hooded parka. "Follow me," she said and led him out the back door, past the shrouded wood shed into a spruce copse. She lay down in the snow and made an "angel" as children do by moving their arms up and down to mark the wings. Then she held her arms out to him. "Come!" she commanded.

She delighted him by verbalizing what she felt, flatteringly specific and graphic when he had pleased her especially. When they had made love in the sun on the *Blue Teal,* she told him, "It was beautiful. When you weren't there, the sun was there." And lying in the snow she had said, "I wanted to feel the warm and the cold so close together." But beyond the descriptions of sensual delight, she also made it plain that their relationship had broader meaning for her. "When I lie with you," she said, "you make me feel like a woman, a *whole* woman. And when we're just together, talking, you make me feel like a *whole* person."

For Hank, too, their affair was liberating. Tensions and restraints that had lain coiled inside him since his return from Singapore were eased. His business life too became sunnier. One morning he found on his desk at the *Courier* a large, fat manila envelope bearing on the outside the rubber-stamped words, Hanson-Portland Bus Lines, Inc. Inside was a bright brochure displaying the excellence of the GM Thirty, a shiny 30-passenger bus with "superb passenger comfort and reliability." Also in the package was a somewhat amateurish press release announcing the purchase of four GM Thirty buses by the Hanson-Portland Bus Line. The second paragraph stated that "recent improvements in management organization and practices have made it possible to reduce bus fares by 10% beginning 1 January. The Hanson-Portland Bus Lines take great pride in offering this new and improved service for citizens of the Portland region."

Hank let out a whoop and called "Pat, come look at this!" Pat came trotting in, eyes wide. When she had finished reading she exclaimed, "We've won, Chief! I told you all along we would." She leaned over as he sat at his desk and hugged him across the shoulders. In his exuberance he patted her on the bottom and she looked back at him coquettishly over her shoulder as she walked out of his office swishing her narrow tail. In a few minutes he called her back.

"Let's have a four-column cut made of this picture," he said, holding up the brochure. "Then write a five or six paragraph piece spicing up this press release a bit. I'll put together an editorial congratulating Joe Harding for his public-spirited action in meeting the expressed desire of the people for better service." He said this with an oratorical flourish. Pat grinned and said, "Right, Chief!"

With the bus line controversy satisfactorily completed, Hank turned the focus of the paper toward a revival of his uncle's campaign to provide college expenses for deserving Hanson High School graduates. He set up a foundation called The James Bladesly College fund, and soon the coffers began to fill, mostly with ten and twenty-five dollar contributions but also augmented with five thousand from an "unknown benefactor" who almost certainly was Helen Bolding and ten thousand from the giant shoe distributing chain which was moving into Hanson. This campaign, together with a juicy murder trial involving a lobster fisherman who came home one day to find his wife beneath another lobsterman and proceeded to perform excruciating surgical maneuvers with his fisherman's knife on the anatomy of the surprised lover, who subsequently died, kept *The Courier's* front page lively and Hank engaged.

The late autumn was now verging into winter, and Hank looked forward to it with the warm confidence of a man who has in balance all the elements essential to his needs. It was in this genial mood one early December morning that he picked a piece datelined Singapore off the UPI ticker. It read: "Singapore: Long simmering tensions between the United States and Singapore surfaced today with Prime Minister Yee Hock Tho's expulsion of three American diplomats. Yee charged that the three were guilty of violating Singapore's sovereignty by acts of espionage inimical to the interests of his government." Hmmm, thought Hank to himself with mild concern, I hope the boys at Langley are able to handle that one. He selected the UPI item for the page three section he had initiated on foreign affairs and leafed through the rest of the file.

It was late afternoon that same day that a man passed Hank's window, paused at the front door, and then came in. It took Hank a moment to recognize him, someone totally alien to the context of Maine and a small town newspaper. It was Pete Risko, his fellow CIA case officer in Singapore.

"Pete! For Christ's sake, what are *you* doing here?"

Risko grinned. "Hello, Hank. Just thought I'd drop by and see how you're getting along." Pete glanced around the worn office.

"Well, I'll be damned! Sit down and tell me what's going on."

Risko shook his head. "Can't do that. But I want to have dinner with you tonight. At the Inn where I'm staying."

"Tonight!"

Risko nodded. "Gotta be tonight. I'm leaving first thing in the morning."

Hank thought a moment. "All right. I'll be there."

"Come to Room 16 about six. We'll have a drink before eating."

At six he climbed the old white-bannistered staircase of the Hanson Inn to the second floor and walked back along the thinly-carpeted, creaking floor to Room 16 on the southeast corner. Risko opened the door immediately to his knock.

"How the hell are you, Blades?" He looked Hank over. "I don't know whether to envy you or to pity you, stuck up here on the northeastern tip of the Arctic. Have much trouble with Eskimos? Or is it Vikings?

"Vikings. But they bring fresh golden mead and long-legged blondes when they come. I'm fine. But Peter, goddammit, what brings you to Maine?"

Risko shook his head as though in resignation. "Pressure of governmental service, Blades. The King's business."

"Yes?"

Risko looked at him seriously. "We're up to our ass in trouble in Singapore. Both State and the White House are giving us unshirted hell for blowing it with Peter Yee." He paused with a sly grin. "I don't suppose the pony express has brought word of it up here yet."

"Read it off the UPI wire this morning." He measured Risko with his eyes. "All right, why aren't you either in Washington or Singapore taking care of it?"

Risko smiled. "The Director, Pick Grant, somehow came up with the notion we need *you.*"

"Me? What can I do after you guys foul it up? Besides, how can I leave my newspaper to bash down to Washington or out to Singapore?"

"We think, especially Pick, you can ease Peter Yee down off his limb. I'm now Division Chief; Jude Welby's still the DD. He wanted to go out himself but Pick killed that. He said you're the guy who recruited Yee and still the one who can handle him best."

"Very flattering. But, Pete, I can't leave here for some indefinite period."

"Pick authorized me to do what it takes to get you. If you need someone to fill in while you're gone we'll detail a top-flight agency editor with newspaper experience to come up here. We'll put you on contract and pay you top dollar. Naturally, we'll cover all your expenses."

Hank shook his head. "I think you're all day-dreaming. What influence can I have with Peter Yee, the prime minister, whom I haven't seen for three-four years.?"

"Hank, will you please at least come down to Washington and talk it over with us?"

Hank paused and then nodded weakly. "All right."

Explaining it to Margaret took a little time and patience. She finally blurted out her chief concern. "But you'll miss Dotty Biddle's Christmas party she's invited us to."

He said he expected to be back before Christmas. She smiled, reassured. "All right, then. Be careful, dear."

Breaking the news to Anne was almost easier than he could have wished. She was in bubbling good spirits. "Oh, Bunny, how wonderful for you!" Her eyes dancing with pleasure, she said, "I've got some wonderful news myself. When I picked up my term paper today — got an A — Professor Witham asked me whether I would be interested in an assistant instructorship in art history next semester. I'll teach one freshman section in the six week art history segment of the Western Civilization course. My academic career is launched!" She reached up on one foot and pecked him on the mouth.

"Great, Anne." After several awkward attempts to continue a conversation which straddled the separate interests of them both, he said, "I've got to pack tonight and take the early morning train down to Boston." Pause. "But I'll be back for Christmas."

"Darling, it's always Christmas with you." She kissed him again, a cousinly or sisterly kiss of farewell. She smiled one of her mischievous smiles. "Just be careful of those Chinese girls. Bob Pintel told me they are made cross wise to us western girls."

"That's Japanese. But I —"

"Goodbye," she said.

Some Work of Noble Note, May Yet Be Done

One

A tall young man about ten years younger than Hank came up to him as he walked into the concourse of Washington's National Airport. "Mr. Bladesly? Let me take your bag."

"Thanks. I can handle it."

"I'll take it sir." He reached for Hank's suitcase and led him across the swarming lobby to a black sedan waiting at the curb. Hank got in the opened door and was preparing to slide across the seat but his young escort slid into the front seat beside the black, neatly-uniformed driver.

"Good flight?"

"Fine." The young man smiled, nodded, and turned toward the front. Hank looked out the window, silently trying to make the too swift transition from provincial Maine to the metropolitan glitter of Washington. He watched as the car moved swiftly up the George Washington Parkway alongside the Potomac River, broad but uselessly empty of working shipping. The arched span of Memorial Bridge, bracketed with two pairs of Italian golden dray-horses, swam past and the noble white marble Lincoln Memorial with the Washington Monument looming high behind it circled forward in response to the car's motion. In the distance were the imposing classical buildings fronting Constitution Avenue, creating the illusion of a new Rome. Then past Roosevelt Island, looking incongruously wild, and then the Francis Scott Key Bridge with the turreted sky-line of Georgetown University behind. The roadway lifted and moved with gentle curves along the palisades fronting the river, crossed the span that suddenly gave a glimpse of historic Chain Bridge below, and led on to Langley and CIA Headquarters.

Pete Risko's secretary, pleasant-faced, middle-aged, and broad of beam, led Hank from the reception center along the broad marbled gallery beside the atrium to the bank of elevators bordered by walls papered with a greatly enlarged map of 18th century Paris, then from the elevators down the battleship grey corridor to the lime green door to Pete's office. Risko came from behind his desk, littered with file folders and loose cables, with outstretched hand, "Glad you're here, Blades. It sure is good to have you back in the spy business. Cup of coffee while I fill you in?" While Dotty, the secretary, was setting down the cups, he said, "By the way, we're putting you up at the Chain Bridge Marriott until you ship out, which we hope will be Thursday."

"Not so fast. I haven't definitely signed on yet."

Risko looked at him solemnly. "Pick Grant is counting heavily on your going." He looked at Hank another moment and then sipped his coffee.

"Start by telling me what went wrong. Is this Buck Jones' foul-up?"

"No, no! We finally got Buck out of Singapore with a shoe horn and ten tons of dynamite. No, this is the work of a guy named Dave Burkhardt."

"That's not a name I remember in Far East Division."

"No, you wouldn't. He was a staff man in WH, running the desk for Costa Rica and a couple more of those two-bit Central American countries."

"Then, what — ?"

"This is one of Jude Welby's new-fangled management ideas." Risko rolled his eyes. "God, don't let me get started on that! The idea is to mix everybody together and to hell with local knowledge or expertise. If a guy knows more than anyone else in the Agency about China, turn him over to Western Europe. If a guy has been hacking around in second level jobs in Far East stations, give him Technical Services. This guy, Burkhardt, knows only the Western Hemisphere and has as much tradecraft as your Aunt Sally. Maybe less."

"Sounds nuts. But what happened?"

"He was running a station program reporting on Communist activities among the Overseas Chinese. It's a region-wide program —"

"I remember it," broke in Hank. "Big Joe handled it."

"That's right. Well, this gives the Singapore station a charter to run ops into adjoining countries, since Singapore is a nerve center and a power base for these activities. So he mounted an op to recruit Chinese in Singapore and send them into Indonesia to infiltrate Communist cadres there working against the local Chinese."

"Sounds ok so far."

"Not bad. But now we come to tradecraft. As you remember, Sing is a very delicate place to operate. It was tough when you were there, with Special Branch calling the shots, but now it's ten times tougher. The Brits did a good job of training locals to take their place when they left, and Peter Yee has the eyes of a hawk. Well, good old Burkhardt managed to break every tradecraft rule in the book, and they caught him dead to rights. Tossed him out. Now, Yee is threatening to break relations with the U.S. and invite the Soviets in to set up a shipbuilding installation."

"My God!"

"So that's why the White House and State are so scourging

us with nettles and whips and why Pick Grant wants you to get out there and calm Yee down."

Hank laughed scoffingly. "Nothing to it, I'm sure."

Risko looked him straight in the eye. "If you can't do it, Blades, no one can."

At Pete's suggestion, Hank spent the rest of the morning reading the case files. He was appalled by what he found. Under Burkhardt's direction, the case officers had operated as openly as though they were selling Girl Scout cookies. No care for secure meeting places, no running of name checks on contacts made, open telephone discussion of meeting times — it was as though they had never heard of the steely efficient Singapore Special Branch. He was on the last folder when Risko came in with two other men. "Time to knock off for lunch, Blades. I brought along a couple of guys who want to meet you. This is Dick Apple and Pat Garrick." Both men were short: Apple dark and intense; Garrick cocky and handsome in a theatrical way. "Pat's here on home leave from Lissane; Dick's the Division's chief of ops. As they shook hands, Apple said, "I've always wanted to greet the man who recruited Yee Hock Tho. One of the great recruitments of all time."

"Doesn't seem to be worth much right now."

"I think that's just a temporary foul-up. It's too bad though. We should have caught it before it happened. We warned the guy once or twice but he just kept blundering on."

"Hank will patch it up," said Risko. "Let's go to lunch."

They drove in Pete's car to an elegant Turkish restaurant at the edge of a shopping mall in McLean. The long, narrow room was decorated with large brass samovars and hanging brass lanterns, their sides perforated with ornate patterns. As he unfolded a large linen napkin, Hank looked around at the other diners. They seemed mostly professional men from nearby offices, narrow ties and slim jackets, and the women, mostly in their 20's and 30's were dressed in tailored suits or trim blouses and skirts. Rather different, Hank told himself, from the Bos'n's Chair on Maine Street.

"How does it feel to be back?" asked Apple.

"Strange."

Garrick laughed, nodding approval. "One word says it all. Headquarters is *strange.*"

Pete grinned at Hank. "Pat is our designated Headquarters hater. He thinks it is unmanly to be here instead of in the field."

Garrick looked amusedly at Pete. "Tell you what, Risko. I took a good look as I was walking behind you to the car. I swear your ass is a good six inches broader than it was when you got back from Singapore. On your way to becoming just another broad-assed bureaucrat. 'Tis a bleedin' shyme to lose a fine case officer o' the likes o' that!"

Risko laughed. "Pat's also the Division Barrymore." he explained to Hank. "Every occasion a star performance."

So the bantering conversation ran throughout lunch. Sometimes personal gibes, then an extended discussion of the previous Sunday's Washington Redskin victory over the San Francisco 49ers, a critique by Garrick of the new play at the National Theater, a chuckle in low tones over a cable from Tokyo about a KGB man caught *delicto flagrante,* a recommendation from Apple that they all read a recent biography of Bruce Lockhart, the British secret agent, the discovery by Risko of an excellent new Chinese restaurant on K Street in Washington. A strong contrast it made to Hank's usual luncheon conversations in Hanson. He had forgotten the good humored camaraderie among CIA people, the close-knit sharing of interest and purposes which is enhanced by the constant need for tight security and the atmosphere it induces of a small, disciplined corps.

As they were leaving the restaurant and walking to the car, Dick Apple said to Hank, "I hope we can talk before you go about how you plan to approach Yee."

"Sure, Dick. Absolutely. I need all the suggestions I can get."

Back in Pete's office, Risko said, "We have an appointment with the Director at 3. Is there anything you want to discuss with me before then?"

Hank pondered a moment. "Well, it's clear from the files that the whole operation was botched." He shook his head, grinning. "I wouldn't be surprised if Peter Yee wasn't just plain insulted by the professional ineptitude."

Risko guffawed. "Good point! Tell that to the Director. I have a hunch he thinks Welby's mix-and-match stuff is crazy." He looked at Hank soberly, thinking. "Does Yee have any confidants you can get next to more easily than to him?"

Hank's heart did an extra flop as the glowing figure of Mai Tin popped into his mind. "His sister, Mai Tin. At least she used to be his confidant several years ago."

"Know her?"

Hank's stone-face came into use. "Met her once or twice."

At three o'clock CIA Director Pickard Grant came around the end of his desk, the same dark, lean athletic figure Hank had last seen when he left for Maine. "Welcome home, Hank. Glad to have you back."

"I'm enjoying being back."

"How's the newspaper business? I always thought I'd like to run a small town newspaper."

"It has its ups and downs. I've just come through a down."

Pickard Grant nodded and smiled across his desk. Outside the large window the dense woods running down to the banks of the Potomac stood sullen and somber in a steady drizzle. Hank reflected that rain in Virginia could well mean snow in Maine. The Director leaned forward, elbows on the desk. "Let me set your mind at ease, Hank. I don't expect you to perform any miracles or have Prime Minister Yee begging for forgiveness. But I think it's fair to say that no one since you left has established the kind of rapport with him you had, and it's worth a try at least to see whether it can be restored."

"I'm willing to try but being prime minister may have made him a different man." Hank paused, reflecting. "One thing in particular I wanted to get your guidance on. You remember that the original recruitment was based on his involvement in the murder of that American newspaperman. That gave me leverage at the time, but my hunch is that it's gone now. Do you agree?"

"Absolutely. The head of a tightly run state like Singapore could quash a thing like that with a flick of the wrist. No, you'll have to make it through personal rapport. Either with him or someone close to him. Wasn't there a sister?"

Again Hank's heart hit two beats where one would do, but his face remained impassive. "Yes, Mai Tin." The name flavored his tongue like the memory of a fine cognac. He hesitated a moment. "What do you think I can offer Yee or provide by way of making amends?"

"I'm tempted to say whatever it takes, but don't make any final commitments without checking back with us."

Just before touching down at Singapore's Palam Airport, the Pan Am 707 made a wide swing over the harbor, its wingtip pointing down at the green water dotted with anchored freighters, lighters towed by launches, lumber junks, and sampans. Slowly the wing lifted again to horizontal, and the skyline of the city came into view with the white cathedral and the old British imperial buildings looking onto the brilliant green of the padang and cricket pitch. The plane settled, the tires making a short screech upon impact with the runway.

As Hank emerged from the briskly efficient immigration and customs counters he was met by a man in a seersucker jacket. "Dick Perkins," he said holding out his hand. Then he muttered in a low voice, "I'm acting head honcho." On the way into town he explained that Headquarters had moved him down from Bangkok temporarily until the dust had settled and Dave Burkhardt was replaced. "So everything's as strange here to me as to you, maybe stranger since you served here before."

"Long time ago."

"I've made an appointment for a courtesy call on the ambassador for 10 tomorrow morning. Thought I'd let you settle in at the hotel and get a good night's sleep."

The hotel was the Benbow Park, a rambling old-fashioned place set in a large park-like setting several blocks north of the city's business section. "Good choice, Dick."

"Hoped you'd like it. To me, it's the nicest. I looked at the others. The Raffles is moth-eaten nostalgia, the Cathay faded 1950's modernity, and the Mandarin all five-star glitter. This looks more comfortable and livable."

After the bright-eyed Chinese bellboy had put down his bags and pulled the drapes, Hank moved onto the balcony that opened off sliding doors. Two stories below, flaming red cannas clustered around an outrageously fragrant frangi pani tree. A soft sea breeze teased the tops of the tall palms at the edge of the garden. The balcony was furnished with a white luncheon table and chairs, a reclining lounge chair, and an egg-shaped wicker swing suspended by a chain. Perfect, he thought, for a young woman in a dressing robe. He tried to imagine Anne, in the pale blue robe she often put on after their afternoon meetings but somehow Anne's persona seemed out of place. He substituted Mai Tin with her golden legs folded beneath the pale yellow silk robe he remembered. Perfect.

At 10 the next morning Hank and Dick Perkins were admitted to Ambassador Glenn Timble's office by a sour-faced secretary. The ambassador remained at his desk without rising. "Come in, gentlemen, what bad news do you have for me this morning?" He was a florid-faced man with a highly pampered mane of pure white hair, an upstate New York lawyer and judge who had won his ambassadorship by extensive service to the political party then holding the White House.

"I came to introduce Henry Bladesly to you, Mr. Ambassador."

"Are you bad news, Bladesly?" the ambassador asked with a smirk and a little shrug that had caused the hearts of several faded blonde admirers to flutter.

"Never by design, sir."

The ambassador grunted. "I assume you're a spy. Do you carry a gat?" Again the smirk and the shrug.

"No, sir." Hank decided to put an end to the cuteness. "I served with CIA here in Singapore about four years ago. At that time I was on fairly intimate terms with Yee Hock Tho. Then I left the CIA. The agency has asked me to come out now on their behalf to see whether I could help smooth things out with the Prime Minister."

"For God's sake!" exclaimed the ambassador. "Haven't you people created enough havoc already?" His already florid face turned crimson. "You want to make it worse?"

Hank paused, then spoke quietly. "Enough trouble has been caused certainly, but our feeling is that since we created it we ought to try to mend it."

"No, by God!" The ambassador thumped his desk with his fist. "Dealing with the Prime Minister is the responsibility of the ambassador, the President's representative. I'm sure as hell not going to let you or any other goddammed spook carry on the Embassy's business."

Hank looked at the florid face reflectively. "Perhaps we could go together, sir."

"I don't like that any better. I'd look pretty damned silly taking a spy to see the Prime Minister of Singapore."

Hank smiled. "Well, at present I'm the owner and editor of a newspaper in Maine. I could go ostensibly for an interview."

Ambassador Timble looked at Hank, his interest piqued. "Maine? Where in Maine?"

"Hanson, a small town north of Portland."

"I know Hanson. I graduated from Yarmouth. Class of 1923."

"I'm class of '52."

A new expression crossed the ambassador's face. Hank could see in the ambassador's eyes that he had quickly been transformed from scorned CIA officer to a respected Yarmouth graduate. "Well, we could try that. But I doubt it will do any good." He called the secretary and asked her to get an appointment, hopefully in the next day or two for himself and Mr. Henry Bladesly, an American newspaper man. Even Hank was surprised when she came back within minutes and said the Prime Minister would see them at 4 that afternoon.

As they walked into Government House, the solid classic-pillared remnant of British colonial administration, and walked the length of a high-ceilinged, terrazzo-floored corridor, the walls lined with long ranks of governor's portraits, most of them wearing the high-plumed hat which was their badge of office, Hank suddenly remembered Peter Yee as the slender, impassioned Chinese youth standing on a rough platform, his face chalky in the light of flaring torches, shouting his cry for independence. Now that stripling was sitting at a broad teak desk just behind the door marked "Prime Minister".

Hank and the ambassador waited for several minutes in the ante room. Then a buzzer sounded faintly and the young Chinese at the reception desk got to his feet and led them to the office door. "You may go in now, gentlemen," he said as he opened the door.

Yee Hock Tho walked slowly toward them, a faint condescending smile on his face as he said, "Mr. Ambassador." He turned to Hank, his glance direct and examining. "Mr. Henry Bladesly. Come sit down, please, gentlemen."

He led them over to a circle of curved bamboo-armed easy chairs surrounding a glass-topped table. To Hank he looked at least six inches taller and twenty pounds heavier, his large head even larger, his shoulders broader. Even his walk conveyed command and authority. "What have you come to see me about?" he asked as they sat down.

"Mr. Bladesly is the editor of a newspaper in America," said the ambassador.

"So my people tell me." Peter Yee turned and looked at Hank, again with that measuring, examining glance.

"Happens to be the very town where I attended college. Just a few years back," said Ambassador Timble with his patented smirk and shrug. "Fine little college."

"Yes," said Peter Yee with a rising, slightly impatient inflection.

The ambassador paused, looking at Hank, as though wondering where to go from there. Yee intervened, "Does this suggest, Mr. Bladesly, that you have come to Singapore to interview me about the crisis in relations between Singapore and the United States?" His look at Hank was now frankly skeptical and edged with irony.

"In part that, Mr. Prime Minister. I would certainly like to hear from you on that subject."

"We both would," chimed in Ambassador Timble.

Peter Yee crossed his legs, his hands joined in his lap, and leaned back in his chair with confident authority. "I think I can meet that request." He then proceeded for the next twenty minutes to give a mercilessly and precisely detailed account of the bungling CIA operation, every step of which had been surveilled and scrutinized by Singapore Special Branch. "In short, he concluded, "what your American secret service has done is to subvert Singapore citizens and bribe or coerce them into conducting espionage operations on your behalf in a foreign country. This is an intolerable affront to Singapore's sovereignty," he went on sententiously. "Moreover, it has endangered the security of my small country, which can exist in the hostile environment that surrounds it only by the most delicate maneuvering. The actions you have taken seem clearly to align us against the dominant force of the region, Communist China. As the leader of this small, unprotected nation, I can not tolerate such interference in our affairs, not even from a nation I once regarded as a good friend."

Ambassador Timble undertook to reply to this indictment. In the soothing syrupy tones he had often used with divorce-seeking Rochester, New York matrons, he said, "Now, Mr. Prime Minister, it certainly was not the intent of the United States to insult your sovereignty or damage your interests in any way. It was —"

Yee Hok Tho's look was steely, his eyes narrowed, "How would you describe it then, Ambassador Timble? Reckless disregard for your host's concerns? Arrogance? Amateurish ineptitude?"

"No, I — Well, I —"

Peter Yee cut him off and turned to Hank. "Perhaps you would like to characterize this operation, Mr. Bladesly."

Hank hesitated briefly. "I would say, Mr. Prime Minister, that it was a poorly conceived, bungled affair."

Yee nodded, his face grim. "Thank you, Mr. Bladesly." He stood up and looked at both the visitors. "Gentlemen, I am a busy man. You have heard my views. Perhaps they will serve as an interview for your newspaper, Mr. Bladesly. Now, permit me to say goodbye."

The two Americans walked silently to the door. In the car on the way back to the embassy Hank listened with half an ear to the Ambassador's excuses for not having handled

Yee Hock Tho more effectively. With the rest of his attention he was seeking some way to reach Peter Yee more personally and privately. He could not ask to see him on his own. Could it be done through Mai Tin? That was possible but how could he reach her? More than likely, she was married and therefore bearing a name he did not know. Could the station's files help? He spent the remainder of the afternoon looking through them and found that Mai Tin's relationship with the station had steadily diminished since his departure. The latest reference to her was more than a year old.

He drove one of the station's cars back to the Benbow and after showering had a solitary dinner in the stately, old-fashioned dining room. He went to his room and poured himself a scotch out of the Ballantines he had picked up on the way to the hotel. He stood out on the balcony, drink in hand, with the warm equatorial night air clinging to him like a lover's caress and the seductively sensuous fragrance of frangipani washing around him. Off in the distance he could hear the sound of traffic on MacGregor Road, and in the still greater distance the faint hoarse hoot of a ship in the harbor. He sipped his drink, feeling himself slowly being absorbed once again by the ineffable allure of Southeast Asia and more specifically Singapore.

He thought he heard a telephone ring and went inside, but it must have been in a neighboring room because his own phone was silent. He was about to turn back when he heard a delicate tapping at the door, almost as though made with a woman's finger nails. He opened it. There stood Mai Tin, glowing in her elegance, wearing the inevitable skin-tight *cheong-sum,* this one a shimmering sea green. To Hank's eye she was entirely unchanged from the day they had said goodbye. "Henry!" she said dropping a small flowered silk bag she was carrying and throwing her arms around his neck to kiss him. Her rich, mysterious scent enveloped him in a bewitching mist.

He reached behind her to flip the door closed with his hand and pressed her slender, supple body to his. "Mai Tin! My God, I'm glad to see you again!" A surge of genuine affection swept through him. They held each other close for a moment. Then she picked up her little bag, fastened at the top with a gold drawstring, and walked into the room.

"Wouldn't it be a charming way to celebrate our reunion if you made me a drink like yours and we went onto your balcony to talk? We have much to tell each other." There it was again, he told himself, that enchanting mixture of a Cambridge English accent and the delicate sing-song Chinese intonation. His ear listened with delight. Being with Mai Tin again was like waking and then returning in sleep to an interrupted, delightful dream.

While Hank was pouring her a drink, Mai Tin explained, "Peetah told me this afternoon you were in Singapore, so I got Special Branch to tell me where you were stopping. I couldn't wait to see if you'd changed."

They walked out to the balcony. "Changed? Well, I'm four years older."

"Oh, I didn't mean that. I'm older too and married. Do I seem changed?"

"Certainly not to the outward eye."

She leaned over and kissed him lightly on the cheek. "Not inwardly either, Henry, as far as you are concerned."

They sat on the balcony exchanging life histories since their parting while the equatorial night sounded with mysterious murmurs and the frangipani tree drenched them with its fragrance. Mai Tin had married a wealthy Chinese importer whose business often took him away. "He's in Hong King now, probably with a mistress he keeps up there."

"You don't mind?"

"Oh, my dear, no. We have a traditional Chinese marriage. Most of the time he lives his life, and I have mine. But you haven't married, Henry?"

"No."

"Do you keep a mistress?"

Hank hesitated, thinking, and realized that neither Margaret nor Anne could by any stretch of imagination be categorized a mistress. "No, not exactly."

"But there is someone."

"Yes." He paused. "Let's say a close friend."

"Good." She sipped her drink, her lovely face with its smooth golden skin pensive. "We have no children. My husband, Wu, says we have no time to raise children."

They sat silently for a time, sipping their drinks until they had drained them. Mai Tin followed Hank as he went inside to replenish their glasses. "I've been wanting so to talk with you about jazz. Have you got the latest Duke Ellington album?"

Hank poured a dollop of water atop the whiskey from a silver pitcher. "No. What is it?"

"It's a collection of last year's hit songs like 'Moon River', 'Charade', and 'I Left My Heart in San Francisco'."

"Doesn't sound like Ellington."

"Oh, but it is." She took the glass he handed her and started back toward the balcony. As she passed a chair she picked up her small silk bag by its drawstring and tossed it onto the bed.

"What's in the bag, Mai Tin?"

She did not answer immediately but walked on to the balcony and sat down. She looked at him with a slight smile. "It has my toothbrush and some other necessaries in case I should miss the last train home."

Hank smiled. "I think I just heard it leave."

"Good." She raised her glass to him, lustrous eyes smiling over the rim. "Here's to us."

They sipped and Hank said, "Tell me about this Ellington album. Doesn't sound like the Duke."

"Oh, but it is. Each tune seems to be arranged around

a soloist. You see, Henry, I remember what you taught me about listening to jazz. In 'I Left My Heart in San Francisco', Lawrence Brown plays a trombone solo. Johnny Hodges plays a saxophone solo on 'Moon River' — I always think of you when I play that — and the backgrounds all have those rich, complex Ellington harmonies."

"I'll have to look for it."

"And, oh, Henry, don't you love Bill Evans' piano?"

"Bill Evans? I don't know him."

"Henry! You *have* fallen behind. He's *the* great new jazz pianist. He's an absolute poet. You'll see. I'll play you some when you come see me."

"Am I coming to see you?"

"Certainly. And Peetah too, some night he is free." She sipped her drink and looked out into the night. Suddenly she turned back. "By the way, how was your meeting with Peetah?"

Hank grinned a little ruefully. "He was very much the prime minister. Very stiff. Very prime ministerial."

"What were you discussing?"

"That recent incident with the three CIA men and the present bad feeling between Singapore and the United States."

She looked reflective. "Is that why you came out here?"

"Yes."

She looked away again into the night. "He's deeply upset about that business, but we've got to find some way to get the two of you together privately." She sipped her drink, tilting her glass to drain it. "Let me work on it. I'll think of something."

Two

Hank spent the next morning reading the station's files on Yee Hock Tho. He found that just as with Mai Tin, the contacts had diminished in frequency until in the last year they had nearly ceased. Meanwhile, the small subsidy for Yee that Hank had established before leaving Singapore had been continued through an indirect banking channel right up to the present time. It was possible, Hank reflected, that Peter Yee had forgotten it still existed, given the small amount of money involved and the indirect way it was handled. But aware or not, and small or not, it represented an obligation that Yee ought to be brought to recognize. It surely was a major irony that Hank's recruitment of Yee Hock Tho, which was regarded as one of the Agency's greatest coups, should have been allowed to bear so little fruit. The value of an agent of influence, a prime minister indeed, lies in his performing some service on behalf of the interests of the United States. This had never happened to date, and Hank vowed that once amity was restored with Peter Yee, he would endeavor to find ways to make the relationship productive.

At the end of the day, Hank went home to dinner with

Dick Perkins who was living alone in the departed station chief's house during his temporary duty in Singapore. Dick had left his wife and children in Bangkok. After dinner they sat over brandy and coffee on the patio overlooking the oval swimming pool. The night air had that soft, velvety Singapore feel that Hank remembered, heavy with unknown and indescribable fragrances, and the fronds of nearby palm trees rustling and whispering in the unfailing sea breeze. They talked in low tones, Dick describing his Agency career and answering questions about the current whereabouts of officers Hank had known before leaving. Hank talked about the life and problems of a small town newspaper editor. Eventually, the talk turned to Yee Hock Tho and the disastrous interview.

"Well," said Perkins. "I've known some politically-appointed ambassadors who were industrial strength nincompoops — some career foreign service officers too, for that matter — but from what I've seen I'd have to put Glenn Timble on a very short list of the very worst. The man is vain and just plain silly. I'm not surprised Yee virtually threw him out. Unfortunately, he threw you out too."

"Agreed. That brings me to something I wanted to tell you, but *only* you. I've made contact" — Hank grimaced inwardly over that word in this context — "with Yee's sister. She has promised to arrange a private meeting for me with Peter sometime soon."

"Good. And if something good comes from it we'll work out how to inform the ambassador later."

When Hank arrived back at the Benbow Hotel that evening the clerk at the desk handed him a small envelope along with his key. Inside, in Mai Tin's artistically precise handwriting, was a brief message. "Come to the villa at 7:30 Saturday. P. and I will be there. M."

As Hank drove the station's Canadian-built Ford across the Causeway into Johore Bahru he recalled other crossings four years earlier. Although much had changed in both his and Peter Yee's lives since that time, the basic situation confronting him now was the same as then. He was soon to be engaged in persuading Peter to do something he did not wish to do. But there was one significant difference. Then he had faced two opponents, Yee and his tense and sardonic sister. Now he faced only Yee with Mai Tin beside him as a sympathetic ally.

He turned the black Ford sedan into the well-remembered narrow driveway through the palm grove. As he turned off the headlights and got out of the car he could hear the gentle wash of the nearby sea, and another similarity occurred to him. The siting of Anne Sawyer Pintel's cottage in Maine and Mai Tin's in Malaya had strong resemblances though half a planet away. But after that the contrasts were stark.

Mai Tin met him at the door, smiling with winning grace. Peter Yee stood up from his chair across the room and nodded crisply. "Good evening."

"Let me fix some drinks before we begin to talk," said Mai Tin.

"Not for me," said her brother. "I have a meeting in my office at 9."

"You'll join me? she asked Hank.

"Please."

While Mai Tin went into the kitchen and began rattling ice trays and clinking cubes into glasses, Hank waited for Peter Yee to speak. He sat looking grim, his large head with hair cut short illuminated brightly on one side by a floor lamp beside his chair. Finally, he spoke. "Mai Tin told me you wished to see me privately."

"Yes. I wanted to discuss how we can repair the damage that has been done. I didn't think it possible in the ambassador's presence. He's unaware of our special relationship."

Yee shook his heavy head. "The man's a blithering idiot. But 'special relationship'? Aren't you speaking historically?"

"I think not. It has not been put to use recently but in my mind and the Agency's it still exists."

"In what sense? I don't recognize any remaining link."

"In one sense, at least, that over the years you have accepted a monthly subsidy from us that still continues."

Peter Yee's face registered as much shock as his Chinese heritage would permit. He got to his feet and met Mai Tin as she entered carrying the whiskies. "Mai Tin. That subsidy that Mr. Bladesly arranged when I was first entering politics. Do you know if it still continues?"

She stopped, a glass in each hand, her piquant face lifted to her taller brother. "Peetah, I would have no reason to know or not to know."

He wheeled around and went back to his chair. "No matter. So far as I'm concerned the connection is dead."

"You surprise me," said Hank calmly, taking his glass from Mai Tin. "I expected you to recognize the obligation incurred by accepting the subsidy, Peter."

Yee glared at Hank. "Mr. Prime Minister, Mr. Bladesly."

"Ah, Peetah!" said Mai Tin.

Yee looked savagely at Hank. He got up and began pacing across the room. "You dare to raise the issue of obligation! Don't you realize your organization destroyed all my obligations to you when you operated in my country behind my back?"

"We recognize it was a mistake. Can't we go —"

"Listen to me, Mr. Bladesly. Let me explain to you something about the politics of Southeast Asia. I couldn't hope for your half-witted Ambassador to understand it the other day, and I feel certain it is not understood in the far reaches of North America."

"Peetah," said Mai Tin, almost crooning in a gentle voice, "can't we be civil to each other?"

"Dammit, you don't seem to realize any more than your American friend how serious this could be for Singapore. No, I won't be civil. I see no reason —"

"I would like to hear your analysis," said Hank coolly.

Yee turned and sat down in the easy chair, leaning forward with elbows on his knees. "It should be obvious to anybody. Communist China looms over the rest of Asia like a massive mountain, a sleeping giant. For the most part its attention is turned inward, at least at present, but without lifting a finger it commands a powerful cultural allegiance from millions of Chinese in Southeast Asia. They are powerful minorities in every country in the region except Singapore. Here the Chinese are a majority and Singapore, more than any other country, could be threatened by Chinese Communist efforts to seduce our citizens.

"That's one side of the threat. The other comes from the Malay states. Singapore is bracketed, north and south, by large Moslem-dominated Malay countries, Malaysia and Indonesia. Both of them have substantial Chinese minorities — Malaysia about 40 percent — and they are acutely sensitive to *any* outside contacts with those Chinese minorities. And they resent Singapore in every respect, our Chineseness and our commercial success.

"So there it is, Singapore, this tiny city-state surrounded by enormous, hostile forces. To survive in this jungle, Singapore must be the Switzerland of Southeast Asia. If possible, we must be *more* neutral than Switzerland. That is why I look at a blundering American spy operation, sending Singapore citizens into a nearby Moslem country to work against Chinese Communist operations there, to be a major threat to Singapore's security. Not to mention the insult to our sovereignty or the treachery of doing it behind our back."

"It was a mistake," said Hank.

"You are correct, Mr. Bladesly," Peter Yee said gratingly. "A terminal mistake." He nodded his large head and leaned back in his chair. "Mai Tin, bring me a short whiskey. I must leave shortly."

Hank restrained a strong impulse to let his eyes follow Mai Tin's lovely figure as she went to the kitchen. Instead he looked steadily at Yee. "Terminal is not acceptable to me or my organization, Mr. Prime Minister. A mistake has been made, I admit, but the relationship between us is sustained by two things: the obligation you incurred by accepting our subsidy over the years and the mutual interest we have, the United States and Singapore, in opposing any Chinese Communist intrusion into Southeast Asia."

Peter Yee got to his feet, his narrow eyes blazing. "I will not listen any more to these absurd claims of an obligation! I do not even know that I have been receiving the money. In any case, it was a ridiculously tiny sum." He took the offered drink from Mai Tin and downed it in a gulp. "I believe you understand my position, Mr. Bladesly. I must go to my meeting."

"I do," said Hank who had also got to his feet. "But you have received the monthly subsidy and to my mind that sustains the obligation."

Peter Yee glared at Hank. He walked swiftly out of the room saying "Good night, Mai Tin" over his shoulder.

Hank sat back down and drained his glass. Across from him, straight-backed on the edge of her chair, Mai Tin gazed at him, her oval face, lovely in its classic Chinese economy. "Well, that apparently is that," said Hank.

"No. You won."

"I *won?*"

"Yes. Peetah doesn't know it yet and apparently neither do you. But you won. My brother has very strong principles. He honors his obligations. He will find out that the money has been coming into his account, and he will be unable to bear not honoring the obligation that imposes. In a day or two he will see you again."

"I would like to believe you are right."

"Don't believe. Just wait."

Hank sighed. "All right. But I'd like another drink, please, while I wait." This time his grateful eyes followed Mai Tin's gleaming, supple figure as she walked into the kitchen.

With no specific duties while awaiting Peter Yee's summons, Hank went into the Embassy to read the daily incoming traffic. He found Dick Perkins looking harassed and muttering to himself. "The Division has sent out instructions to maintain contact with several key agents during this interim period, and I'm goddammed if I can cover them all."

"Why don't I give you a hand?"

"You don't mind?"

"Glad to help."

"Great. Here's one, the file on FOX. I think the MO calls for a meeting every third Thursday. That's today."

"Okay." Hank took the file into a nearby office and began to read. FOX was a Chinese engineer at the Naval Dockyard with access to top management decisions and communications. Headquarters had levied a standing requirement for intelligence concerning a deal with the Soviet Union for ship repair service at the dockyard. The designated meeting place on this date was the Golden Flower Cafe, the site of his first meetings with Peter Yee. The time set was 4 p.m.

He set out shortly after 3 on a twisting, turning stop-and-go route that put him at the Golden Flower just before 4. En route, he discovered he was enjoying himself more than he had in months, even years. It was also fun to find the Golden Flower unchanged, clattering with high-pitched Chinese voices and teeming with bustle.

The coarse-grained file picture of FOX had been taken at some distance with a telephoto lens but Hank picked out a 35-year old Chinese sitting alone as a likely man. He approached and gave the parole. "I'm a friend of Sun Lee Wat. Mind if I join you?"

The Chinese looked around, startled. "Mr. Winthrop not coming?"

"No, he's out of town."

"I see." FOX looked anxiously at Hank. "How do I know. . .?"

"Because I greeted you properly. And I have in my pocket an envelope with 500 Singapore dollars which I will hand you before I leave."

The Chinese breathed deeply. "I see. Sit down. What can I tell you?"

"What have you heard about negotiations with the Russians for ship repair service at the Dockyard?"

FOX shook his head. "Nothing. My boss thinks it's just propaganda by Yee Hock Tho to scare the Americans."

"Who is your boss?"

The answer FOX gave was, as Hank knew, already recorded in the file but he asked it, as he did several other questions about personnel and organization to check for consistency and reliability. Finally, Hank asked, "Is anything unusual happening at the Dockyard?"

FOX pondered, sipping his Tiger beer, and said, "The Malays, the Moslems, seem restless. Meeting in small groups and arguing with each other." Hank nodded, passed the envelope with the 500 Singapore dollars under the table, and left.

Next day Dick Perkins came into the office where Hank was sitting, still awaiting word from Peter Yee or Mai Tin. "I've got two blips from agents asking for meetings today. One is at the bar just outside the air base at Changi. The other is on the company ferry to Blakun Mati Island. Which do you want?"

"I'm a boat lover. I'll take the ferry."

"It's yours." Hank opened the manila sleeve and discovered

to his great surprise that the case was his old agent, DAMASK, the Malay student at the University of Malaya. He had gone on to graduate work after Hank's departure, was now an instructor in political science. The file showed that DAMASK had advanced from a sort of handyman to a productive and reliable informant on Malay dissidence, especially fundamentalist Moslem groups.

Shortly before 4:30, the time DAMASK had set for the meeting, Hank arrived at the gate for the ferry operated by a fish processing plant on Blakun Mati Island. The service existed to transport the processing company's employees but it was open to all comers. Hank was wearing a sport shirt and shorts and carrying a small bag with swim trunks and towel. He spotted DAMASK with no trouble, the same ingratiating manner of an Indian jewelry salesman but gone a little to pot in figure. He did not immediately recognize Hank who had gradually made his way to a place at the rail beside him. "Do you know," asked Hank using the stipulated parole, "whether this ferry runs every hour or half hour?"

"Every hour," said DAMASK. He glanced sideways at Hank and whispered, "My God, it's you!" Then he turned, executed the niftiest brush pass you would ever want to see — or as Hank inwardly corrected himself, the *niftiest pass you couldn't see* — and walked slowly toward the gangway for departure.

While most passengers turned left toward the processing plant, Hank turned right toward the beach. He climbed over several grassy hillocks and down through the palm grove lining the beach to the sandy strip beside the pale blue water. The hazy atmosphere made the distant horizon on the Straits of Malacca shimmer and off to the west towering white cloud cliffs assembled for the late afternoon tropical thunderstorm. He looked around. He was as alone as though standing on the edge of the universe.

He opened the tightly folded paper DAMASK had passed. The message was stark: "MOSLEM REVOLUTIONARY

LEAGUE PLANS ASSASSINATION PRIME MINISTER THIS AFTERNOON OUTSIDE OFFICE." Hank looked at his Omega watch. It was 4:51. As he remembered, Government offices closed at 5 and the Prime Minister usually left between 5:30 and 6. Hank had to get back into town as fast as possible.

He trotted back along the path over the grassy hillocks and down to the ferry dock. The ferry had gone. He walked up and down the wooden jetty looking for a water taxi. None in sight. He ran back and forth looking for a skiff or any kind of boat he could commandeer. None to be found. After several minutes, his watch now showing 4:59, he spotted a water taxi leaving the ferry pier and coming across. He waited impatiently, time moving with leaden feet, until the boat docked. A round, cherubic-faced Englishman stood up in the boat and fished in his white shorts for the fare. He pulled out a large bank note. The water-man, a dark-hued Hainan Chinese wearing a battered hat, watched impassively while the engine of his five-seated skiff chugged uncertainly and vented puffs of blue smoke. "Bother!" said the Englishman. "All I have is this 50 dollar note. I don't suppose you have the change?"

The boatman looked at the bill the Englishman was waving before him and shook his head. "Well, hold on. I'll just pop up to the office and get change."

"Here," said Hank, pulling out three dollar bills. "I'll be glad to pay it. I'm in a hurry."

"No, my dear chap. Thanks awfully, but I couldn't dream of letting you pay my fare." He turned to the boatman. "Just hold tight like a good fellow. I won't be a sec."

He had taken no more than a dozen steps when Hank, nearly jumping out of his skin with tension, jumped into the skiff and shoved the money into the Chinaman's hand. He gestured strongly toward the opposite shore. "Go other side. Quick, quick!"

The boatman nodded, turned and opened the throttle on the ancient engine, and swung the boat in a half circle away from the dock. From his seat in the bow Hank could see the round Englishman waving his 50 dollar note and shouting something indistinguishable, his mouth opening into an O and closing. Hank glanced again and again at his Omega as the skiff made a bare three knots toward the ferry dock. The hands stood at 5:11 as the boat bumped the jetty. Hank quickly shoved five sweaty Singapore dollars into the Chinese boatman's hand and jumped onto the dock.

The inside of the old Austin, which the station had still kept for operational use, was at oven baking temperature when Hank got in and tossed his bag in the back. In his impatience he pushed down hard on the accelerator and flooded the engine, already super-heated by the equatorial sun. He pushed the accelerator all the way to the floor and kept the starter cranking with a sound like a worn electric can opener. At last the engine coughed, sputtered, barked a backfire, and burst into full 30 horsepower song. Hank jammed the car into gear and headed through the thickening late afternoon traffic toward the embassy.

He stopped the car at the curb and ran past the marine guard, ignoring the leisurely elevator, and vaulting the marble steps two at a time. He burst into Perkins' office. It was empty, the safe locked. In the bookcase across the room he found a Singapore telephone directory and riffled through the pages to locate government office numbers. There was a listing, "Office of the Prime Minister." He dialed the number, watching as the rotary selector moved slowly back after each turn. While the number was ringing he looked at his watch: 5:25. After three double rings, a cool, modulated Chinese voice said, "The office of the Prime Minister."

"This is Henry Bladesly. I must speak with the Prime Minister at once."

"I'm sorry, Mr. Bladesly. The Prime Minister is taking no

more calls today. Perhaps you will call back tomorrow or make an appointment to see. . ."

"This is urgent! An emergency. I must. . ."

"I'm sorry, Mr. Bladesly. The Prime Minister's instructions were strict."

Hank slammed down the telephone and turned back to the directory. Special Branch, Special Branch — there it was. He dialed the number, his impatience now just short of a scream. A crisp voice answered on the second ring.

"This is Henry Bladesly at the U.S. Embassy. I have some urgent information concerning the Prime Minister."

Without hesitation the voice replied, "I'm sorry, Mr. Bladesly, I cannot receive information from unknown callers by telephone. Perhaps you could come to Headquarters and be interviewed."

"No, damn it. This is urgent, an emergency. I tell you, I am Bladesly at the U.S. Embassy."

There was a brief pause. Hank's watch now read 5:29. "The U.S. Embassy," the voice mused. "Perhaps I could call you back there."

"Fine. Do it right away!"

"Righto."

Hank sat then, staring intently at the telephone, willing it to ring. He watched the silent phone while the sweep second hand on the Omega made two and then three full turns. It was then 5:35, and he jumped up and ran out the door.

Galloping down the steps he realized that the Special Branch duty officer had undoubtedly called the embassy number and the switchboard was closed for the night. Only the CIA office telephones remained operative, and he had not thought to provide the Special Branch man with the number. The marine guard tried to get Hank to sign the night register, but Hank rushed past him saying, "Later!"

This time he approached the temperamental Austin

engine delicately, and it started at once. He bulled his way into the stream of traffic passing the embassy entrance, and drove the three blocks to the Government building. There seemed to be a clot of cars around the entrance so he double parked about two hundred yards back and ran on. He was just halfway there when a brilliant orange flash and a rocketing blast slammed him sideways onto the grass beside the walkway. He lay sprawling and stunned for a moment and then got to his feet, his ears ringing and sounds muffled. He walked slowly forward. At the curb stood two cars. The one ahead, smoke pouring out of the blown top and blasted windows, was a mere hulk. The one behind was intact except for shattered windows, and beside it two figures were lying, seemingly through the smoke a white uniformed syce and a woman in a pale blue dress. Before he could get closer he was stopped by a Singapore policeman, one of a dozen who came running to the scene from all sides. "Stay back, sir!" Over his shoulder Hank could see two guards run out of the Government Building and kneel beside the bodies on the ground. "Keep moving, sir. Move on!" The policeman tapped his baton smartly into his palm for emphasis.

Hank went back to the Austin and drove to Special Branch Headquarters. He might as well have gone to Exchange Alley for all the information he could get. The tight-lipped desk officer kept repeating, "I have nothing to tell you, sir. Nothing at this time."

"Was the Prime Minister injured?"

The white uniformed officer hesitated, seemed almost on the verge of saying "no", and then said, "I have nothing to tell you, sir."

Frustrated, Hank left. At the Benbow Park he ate a solitary dinner after two double scotches. Later in his room he paced up and down trying to think of ways to get through the impenetrable screen of silence Peter Yee's government had thrown up. Somehow he would find Mai Tin. She would tell him the facts. After futilely trying to read a paperback of one of John LeCarre's recent fantasies about the spy trade, he drank two more scotches in quick succession and went to bed. Before he fell asleep he once more visited, like a tongue testing a sore tooth, the chagrin he felt for not giving the warning in time. He sighed deeply and thought that at least he was morally certain Peter Yee was not the victim of the bomb blast.

Next morning's *The Straits Times,* which arrived together with his papaya and coffee, ripped even that consolation away. "BOMB BLAST INJURES PM'S KIN" screamed the banner headline. And below it, "SISTER STRUCK BY CAR BOMB." The story under the headlines detailed the facts: a bomb inside a car parked in front of the Prime Minister's office had exploded at 5:41 p.m., just as Madame Wu Mai Tin, sister of Prime Minister Yee Hock Tho, was alighting from her car at the entrance. Madame Wu was "in hospital", her condition as yet unknown.

It was noon before Hank could get through to Peter Yee's office. He had tried the Seventh Day Adventist Hospital three times but each time he was told by a crisp British-accented voice that no information regarding Madame Wu's condition was being provided outside the immediate family. At last, a male Chinese voice in Yee Hock Tho's office informed him the Prime Minister would receive him at 4 p.m.

Peter Yee's face was somber and grim. "I have very little information to give you but sit down a moment if you like."

"Thank you. How is Mai Tin?"

Yee shook his head. "The doctors are still uncertain. The blast blew shattered glass across her face. They are concerned" — he stopped and looked across the room out the window — "about saving her sight."

"My God!"

The two men sat silently for several moments. Peter Yee shook his head. "Obviously, the bomb was meant for me.

Special Branch believes it was the work of Moslem terrorists — probably from Indonesia."

The reference to Indonesia and its connection with the blundered CIA operation was not lost on Hank. Again the men were silent with only the faint sound of outside street traffic faintly audible. A ship in the harbor gave out a hoarse bellow. At last Hank spoke. "I want to help somehow or other. Any resources my Agency or my Government can command I offer." The slight twinge that Hank felt over this unsanctioned offer was muted by his recollection of Pickard Grant's instruction, "whatever it takes."

Peter Yee looked up, his eyes softer than Hank had ever seen them. "Thank you, Henry." He paused and looked away. "I will get in touch with you tomorrow. You are at the Benbow Park? You will hear from me sometime tomorrow."

The next morning, after a quick breakfast and a brisk walk around the grounds of the Benbow Park, Hank sat in his room and waited. Through the open door to his balcony he could hear the morning calls of birds, some were raucous but one was remarkably like a flute obligatto. Now and then a bright-eyed mynah bird dropped onto the arm of the chair and then onto the table, all the while cocking its head and appraising Hank. The breeze flowing into the room had that magically enchanting Singapore mixture of clinging softness and exotic fragrance. At last the telephone rang. Again it was the male Chinese secretary. "The Prime Minister would like to see you as soon as possible."

Peter Yee was standing at the window behind his desk, his back to the door, as Hank was ushered in by the young Chinese assistant. Yee turned around, his face ravaged with worry and lack of sleep. "Good morning, Henry. Sit down. The news I have is very bad."

"Not blinded!"

"No. At least not yet. The doctors have concluded that

several shards have penetrated deep into the eyeball. So deep that the optic nerve may be 'compromised', as they say."

"Can they operate?"

"They are uncertain. It would be an extremely delicate operation. They are searching the region for a skilled specialist — Hong Kong, Bangkok, even New Delhi."

"Peter — uh, Mr. Prime Minister —"

"Peter."

"— let me see what I can do. I will be back to you before the day is over."

On his way to the U.S. Embassy and the CIA office he checked his wrist watch. Eleven-ten a.m. That meant elevenish, close to midnight, at Langley. No matter. In the office he filled Dick Perkins in on the situation and got his approval to use "Flash" precedence on a message to Headquarters. The cable was short and bold. He requested an immediate appointment with the best eye surgeon in the United States and the use of a CIA charter aircraft within the next 24 hours to fly the patient.

Then began the wait for a reply during which he imagined the stir he had created in Washington: the Watch Office call to check with Pete Risko or Jude Welby before waking the Director, the midnight ride by an Agency courier down across Chain Bridge and up Arizona Avenue to Pickard Grant's house, and then — Well, beyond that there were too many variables. He could only wait. And wait.

At three in the afternoon he got a reply. "REQUESTS APPROVED. CONTACTS BRANCH BOSTON SEEKING SERVICES MORRIS HALSTEAD, PREMIER EYE SURGEON. AGENCY REQUESTING AIR FORCE PROVIDE SPECIAL AIR MISSIONS JET FROM CLARK. STAND BY."

"Stand by" meant sitting in his office while the staff closed up and went home. It also meant eating cardboard-flavored fried rice he had induced one of the char force to get for him from a passing Chinese food cart. By 10:30 p.m. he had read every scrap of reading material in the CIA suite and was contemplating raiding one of the nearby Embassy offices when he heard the step of Jake Artson coming down the hall. He got up to meet him. "'FLASH' for you, sir," said Jake.

He ripped open the envelope and read "SERVICES HALSTEAD OBTAINED. SAM JET ARRIVING MORNING LOCAL TIME. MANILA WILL CONFIRM ETA."

It took over 45 minutes to reach Peter Yee. He started by calling the Special Branch duty officer. "I understand it may be urgent, Mr. Bladesly. And yes, your name is known to us. But first I must locate the Prime Minister's P.A. and get his approval for putting you through to the P.M."

The increasingly familiar young Chinese voice of the personal assistant came through the phone shortly after 11. He grasped the situation quickly. He explained he was at least 15 minutes away from the P.M.'s residence but he would leave for there immediately and arrange for a return telephone call. True to his word, the phone on Hank's desk voiced its *Br-ring–br-ring* 20 minutes later and the voice said, "Mr. Bladesly? Here is the Prime Minister, sir."

Peter Yee's response to Hank's information was a prolonged, perhaps shocked, silence. At last he spoke, using his stiff, prime ministerial voice in the presence of his personal assistant. "Those arrangements sound excellent, Mr. Bladesly. My office will be in touch with you early tomorrow morning to make plans for moving the patient to the airport to meet the aircraft."

By noon next day the silver USAF jet was lifting off Changi Air Base strip with a heavily bandaged Mai Tin aboard. Accompanying her were three medical people from the Singapore Seventh Day Adventist Hospital and an Air Force doctor and nurse from Clark Field. Hank wanted to squeeze Mai Tin's hand, her form looking remarkably small on the wheeled stretcher as she was passed from the ambulance to the airplane, the noonday equatorial sun dazzling as it struck the white bandaged head, but he hung well back, not wishing to be seen in intimate relationship with the Yee family. As he walked to his car he mused that with stops at Guam and San Francisco, the big jet ought to arrive at Logan in Boston in 24 to 26 hours. Midnight in Boston where she could be transported to the hospital, received and prepped, and operated on the following morning. Now to go back to the waiting.

Clearly, no further progress could be made in the reconciliation with Peter Yee until Mai Tin's situation was resolved. How long this would take no one could say, but it was already mid-December and his promise to Margaret to be back for Christmas was threatened. He needed to be in Singapore to receive the news from Contacts Branch Boston and pass it along to Peter. He was snagged by circumstance, prisoner of a surgeon's verdict.

The initial news from Boston was cautious. The glass splinters had been successfully removed but some days must go by before all danger of infection had passed and before Mai Tin could be examined to determine whether vision loss through nerve damage had occurred. The indeterminate phrase, "some days," decided Hank. He sent a cable saying "unavoidably detained" and tried not to think about Margaret's disappointment.

Ten agonizingly slow days went by. He ate Christmas dinner alone at the Benbow Park and afterward went for a long, aimless walk in the Botanical Gardens, the scalding sun like a searchlight through the heavy shadows of the gigantic trees. Late Christmas night he tried for two hours to telephone both Margaret and Anne but each time the British voice informed him "all circuits are engaged, sir." Some time after midnight he went to bed, heavy and stupid from too much scotch.

Three

At last came the long awaited word: the operation a success; patient recovering. Vision in the left eye, 85%; in the right, 50%. Some improvement during convalescence could be expected. Slight plastic surgery desirable but could be performed in Singapore. Patient to be released the following day.

Hank asked and was able to see Peter Yee immediately. The eyes in the solemn, pock-marked face never left Hank's as Yee listened to the message. Then he looked away without speaking. He got up and walked to the window, gazing down on the emerald green padang below. There was a long silence in the room, broken only by the faint tapping of a typewriter outside the office door. Yee turned back toward Hank, his large head luminous in the light from the window, his face in shadow. "Henry," he said slowly, " I will have something to say to you in a day or two. Let me arrange a meeting then. My office will reach you."

That was Monday afternoon. On Wednesday, while a late afternoon thunder shower dropped sheets of water onto the macadam hardstand as the big jet pulled in and the downpour brimmed to overflowing the deep monsoon drains surrounding the building, Hank stood quietly in the crowd at the airport arrival area and watched as Mai Tin passed slowly by on the arm of a Chinese nurse. She was wearing dark glasses, so dark as to approach opaque, and she walked slowly, looking neither right nor left. But she was back.

On Thursday evening Hank was sitting with Peter Yee in the aft cockpit of the Singapore Harbour Patrol cutter, *Kris*. Off to the starboard lay a dozen or more freighters, anchored and waiting to be lightered off, their light-tipped masts dotting the harbor in a random pattern. Occasionally a ship uttered a short hoot in signalling to one of the lighters, and the sound came to Hank's ears through the steady wash and hiss of the sea along the cutter's side and her tumbling wake. But Hank was only dimly aware of the sight and sounds in the night of the fabulous harbor. His mind was too engrossed in absorbing the reach and significance of Peter Yee's just concluded remarks.

Yee had begun by describing his deep isolation as leader of the infant city-state. Aside from Mai Tin he had no confidants, no right hand man. "In governments, political organizations, every man is a politician," he said. "Everyone is either a momentary ally or a foe. I have no one I can trust, really trust, to act at all times in my interest."

Then he had turned to the CIA operational fiasco. "That should never have taken place, Henry. If I had someone around me who was thoroughly versed in security affairs it would not have happened. He would have been alert and put a stop to it before it got well underway."

Peter Yee paused then and watched as a mahogany-hued junk passed on *Kris's* port side, her masthead lighted by a kerosene lamp above her slatternly sail. "I have thought carefully about what I am about to say to you," he resumed. "I have discussed it with Mai Tin. And I have decided to offer you a post in my government. Wait!" He held up his hand as Hank started to speak. "Hear me out. Together we can negotiate your title and duties, whether they would primarily involve security affairs or press relations, either of which you could perform. And I know there are some legal technicalities, all of which I can deal with. As for stipend, I will double, no, triple, your present income. But what I want, and what I am confident you can give me, is the service of someone I can trust, someone who has proved his trustworthiness and his loyalty to me and my family."

Too astonished to reply, Hank had looked at the powerful Chinese across from him in the cockpit; his elbows on his knees and his large head thrust forward. "Peter, I can't —"

"It will take time. There a number of things to consider."

A number of things! They were so many and so various that for the first time he could remember Hank felt overwhelmed. To accept Peter's offer would cut Hank's life in two like a meat cleaver. His roots in Maine, the family obligation to the *Hanson Courier,* his personal relationships: these were just the heads of a longer list. And yet, and yet. . .The magical lure of life in Singapore, the magnificent jewel of Southeast Asia, the sensuous color and alluring strangeness of the streets, the people, the nose-tingling fragrances of flowers and trees and the harsh but exotic smells of the river, sour charcoal fires, and acrid curing rubber. Singapore was enchantment. Life there could be a romantic dream realized.

Peter Yee began talking again in a low voice, going back over the ground of his isolation and his need for impartial, disinterested advice, but Hank scarcely heard him and did not reply. The names of those who held key positions in the pattern of his life rolled by in his mind like the final credits in a film: the *Hanson Courier;* Margaret, his demi-fiance; Anne, his lover; Mai Tin, his — friend. Then there were the men in CIA who were depending on him to restore good relations in Singapore. The task he had been assigned by CIA at the moment seemed a tangential consideration but at least it gave him something to discuss with Peter Yee. Always, the secondary aspects of a problem are easiest to handle.

"Peter, what about the CIA relationship? You remember, the Agency sent me out here to resolve that problem."

"If you accept my offer that will resolve itself."

"And if I don't?"

"Ah, well, Henry." Peter looked down at his shoes on the greyish teak deck. "I suppose you will charge me once again with being un-Chinese, but I don't feel I can make that a hostage to your agreement. If you do not accept my suggestion we can still work out something."

Hank nodded. "Thanks, Peter."

Both men remained silent then as the twin diesels beneath the deck of *Kris* lowered the pitch of their drone. Ahead off the starboard bow loomed the white stone tower of Raffles Light, the historic beacon marking the passage from the Straits of Malacca into Singapore Harbor. The cutter slowed as it approached the wooden jetty, the engines idling and then surging in reverse as the foam thrashed around her stern. Above them, in the heavy air of the night sky, the great light silently threw its beam in a perpetual circle. Two seamen leaped onto the planked dock and snubbed the cutter's lines fast.

"Let's go inside and look around," said Peter. Inside the broad-based stone tower they climbed steps made of stone jutting out from the side of the tower in an ascending spiral. They were greeted by the lighthouse keeper on the platform just below the swinging light. The incandescence was blinding as the great light swung by on its endless round, the glare of the lamp intensified by giant glass prisms. The keeper described the mechanism that turned the light and enlarged on the beacon's capabilities. Hank tried to focus his mind on the historic resonance of the name, "Raffles

Light," as he looked about at the old tower, but instead he found himself rolling over the names that bound his life together: Margaret, Anne, the *Courier,* Mai Tin, CIA, Pickard Grant, Pete Risko. And then again, Margaret, Anne...

It was just before midnight when *Kris* slid into her slip at Singapore Harbour Patrol Headquarters. As the Prime Minister's Mercedes 600 limousine stopped before the Benbow Park entrance, Hank said, "I'll make an appointment to see you in a day or two, Peter." Then he went to his room, poured himself a stiff scotch and walked onto the balcony through the glass doors. Awaiting him as always was the magical equatorial night: the strange sounds of unknown night birds, the sizzling, zinging noises of unfamiliar insects, and forever and ever the heavy, mind-numbing fragrance of frangipani. Without bidding, his mind recollected a winter night in Maine, as it would be in Hanson in another twelve hours: the frozen silence, the tingling, arid, odorless air, animal and human life all huddled into some kind of protective warmth. Both surroundings held places of importance in his life and certainly at present Maine held the central core of his life's meaning. And yet, and yet...

Sleep proved impossible to achieve, and he spent the night staggering from one set of considerations to another. In the morning, he knew only for certain that he could not make the decision by himself in Singapore. He made an appointment to see Yee Hock Tho and entered his office shortly before noon. The Prime Minister greeted him quietly. "Peter," Hank said, "I am flattered more than I can say by your offer, but I can't make a decision now. I need time to think and to talk with others back in the States."

"I understand. How much time do you need?"

Hank hesitated. "I can't answer that. Days or weeks..."

Peter Yee nodded. "You know, Henry. I have found it useful when making a difficult decision to set a deadline for myself. What do you say to thirty days from now?"

"That's fair. Thirty days." Hank pondered a moment. "I will be talking with my people at CIA Headquarters. What can I tell them about our relationship with you?"

"Tell them we can resume as before — with different people on your side, of course. You understand my concerns. I will trust you to represent them for me."

"All right. I will." Hank paused, hesitant. "Peter, do you think it possible for me to see Mai Tin before I leave?"

"I am quite certain she would like it. I'll ask her to ring you up at the hotel."

After a solitary lunch, Hank waited in his room for Mai Tin's call. At last the telephone on the side table rang and through the instrument came that enchanting, lilting voice, diminished and attentuated by trauma but still unmistakably that familiar beguiling sound. "Henry, could you come have tea with me at 4 o'clock?"

"I would love to."

"At four, then." The telephone gave a definitive click.

In her large living room, richly but quietly furnished and decorated by masses of flowers, sat Mai Tin in a long, white flowing robe. She did not rise as the Chinese maid announced Hank but held out her fine-boned hand, her lustrous eyes barely visible through the dark glasses. "My dear friend," she said. "My *dear* friend."

Hank would have liked to have kissed her but her figure and her manner gave off an aura of fragility, as delicate as translucent Chinese porcelain. He took her hand gently and then let it slide slowly away. "Mai Tin," he said. "I'm glad you're back."

Four

If CIA Director Pickard Grant was caught by surprise when Hank told him of Prime Minister Yee Hock Tho's remarkable offer, it did not register on the lean, hard-jawed face. He listened intently as Hank related Yee's agreement to return Agency relationships in Singapore to their previous status and nodded as if with satisfaction. He sat quietly behind his desk for several moments and gazed out the window wall of his office. "Well, Hank," he said at last, "we sent you out to Singapore to restore relations there and that you have done. From my point of view and the Agency's that completes the mission. But now, as for this other thing, Yee Hock Tho's offer to hire you, that's really outside our jurisdiction. I admit that having a former Agency officer in the employ of a foreign government, and looking down our throats, would present real problems. But we're all grown men, rational fellows. I think we could deal with that somehow."

"But do you have any advice about whether or not I should accept the offer?"

"No, none." Grant smiled a thin smile at Hank. "I don't know anything about your family situation or your connection with the newspaper in Maine, but I imagine that those are the considerations that will weigh most heavily. I can't help you there."

"No, I guess not."

There was a prolonged silence while Hank stared at his shoes and Pickard Grant watched impassively. Then he spoke, "I suppose you will need to go back to Singapore to talk with Yee after you've made your decision. We'll pick up the tab on that, no matter which way you decide, if you'll do what you can to get our fellow off on the right foot. The only other thing I can say is good luck!" He stood up behind his desk and held out his hand.

"Thank you, sir." They shook hands and Hank made his way to Pete Risko's office.

"Jesus, Blades," said Risko when Hank told him about Peter Yee's proposition. "You'll be richer than stink! I wish one of those oriental potentates would make me an offer like that. I'd snap at it!"

But snap at it was precisely what Hank could not do, he realized afresh as he flew to Boston and then boarded the Boston and Maine train for Portland and Hanson. The lure of Singapore was strong but the threads that tied him to Maine were almost innumerable. Each would need to be traced back to its anchoring point and its strength tested before a decision could be made whether to break it.

Margaret met him at the train station, and Hank realized as he received her kiss that she had carefully prepared for the meeting. Her clothes and her grooming were up to "party" caliber. She looked like a very well turned out young American matron, and her Tweed perfume that reached his nose as they kissed bespoke demure restraint. Indeed, it seemed something more than restraint. There was a faint brittle edginess in her voice as she said, "I'm so glad you're back, Henry. At last."

Next morning as Hank stepped off his front porch on his

way to the *Courier* office, the biting cold air struck at him like a blow. The bone dry, frigid air stiffened and clogged his nostrils, and the breath came out of his mouth like steam. The soft, caressing air of Singapore seemed like a vanished dream, one he would give much to recapture. But, he thought to himself as he walked with care, avoiding the icy patches on the walk, the decision to return to Singapore as Yee Hock Tho's assistant was not a simple, one-dimensioned one. It was compound. If he were to go to Singapore, would he take along a wife? Could he imagine Margaret moving amidst the social circles he knew in Singapore? Or was this the occasion to break up a relationship which seemed to give so little substance to either of them? And if he did decide to break with Margaret, would he then go to Singapore alone and seek to establish some kind of an ongoing intimacy with Mai Tin? Or would he instead use his separation from Margaret as the occasion to deepen, and perhaps formalize, his relationship with Anne? He could imagine Anne moving with ease and grace in Singapore more readily than he could Margaret. He could even imagine Anne and Mai Tin becoming friends.

He crossed the Boston and Maine tracks leading west from the station and saw ahead of him the familiar buildings of the Hanson business district: the hardware, the red brick bank, the pharmacy, and just beyond, the well-worn face of the *Courier* office. The disposition of the *Courier* was also part of the compound decision. Would he hire someone to run the newspaper and cut the Bladesly family ties to a long-standing Maine institution? There were so many considerations, so many balances to make and adjust, that he began to feel that Peter Yee's thirty day period was scarcely enough.

As he walked in the door of his office there was a feminine squeal and Pat Long threw herself into his arms. "Chief, you're back!" She pulled away and turned to a thin, pale man behind her. "Let me introduce you to Winton Jackson who has been running the place in your absence."

After shaking hands the two men sat down in Hank's office where Jackson insisted on Hank's taking his old chair at the desk. "Yours now," he said. "I give it up with some reluctance. I've enjoyed playing newspaper editor far more than I expected to." Jackson went on then to describe himself as "a Maine boy. Born and grew up in Farmington. Went to Yarmouth. A class about ten years ahead of yours. Drafted in the Army in World War II, did some public relations work, and after the war ended up as an editor in CIA's Office of Current Intelligence where I was when Pickard Grant plucked me out to come up here while you took on some derring-do for the Agency."

Hank nodded. "How has it gone?"

"All right so far as I know. I don't think I broke any crockery. I kept the editorials pretty bland except that I have launched a campaign to get the highway people to do something about that bad intersection where Route 1 and 1A come together just south of town. There was a lulu of an accident there last week, car and a cement truck, two women killed. I thought you'd approve of that."

"Absolutely."

They spent the rest of the morning leafing through back issues of the paper while Jackson explained the considerations that lay behind his decisions. It became clear to Hank as the morning wore on that a very creditable job had been done in his absence. "Looks great to me, Winton," he said. "I can't see that you missed a beat." Inwardly he was thinking that the *Courier* if left to Jackson to run would be in very capable hands indeed.

They lunched together at The Bos'n's Chair while Hank tried to stifle the contrasts that arose in his mind between the surrounding New England bare simplicity and the exotic elegance of restaurants in Singapore. "Working up here on *The Courier,''* Jackson was saying, "has given me a chance to think about my own future. I can retire now at any time, and I think I want to get out of the mad race in Washington and get back to some place more wholesome and normal. Like Maine. Like here." He paused and looked directly at Hank. "You've got a nice operation here. One I'd be happy to get involved in, either as an assistant editor — with my annuity I won't need much salary — or take it over for you while you go off and do something else for a while."

"It's something to think about," said Hank. Something indeed. One of those elements in his compound decision had been spoken for.

Five

The wind from the sound blowing across Summer Point was arrow-sharp and made Anne Sawyer Pintel's right ear tingle as she strode along the road leading into town. Patches of ice on the road that came with erratic frequency made bicycling too hazardous so she had decided to walk the nearly three miles into the College to meet her 10 o'clock class. Despite the cutting wind that whipped her skirt against her knees and numbed her right cheek, the inner Anne was warm and content. She hummed the Allegro to Mozart's Clarinet Concerto, matching the rhythm to her stride. "Bum-tiddley-tum-tum-tum."

Life had taken on a sunshine-in-the-morning flush for Anne over the past several months. From the black nadir she had hit after Bob Pintel had told her their marriage was over, there had been a steady succession of upbeat changes, beginning with her friendship and lighthearted affair with Hank, her appointment to the faculty of Yarmouth College, and now most recently the slow, steady, solid development of her relationship with Bruce.

Bruce Goddard was an associate professor of philosophy at Yarmouth. In his early forties, a widower of three years, blocky of build and almost exactly Anne's height, slow and thoughtful of speech with gentle, teasing humor, he had instantly captured her attention when they had first met at lunch in the company of Ogden Witham, her history of art professor. It was the deeply bedded assurance he exuded in manner and speech that was so winning. It was an assurance not unlike Hank's but different somehow in its expression. Hank's seemed to rest primarily on pure masculinity, masculine strength and muscular confidence. Bruce's was more intellectual, more inward, more philosophically based, undoubtedly the product of his years of philosophical study. Besides, he had curly, blondish hair and deep blue eyes.

A few days after they had first met, Bruce had asked her to lunch with him again. It was then she had learned of his wife's death from cancer three years earlier. She also learned then with that sensitively-tuned intuition of women that he was attracted to her. She had warmed to it as a woman does to any presentable man's interest but she soon realized that something deeper, more fundamental was happening to her. Something more than the comforting glow she had first felt in the presence of Hank's assurance, something more than the stabilizing, gravitational pull of Hank's companionship, something more permanent in its implications than her sexual romps with Hank. She did not even let the word, "love", reach the surface of her consciousness, but she was aware that somewhere in the deepest recesses of her being it had begun to bud.

After that luncheon they had been together with increasing frequency: afternoon walks, lectures and plays and concerts at the college, a dinner or two at a fine restaurant in Portland. Once as he took her to the door of her house, Bruce had kissed her, warmly but respectfully. She had responded with an almost maidenly restraint that made here giggle at herself after the door had closed behind her and Bruce was walking out to his car. But she had liked his kiss, its strength and its sincerity.

Her fingertips within her fur-lined gloves had all gone numb by the time she had finished walking across the campus under the bare-limbed elms and reached for the brass-handled door of Dunlap Hall. She was still hanging up her coat, stamping her feet to bring back feeling, and touching her crimson cheeks with tingling fingers, when the door of the office she shared with another assistant instructor gently opened behind her. It was Bruce on his way to his own 10 o'clock class, sticking his head around the door, blue eyes warm and merry. "Lunch today?" he asked.

"Love to," said Anne. "I'd love to!"

Margaret Rawlins' mind was a weltering sea of cross-currents and riptides as she drove out of Portland going north on Route 1 toward Hanson. Mingled pleasure and self approval surged back and forth against uncertainty and self-reproach. She had lunched with Guy Boudreau for the third time in as many weeks, but this time they had lunched at his house, and she had joined him in lovemaking up to the point where he had taken her hand, moist and trembling with deep arousal, and had started to lead her upstairs to his bedroom. Then something within her had said no, and she pulled her hand free.

That part she was proud of. But was she? She welcomed Guy's admiration; she drank it like a parched traveler in the desert. She found his lovemaking thoroughly pleasurable, a beguiling mixture of hesitant advances and unexpected audacity. And she had known Guy for years, since their first year in high school when they had gone out on several innocent dates. He was an old and trusted friend, and he seemed to want her with open and deep sincerity. Then why. . .?

Margaret had been going to Portland once a week for the past month, the period when Hank was in Singapore, for hormonal testing. "I could do it here," Doc Hanley had said, "but Bill Pearsall is the specialist in this field, and you might as well have the best." By accident that first week she had met Guy Boudreau at a small French restaurant on Front Street. He had joined her at her table, learned of her scheduled weekly visits to Portland, and made a date for the following week.

Guy Boudreau was the rich boy in her high school class which is to say that his father was the owner of a string of hardware stores in Maine. Guy had never seemed spoiled by his family position. He was modest, gregarious, warmly friendly, but he was the only boy in the class to get a new car upon graduation — a yellow Plymouth convertible — and, unlike his college-bound classmates who went to Hanson's Yarmouth, he went away to Dartmouth.

At a Dartmouth Winter Festival, Guy had met a dark and voluptuous Vassar girl, Rebah Goldsmith, daughter of one of the oldest Jewish banking families in Manhattan, whom he married the day after graduation. It took just two years for Rebah, raised in the luxury and cascading variety of Manhattan, to find that she and Portland did not like each other much. She announced one morning she was leaving, got a divorce, and settled down in New York as the wife of a successful young broker. That had been five years ago, and Guy had never remarried.

In the dining room of Guy's house, poised on the southern edge of Portland harbor, they had sipped clam chowder served by Guy's housekeeper who discreetly retired after putting their waxed paper wrapped sandwiches before them. Margaret felt the hot chowder nestle down contentedly beside the vodka martini Guy had served her upon arrival. She had felt very luxurious in the richly furnished room, watching out the broad window as a small coastal tanker up from Boston passed slowly by accompanied by an anxious, fuss-budget tug. It almost seemed as though the years had silently slipped away, and with Guy she was once again a young girl. Under Guy's admiring glances and gentle banter her neglected femininity awoke, became aware of itself, and purred softly like a stroked cat.

It was on the silk-cushioned sofa, while they were sipping their coffee, that Guy had said, "Being with you again is like being 18 again. Even after you turned away from me for Hank, I went on admiring you. Wanting you."

She squeezed his hand. "That's sweet."

He sipped his coffee from the delicate white, gold-edged cup, his dark eyes watching her over the brim. He set the cup down. "Something tells me, Margaret, that you are not really very happy these days. That saddens me. I know *I* could make you very happy indeed."

She gulped. "Don't," she said. "Don't spoil this."

It was then that he had leaned over and kissed her. Gently at first and then more and more intensely. Restrained at first, she had responded with mounting warmth until he had risen, holding her hand, and began to lead her to the stairway.

She was right to stop. Then. Wasn't she? But now, here in this swiftly running car that was taking her back to the uncertainties of her relationship with Hank and her humdrum life, she was not so certain she would stop next time. She had never admitted it to herself before, but Guy's remark about her unhappiness had flushed the thought to the surface. She and Hank were going through the motions. Their interest, their orientations, were widely different. Her universe was bounded by Hanson and her circle of lifetime friends, Dottie, Betty, and Sue. His was cosmopolitan and stretched, literally, half way around the globe. Her world and Guy's were intrinsically more compatible. She asked herself, hesitantly, almost shrinking away from formulating the thought, why shouldn't she take what Guy offered? Why should she trudge on, making a life so half-heartedly. . .

Suddenly into her vision to the right a huge dump truck loomed, massive and menacing, speeding into the intersection where Route 1-A joined Route 1. The truck was moving too fast to stop even if he had intended to. She jammed on her brakes and swerved hard to the left. Out the right window she could see the enormous spinning front wheel and the massive steel fender, huge and deadly. Then there was a sharp double bang as her front wheels struck the high curb of the median island marking the intersection. The impact threw her up off her seat and hard against the steering wheel. Suddenly there was silence, and she realized the truck had not struck her. She had managed to miss it.

Quickly two men were at her window. "You all right?"

"I'm okay. Give me a minute to catch my breath, and I'll go on."

"No," one man said. "You can't. Both tires are blown."

Hank arrived within ten minutes after her phone call from the nearby service station where her car was towed. As usual he was very calm. He quickly made arrangements for having the car checked for damage and for replacing the front tires. Then he drove her home in the green *Courier* truck. He was very solicitous with Margaret, very gentle and understanding, but beneath it all Margaret seemed to sense the feeling that somehow she was not entirely free of blame. Had she been day-dreaming or in some other way inattentive as she approached the dangerous intersection? Whatever it was, her intuition told her, she had somehow failed to meet the standard.

Six

It was well into the second week of Hank's return from Singapore, and the eleventh day of his allotted thirty days before making his decision known to Peter Yee. It was also the third consecutive day of extremely foul weather. Sleet, freezing rain, wet slushy snow, all dropping out of a heavy, lowering sky that seemed to suggest the sun had lost its way and would never appear over Maine again. Hank's mood, already ragged from tension and uncertainty, turned savage.

He began his day at the *Courier* office by berating Pat Long at great length for not following up a lead on a commercial real estate transaction, and then savaged meek, old Agnes for having missed payment on a shipping bill and losing the two percent discount. He stormed back in his desk, feeling aggrieved by unseen, ill-defined forces. But as he tried with minimal success to write an editorial on the need for improvement of the municipal sewer system, he began to realize what was eating at him. It was simply that he was approaching the edge of decision, an instant when he would either have to jump or remain rooted to familiar terrain. The decision was tearing at the sinews of his life. It was painful.

It was also unavoidable, not to be shirked. By lunchtime he had determined to make a beginning and to begin by settling his relationship with Margaret. It had to be either permanence or a break. But permanence, marriage, seemed the only reasonable, and fair choice. Time establishes its own obligations, and they had been a couple for a long time.

Walking home through the misty, cold drizzle, he realized that an undercurrent of resentment set up whenever he thought about Margaret. Her hold on him seemed somehow unjustified, unwarranted. But then he thought of the day she had met him at the train station, having made herself wonderfully attractive but wearing beneath the handsome surface a slightly defensive armor in her awareness that she did not completely please him. His feeling for her softened. It softened still more when he remembered her brave but shaken demeanor the day he had gone to get her after her near miss with the speeding truck. And then the thought followed that his resentment was itself unjustified. Margaret was an attractive, worthy woman who had long occupied a place in his life. She belonged in Maine, in Hanson. She was a center around which his future in Maine could revolve. Children, a family, and his career with *The Courier.* The decision seemed inescapable.

He took her to dinner that night at *The Yarmouth Inn.* She was wearing a fuzzy, pale blue sweater suit that made her eyes glow and delineated her womanly bosom with loving care. At dinner, over the table lighted by a small brass lamp holding a candle, he told her of the offer made him by Prime Minister Yee, and she said, "Oh, Hank, you must be so proud."

"Yes, but I don't think I will accept." In response to her querying expression, he added, "Partly, it depends on you."

Dinner arrived then in the hands of a chubby, blonde girl, and the subject was dropped. She told him that Midge Oliver's baby, her third, was due next month. After dinner he took her through the icy drizzle back to his house, and after dropping a half dozen old Dorsey and Artie Shaw ballads on the turntable he walked across the room and sat beside her.

He plunged in. "Margaret, I should have said this long, long ago." He looked down at the floor. "We talked at dinner about the fundamental decision I've got to make — go to Singapore or stay here. This is a real crossroad. If I decide to stay here, which I think I am leaning toward, it will be a final decision. Permanent. I will devote myself to making a life in Hanson. And so, knowing that, I want to ask, will you marry me?"

She burst into tears and put her arms gently around his neck and kissed him on the cheek. Then she leaned back and dried her eyes. "Oh, Hank, I'm so glad you asked. At last." She blew her nose and dabbed at her eyes again. "I've waited so long." She smiled gently. "But I'm not going to marry you."

Her answer struck Hank like a blow. *Not marry him!* His surprise was massive. He fished around within for some other emotion — chagrin, relief, disappointment were obvious candidates — but found none. He felt only surprise. His ear caught and noted Tommy Dorsey's trombone, muted, close to the mike, and sounding more like a cello than a horn, tracing the melody of "I'll Never Smile Again."

"But why?"

She kissed him again on the cheek and crossed the room to the easy chair. The lamp beside the chair made her head radiant, her ash blonde hair glistening and her high cheekbones highlighted. "For lots of reasons. I've been doing some thinking, and facing facts lately. While you've been gone."

Quietly then and without tears, looking more assured and handsome than he had ever seen her, she recounted how they had been in love in school and how since those early spring days of their youth they had grown slowly and steadily apart. "I've remained a Maine girl, a small town girl. I like my friends and my home here. You've become very worldly, much more worldly than me. You're a cosmopolitan. You've outgrown Hanson. And" — here she gulped — "me."

"But I told you I'm about to decide to stay in Hanson. Run *The Courier.* And marry you."

She shook her head. "No, Hank. You'd regret it the rest of your life." She shook her head again. "Hank, I don't think you're being honest with yourself. Maybe you're trying to make it up to me. Or you're — oh, I don't know, but whatever it is, it is not right for you. Or for me."

He was silent. Baffled. Some part of his mind said Margaret was right but another part was reluctant to accept it. But Margaret's explanation had caused the surprise to evaporate. What was left in its place? A blank, too neutral even to be called "numbness."

After a moment she looked up, smiling shyly. "Do you remember Guy Boudreau?"

"Of course. In our class."

"I saw Guy several times while you were away. We had fun. I think he wants to marry me." She looked down at the floor. "Maybe in time I'll let him. He belongs in Maine, like me. Maybe we would be right together."

Two days later, when Hank drove the green *Courier* truck out to Anne Pintel's house on Summer Point, the sun was melting the tiny globes on the tips of the tree branches and prismatic drops fell flashing in the brilliant rays. It was a late winter thaw, a false harbinger of spring, but it lifted the heart with expectation.

Hank had seen Anne only once since his return, a quick lunch at the Bos'n's Chair between her 11 o'clock class and

1 o'clock student conferences. He had told her about Peter Yee's offer, and she had responded enthusiastically. "Oh, Bunny, how wonderful for you! You'll be an oriental prince with a villa by the sea and Chinese maidens hovering around you!"

Today, as he entered her house he found her sitting in her chair beside the phonograph, surrounded by books, a pencil stuck in her hair over her ear. "Hi," she said. "I'm busier than stink. I've been asked to give an evening lecture at the Faculty Club on French Impressionist music."

He paused in the doorway. "Maybe I'd better leave you to Debussy and come back."

"No. Come in. I could use a break. I'll get some sherry." She leaped to her feet, kissed him briskly on the cheek as she passed on her way to the kitchen.

Sitting beside her on the sofa, sherry in hand, Hank saw that Anne was all crisp efficiency. Not the hesitant, uncertain young woman of last summer. Her movements were always quick but today they were also edged with decision. "Anything new about your 'Singapore chance'?" she asked.

"Not really. I'm still hanging fire. But I'm leaning toward staying here. Not taking the offer."

She cocked her head thoughtfully. "Not bad. Then you can marry Margaret Rawlins, raise a family, and run *The Courier.*"

"Margaret won't have me. Turned me down."

Anne's eyebrows arched high over her deep-set eyes "Oh?"

"She says we've grown apart. She's small town Maine and I'm cosmopolitan. Something like that."

"Smart girl. She's right though the reasons may be wrong."

Now it was Hank's eyebrows that lifted on his forehead. "What does that mean?"

Anne took a sip from her sherry and set the glass on the coffee table. She turned and put both hands on his shoulders. "I'm not sure I can say this without wounding you. But you know how genuinely fond I am of you. You've been very good to me. Good *for* me. You've carried me across a Slough of Despond and put me safe and dry on the other side. So I am speaking now as a friend and" — she nodded her head in affirmation — "a lover."

She got up then and stood before him, hands on hips. "I'm no psychiatrist, though I've waltzed a few rounds with one, but my feeling is that you, for whatever reason, come up short where commitment is concerned. Tying yourself to a person, or possibly even to a place, is not something you can easily do. Something inside you holds you back, keeps you separate."

Remembering their passionate and draining love-making, Hank asked, "Do you think that has been true with us?"

She nodded. "Essentially, yes. Oh, we've had some glorious romps in bed, and you're a fabulous lover. Strong, dominating, overwhelming — I'm getting a little weak in the knees just remembering — but I came gradually to realize that some part of you was standing aside. Not giving yourself to me."

"Would you like to try again right now? Let me show you you're wrong?"

She sat back down beside him and patted his hand. "No, dear. That's finished. I don't regret a single moment, not one. But now it's finished."

"Just like that?"

"Yes." She patted his hand again. "Not bitterly. With great affection rather. But it's time to move on."

"Move on?"

"Do you remember that man who came up to the table at the Bos'n's Chair and said hello?"

"Bruce Something or Other?"

"Goddard. Bruce Goddard."

"What about him?"

"We're engaged." Anne smiled softly. "I think I'm in love."

Hank leaned back on the sofa and rubbed his hand across his forehead. Twice in two days was too much. His capacity for surprise was now exhausted.

She patted him again, this time on the knee. "Aren't you happy for me?"

"Well, yes. But I was hoping that we — uh, you and I —"

Realization slowly dawned in her eyes. She knelt down on the floor beside him. "Oh, Hank. Bunny dear. That was never meant to be. We were just playmates. We're marvelous in bed together but there's more to life than bouncing on a mattress. We're really very different people. You've got a life to live completely unlike mine."

"Doing what?"

"Going back to Singapore."

Seven

Dick Perkins met Hank as he emerged from the customs area of Don Muang Airport in Bangkok. "Greetings," said Dick. "Seems like I'm making a career of greeting you at airports."

"Yeah, we really ought to stop meeting like this."

"I've been back from Singapore less than a week."

Perkins gestured to the porter carrying Hank's bags to take them to the white-uniformed driver standing beside the black Embassy sedan at the entrance. "Understand you're the new chief here in Bangkok. How did that happen?"

"It's a long story."

Well, really not so long, Hank mused, as Perkins saw to stowing the luggage and tipping the porter while Hank climbed in the back of the sedan. Only a little over three weeks ago he was still balancing whether to leave Hanson or stay. The morning after his talk over sherry with Anne, he found he knew exactly what he wanted to do. He telephoned CIA Headquarters in Langley and with only a slight delay got Winton Jackson. "How soon can you come up here and talk about taking over *The Courier* for an indefinite period?"

Jackson coughed. "Will tomorrow do?"

A week later Hank was standing in Pickard Grant's office. "And that's your decision?" asked the Director.

"Yes, sir. I decided I didn't want to tie my future to a politician, not even one as enlightened as Peter Yee. Besides, I would always be wondering whether I owed my position to gratitude or my own merit."

Grant had looked down at his desk as he tapped the eraser of a pencil on the blotter top. He looked up and smiled. "I must say I'm relieved. It would have been a bit awkward for us having you working for Yee Hock Tho in Singapore. Manageable, but awkward." He smiled again. "Sit down, Bladesly. Would you like a cup of coffee?"

"No, thank you."

"I assume you want to go out to Singapore to break the news to Yee in person. As I told you, we'll finance that. Our new man, Collins Champion, has just arrived. You can set him up." He leaned back in his arm chair. "And then what. Back to newspapering in Maine?"

"No. I've decided to put that aside, at least for a while. I'd like instead to go back overseas for CIA."

"Oh? Singapore?"

"I don't think that would be a very good idea. No, not Singapore, but I'd like to be posted somewhere in Southeast Asia."

"Ummm." Pickard Grant had looked at Hank reflectively and silently for a moment. "Maybe something can be worked out. I've got an idea I'd like to check out."

Next day the CIA Director had called Hank back in. "How would you like to take over the station in Bangkok?"

"Nothing could please me more."

"Good. I think you're the man for the job." He looked out the window at the woods along the Potomac where spring was tentatively trying on new apparel, tiny green leaves and timid red maple buds. "We've got a lead on a topflight KGB general who's just been sent there. Exiled there, apparently. We think he's ripe for recruitment as an agent. We want you to give it a try."

That was the long story of how he had been sent to Bangkok, only part of which Hank told Perkins as they rode from the airport to the U.S. Embassy. The exiled KGB general was left unmentioned. "What about the paper you owned in Maine? Did you sell that?"

"No, I couldn't do that. It's been in the Bladesly family for three generations. I worked out a caretaker deal with the OCI fellow who took over when I came out in December."

The rest of the day was spent settling in, meeting the case officers and the clericals at the station, being introduced to the ambassador, and inspecting the station chief's house he was taking over.

That evening, Hank and Dick Perkins sipped drinks as they lay in lounge chairs beside the swimming pool which was encircled on two sides by the living room and bedroom wings of the low-roofed, pleasant house, Hank's new home. A brilliant yellow bird flitted in and out of the shrubbery, and the mingled fragrance of bougainvillea and frangipani lay heavy on the humid evening air.

"You'll find the work heavy but not overpowering," said Perkins. "And there's plenty of recreation here. There's golf and tennis at the Race Track Club, sailing at the Krung Thep Sailing Club on the river, and weekend beaching at villas you can rent down at Songkhla. What's your pleasure?"

"I think I'll go for the Sailing Club and weekends at Songkhla."

Several weeks passed before Hank spotted Sergei Zablonsky, his KGB target. His instructions had been not to seek out the Russian. "If possible," the guys in the

Soviet Division at Langley had said, "let him come to you. He's a cocky, arrogant, aggressive son of a bitch, and we suspect he'll make the first move."

It was a Sunday afternoon at the Krung Thep Sailing Club. Hank had taken out one of the Club's Lightnings with a guy in the Embassy political section as crew and was heading downriver on a starboard tack against a good south wind when another Club Lightning came astern on a port tack. The man at the tiller, wearing a blue shirt and a gold-trimmed yachting cap called out, "How about a race down to the Point?" The voice was pure Oxford English. Hank looked narrowly at the face beneath the yachting cap and saw that it was Sergei Zablonsky. It matched the picture in the Headquarters file. He remembered also being told, "He speaks with an English accent. *English* English. He sounds more English than lots of Limeys you'll meet."

"You're on. What are the stakes?"

Zablonsky shrugged. "Drinks. Whatever you say."

"Let's go."

Hank swung the tiller over to the port rail to bring the Lightning about. He hoped to blanket Zablonsky's wind on the port tack but was only partly successful. The two boats moved downriver side by side on the port tack until they came to a bend to the right, toward the west. Zablonsky held his tack by pinching until he had cleared the bend but Hank came about and headed across to the other side of the broad, brown river. His years of sailing in the nooks and crannies off Casco Bay with its 10 foot tides had taught him that the current is strongest on the outside of the curve. Sailing with the current as he was, it was therefore best to take the outside going downriver and the inside going upriver.

His tactics were right and when they came to the next bend, this time to port, Hank crossed over again and passed Zablonsky a good two lengths ahead. By the time they reached the Point, Hank's lead was nearer four lengths.

He jibed about and passed Zablonsky who was still heading downriver. "All right, mate. You win that round," yelled Zablonsky. "How about racing back for the other half?"

"Fine." Hank slacked off and let Zablonsky come up even. "Go!"

The outcome when sailing against the current was even more decisive. Hank hugged the inside of the bends while Zablonsky, believing mistakenly he was gaining the advantage by having unobstructed wind, stayed out in the heart of the current.

In the clubhouse, after the boat boys had taken over, they sat down for drinks. "I must admit, old boy," said Zablonsky, "you're a good sailor. Where did you learn your sailing?"

"Growing up as a boy in Maine."

Zablonsky's rugged, Slavic face took on a superior, sardonic expression. "Maine? Where's that, part of California?" He guffawed raucously.

"No, it's —"

"I know where it is, old son. That's a joke. Maine is on your northeast corner, just below Canada and east of New Hampshire. I probably know the geography of your country better than you do." Again his expression was superior and sardonic. "Let me ask you, where's Hoisington? H-O-I-S-I-N-G-T-O-N."

"Never heard of it."

"Aha! It's in Kansas. Middle of the state."

Remembering another instruction he got from Soviet Division — "he'll never stop trying to one-up you, the arrogant bastard; don't let him do it to you" — Hank decided to try to match him. "Here's one for you. Where's Moscow?"

"That's a joke, eh? The Soviet Union, of course."

"No, in the U.S. We're discussing U.S. geography remember?"

Zablonsky pondered briefly and then his broad face

broke into another sardonic smile. "Washington, D.C.!" He guffawed loudly.

"No. Actually there are ten Moscows in the United States: Idaho, Indiana, Kansas, Kentucky, Michigan, Mississippi, Ohio, Pennsylvania, Tennessee, and Vermont."

The Russian nodded, lips compressed. "You know a little geography, too."

"I learned that for a geography test in school."

The KGB general looked at Hank appraisingly. "Do you come here each weekend?"

"Most of them."

Zablonsky nodded. "Let's meet and race again." He raised his glass to Hank. "Drink too."

Next weekend Sergei Zablonsky was not to be found at the Krung Thep Sailing Club but Hank encountered Ian Ainsley, instead. He had known that his old British MI-5 contact in Singapore was stationed in Bangkok but had not felt any particular urge to resume the relationship. Meeting him face to face was another matter, however, so he stopped by the table where Ainsley was seated, elegant in a white oxford cloth shirt, white flannel trousers, and white boat shoes. "Hello, Ian," he said.

Ainsley looked up languidly, putting down a long greenish drink he was holding. "Why, Bladesly, old chap! What a lark to see you again!" He got slowly to his feet and gave Hank a limp handshake. "Sit down a moment, won't you, and have a bit of a natter."

Hank signaled to the Thai waiter to bring him a beer and sat down. "I'd heard you'd left the Service," said Ainsley.

"I did, to take over the family business for several years. But now I'm back."

"Couldn't give up The Great Game, eh? Or was it the lovely

Chinese ladies of the region that brought you back? I heard at one point that you and Yee Hock Tho's sister were making sweet music together."

"Now, Ian, no one can beat you in enjoying the charms of the lovely Chinese ladies."

Ainsley smiled a drooping smile. "I *have* had my little successes."

They chatted for half an hour about old Singapore acquaintances. "You remember Jill Beamis, my P.A. at Phoenix Park? She's married now, lives in Hampshire, mother of bouncing twin boys."

"Good for her."

Just before they parted Ainsley asked, "I say, Bladesly, you don't play bridge, do you?"

"A little, now and then."

"A couple of my chaps and I are sometimes looking for a fourth. I'll ring you up some time and we'll give it a try."

Not a relationship he was especially eager to nurture, Hank thought to himself as he walked away, but in his profession it was sometimes useful to be able to call on a friendly Service for assistance. It was a decision he later came to value.

Hank's meetings with Sergei Zablonsky continued sporadically at the Sailing Club over the next several months. Usually they raced and invariably Hank won. Finally, he explained to the Russian, who had done all his previous sailing on lakes or the open sea, about the differing speed of the current on the inside and outside of the river bends. "I say, old boy, that's awfully decent of you. I don't believe I would have done that for you." He guffawed his usual ceiling-cracking laugh.

One day after a race which Zablonsky had won by a hair

and he had had an extra drink to celebrate, he said in a low voice, looking down at the table, "I say, Bladesly, old chap, I believe I know what you do and I expect you know what I do. Why don't we get together sometime for a private professional chat?"

The break had come at last. Hank's face did not change a millimeter. "Fine with me. Where?"

Zablonsky looked around slowly and casually. "I could come by your place some night around midnight."

"Okay. Name it. When?"

"I'll try Tuesday. If I don't make it Tuesday, the next night."

It was Tuesday night and 12:16, Hank's Omega said, when he heard a car engine in the driveway. He had left one of the garage bays open so that Zablonsky could put his car inside out of sight. The Russian came up the path from the garage and into the light streaming out of the living room and across the patio and over the pool, making ripples in the pool shimmer. Zablonsky glanced around. "Nice place," he commented. "Do you live this well in the States?"

"Certainly." He gestured toward a chair. "You'd prefer to sit outside here, wouldn't you?"

"Yes, but a little back out of the light, if you don't mind, old boy."

They moved the chairs back from the side of the pool, and Hank turned to a table set up as a bar. "How about a drink?"

Zablonsky peered searchingly at the labels on the bottles. "Ah, Bell's 12-year-old scotch. I see you have good taste. I'll have some of that. On the rocks as you Yanks say."

Hank handed a glass to the Russian and sat down. "Success!" said Zablonsky raising his glass.

"Success."

Neither spoke for several minutes while the tropical night sounded about them, chirping tree toads, rasping and buzzing insects, and a raucous gecko uttering his insistent cry somewhere in the darkness. "Tell me, Bladesly, how do you happen to be posted to Bangkok?"

"Chance. I had a previous tour in Singapore, and I wanted to come back to Southeast Asia. Bangkok happened to be open."

"I see." Zablonsky sipped heavily at his drink, nearly downing it. "I can tell you how I happened to come to this back corner of the world. I was skewered by a fellow officer."

"Oh?"

"Chap I served with in London." He finished off the drink. "I must say, old son, that's frightfully good scotch."

"Have another."

"Other *half,* my boy. Other *half.* You must adopt that special British courtesy."

"Right." Hank poured a stiff dollop into the glass and set the bottle down on a table beside the Russian.

"Dimitri Kazov is the bastard's name. You may have heard of him."

"I've seen his name on an organization chart."

"Big shot. Probably headed for the top. Over my bloody body, the son of a bitch." He emptied his glass again and reached for the bottle.

"Jurisdictional fight of some kind?"

"No. Over a woman. One we were both banging." He took another swallow of his drink and turned to Hank, a leer visible on his face in the semi-darkness. "Tell me, old boy, how many women have you screwed?"

Hank, recognizing the ploy, lied generously.

"Fifteen, sixteen."

"Oh, my God! You're just a boy! I've had 53, the youngest 16, the oldest 56. Forty years of joy in between!" He chuckled a low volume version of his usual guffaw.

Silence fell again except for the myriad night noises in southern Thailand. A bird out near the garden wall uttered a frightened squawk. Zablonsky's mood switched back to anger. "That bastard Kazov. Some day I'll pay him back."

Hank moved in. "How can you do that when you are out here and he is in Moscow?"

Zablonsky looked up quickly, a knowing and secret smile on his face. "I don't know." He had refused to take the jump. After a moment he said, "God, that pool looks good. Hot night. C'mon, Bladesly, let's have a swim." He quickly stripped off his clothes, his barrel chest hairy over a large belly, his shoulders and thighs heavy and muscular. He plunged in with a huge splash. Hank slipped in at the other end, keeping a safe and wary distance from the KGB man. They climbed out after several minutes of thrashing about in the tepid water and dried themselves with towels Hank fetched from the poolside cabana.

"Tell me, Bladesly," said Zablonsky as he poured another stiff dollop of Bell's 12 in his glass, "are politics rampant in your organization too?"

"I would say not. Not in my experience anyway."

They exchanged comments for some time about bureaucratic practices in the rival organizations, Hank trying all the while to seem candid while masking precise organizational connections. Zablonsky's comments were punctuated at regular intervals with expletives aimed at "that bastard Kazov. Everybody knows I'm the best agent in the KGB, and he fucks up my career and gets me buried out here."

"How can you pay him back? There ought to be some way."

Again the Russian smiled his secret smile. "I'll find a way some day." He downed his drink and got to his feet. "Let's do this again, old son. I'll see you at the Sailing Club." He shook hands with a courtly gesture and slipped off into the night.

There were six more of these sessions over the next three months. Each time Hank opened the way for Zablonsky to take the hurdle with some variant of "How can you get revenge?", the KGB general smiled his secret smile and gave a noncommittal answer. It was like having a fighting, plunging gamefish on the line that had taken the bait but refused to come to the boat.

At last, one night by the side of the pool after several good belts of scotch, Zablonsky responded to Hank's question. "I'll tell you how. I got a general instruction the other day from Kazov's directorate about a new anti-U.S. campaign in the Middle East: propaganda, terrorism, sabotage. They won't send any specific operations messages out here to me in this dismal privy of creation but I know enough about KGB M.O.'s to guide you in defeating them. We can knock Kazov back on his ass, and then they'll find out the mistake they made in choosing him over me, the best operational man in the KGB!"

Hank was silent for a moment. Cautious. He did not have the net under the fish yet. "That might work, Sergei. But can we come up with enough specifics to mount counter-operations?"

"You're damned right! I know KGB operations inside out. I trained most of the young guys they're using. Ungrateful bastards!"

Hank nodded. "I'll have to try it out on my organization."

Zablonsky exploded in anger. "See here, Bladesly. You're not dealing with some little raw recruit off the streets. I'm a KGB general! You know who you're dealing with. Your Headquarters knows too. Let's not get into this routine procedure crap — I give you information, you pay me something, you ask me to sign a receipt and some kind of contract. None of that shit. I'm a professional. The best. You know what you're getting. So don't piss around!"

Hank grinned at the furious Russian. "Okay, Sergei. Okay. Here, have some more of 'the other half'." He raised hs own glass. "We understand each other. Success!"

Slowly the anger softened on Zablonsky's face. He slowly raised his glass too. "Success," he growled.

At their next meeting Zablonsky brought lists of likely propaganda themes and the probable vehicles for promoting them as well as probable terrorist targets, sabotage sites, and local groups likely to be the action elements. Hank looked the list over and said, "This looks very good, Sergei. I'll zip this back tomorrow morning."

"You had better zip this along too. This is a statement of the return I expect from your side."

The statement was brief and precise: 25 thousand U.S. dollars to be deposited immediately to Zablonsky's account in a Swiss bank; five thousand dollars additional to be deposited each month the relationship in Bangkok remained active; safe passage and lifetime safe haven in the United States in the event of a contingency requiring termination of the Bangkok relationship; and a stipend sufficient for him to "live like a gentleman" during his residence in the United States.

To Hank the price looked steep but remembering the Russian's angry outburst during their previous meeting he did not comment. Instead, he asked, "What contingencies might break it off?"

"There are two. First, I might be called back to Moscow. Second, our connection might be blown. As for the first, considering that bastard Kazov's hatred of me, it's not likely to happen for a long time. He'd like to keep me out here in the jungle the rest of my life. The second, well, if you Yanks can exercise any good security — which would be a bit uncharacteristic, I must admit — it won't happen ever. I'm too smart for the lads the KGB has out here. They'll never suspect me."

Headquarter's response to Hank's back-channel cable announcing the recruiting of Sergei Zablonsky was enthusiastic. Pickard Grant's private message to Hank was:

"WELL DONE. (CORRECTION) VERY WELL DONE. For the next three months the recruited KGB general was a fountain of excellent intelligence. He pinpointed repeatedly the targets and sites of planned terrorist operations. U.S. counter-terrorist activities had one unheralded success after another. Unheralded, that is, to the world press but recognized and recorded by KGB Headquarters in Moscow.

For Hank, life in Bangkok settled down into an enjoyable and busy daily rhythm. He knew that his work with Zablonsky was effective and highly useful. He felt, in the words of Ulysses in Tennyson's poem, that "some work of noble note" was being done. He made a number of friends, both in the American and foreign diplomatic community and some among Thai professional and business people. He had found and rented a lovely villa on the edge of the South China Sea in Songkhla, and had bought half interest in a 36-foot cabin sloop with the chief of the U.S. Embassy political section.

He had also made, despite the scornful reluctance of Zablonsky, a set of contingency plans to get the KGB general out of Thailand and on his way to safety in the event his cooperation with Hank was discovered. The first step was a telephone signal that the time for escape had come.

It was three months and six days after the night of Zablonsky's recruitment when the telephone at Hank's bedside yanked him out of deep sleep. In the dark he fumbled for the phone and heard when he got it to his ear a deep voice saying softly "64" followed by a click. It was the signal and unless he was intercepted by Soviet security agents, Zablonsky would be arriving in fifteen or twenty minutes.

Before he threw on his clothes Hank consulted his bedside telephone directory and dialed a number. A sleepy, languid voice answered, "Hullo."

"Ian, this is HB. I need that notebook. Now. Immediately."

"Oh, Gawd!" There was a long, audible yawn. "My dear chap, it's 2:15. I'll have it for you first thing in morning. Say, about 10."

"*Now!* I need it *now,* Ian." His voice was hard with tension.

There was a long pause. Hank was fearful Ainsley had gone back to sleep. But at last the languid British voice said, "Damn you. I'll meet you there in half hour."

Hank threw on a sport shirt and slacks. He grabbed the small duffle bag in the closet, already partly packed, and stuffed his razor, toothbrush, and other toiletries in it. Oh yes, fresh shorts and socks. On his desk he picked up his wallet, a folder of American Express traveler's checks, his diplomatic passport, and his CIA identification badge. These he put inside a waterproof zippered sheath and placed them in an inner pocket of the duffle bag.

He crossed the long open living room and turned on the kitchen light. Then he went to the sliding door opening onto the patio by the pool and opened it. Outside the night was dark, lighted only dimly by a grotesquely shaped waning moon riding through scudding clouds. The palm trees rustled mysteriously in the night wind. He went back to the kitchen to make coffee and had just finished putting out cups when he heard Zablonsky's step on the patio. He came in, his face drawn, muttering, "The sons of bitches. I don't know how they got on to it."

"Tell me about it later. Give me your passport."

"What?"

"Your passport. I need it for the picture."

Still seeming stunned, Zablonsky pulled the Russian passport out of his pocket and handed it to Hank.

"Did you have time to pack a bag?"

"No, the bastards were surrounding the house. I got out through a back window and across the garden."

"In the closet in the bedroom you'll find a Pan Am flight bag. Pack it with whatever you need. Things will be tight but they'll do. And make some coffee. I'll be back in 20 minutes.

Before the Russian could answer Hank slipped out the patio door and trotted to the garage. He backed the Mercedes 250 quietly and headed down the boulevard to the British Embassy. Ian Ainsley, wearing a rumpled shirt and black slacks, let him in. "Fucking inconsiderate, old boy," he said. "Just regaining my strength after a bout with a lovely lady."

"Spare me the details. Here's the passport with the picture to transfer to one of yours. Your tech here?"

"Yes. Come on back to the office."

In ten minutes, Hank had a British passport bearing Sergei Zablonsky's picture and the name, "Geoffrey Boggs."

"Boggs, Boggs," said Ainsley. "Believe I knew him at Harrow."

"Unlikely," said Hank turning to leave. "I owe you one, Ian. See you in a few days."

Twenty minutes later, Hank and Zablonsky were moving swiftly through the night in the Mercedes 250 down the coast road on the east side of the Isthmus of Kra. Traffic was nearly non-existent at this hour, and aside from the rising and falling and twisting of the black macadam surface in the long, searching beams of the Mercedes headlights, the only thing to be seen was the occasional flash of yellow eyes of some wild creature in the bushy verge. Zablonsky had recounted to Hank that he had recently become aware of unusual activity in KGB security traffic and then had spotted a top-ranking KGB security man of his acquaintance in a downtown lobby. The coincidence was telling and his suspicions were confirmed when he had seen several men moving in the darkness out a window after he had gone through obvious signs of going to bed. "They thought they had me, the dumb bastards."

Hank said nothing, intent on maintaining as high a speed

as possible on the narrow, high-crowned road. After a while Zablonsky asked, "How far is it to Songkhla?"

"Three hundred miles. With luck we'll be there between 8 and 9."

"Three hundred English miles," Zablonsky mused. "That's just under 500 kilometers." He was silent again. Then he said, "I say, old chap. I doubt you know what the English call a road surface like this."

"They call it 'metalled'. It's a metalled road."

"That's right. Damned odd language those chaps use."

"That's no way to talk about your countrymen, Geoffrey Boggs. Not *pat* — as in 'spat' — triotic."

"You're right, old boy. Bloomin' bloody right."

A blood red sun had lifted two hours above the rim of the South China Sea when Hank turned the Mercedes into the lane that ran down to the villa. He put the car in the tiny garage behind the house and locked the door. Over a pick-up breakfast of two-week-old eggs and stale muffins out of the refrigerator, he and Zablonsky discussed their next move. "I think we ought to lie low all day and set sail after dark," said the Russian. "The less anybody around here sees us the better."

"It doesn't matter," said Hank. "They'll spot that the sloop is gone in the morning anyway." They sat at the red painted kitchen table looking out the window at *Black Tern,* lying some three hundred yards offshore, tugging and yawing on her anchor roding like a spirited horse, the greyish seas under the driving wind washing along her sides and leaving a wake under her stern as though she were under way. "Besides that's good wind out there, put us on a beam reach for a southerly course. We've got a 100 mile run down to Kota Bahru, the nearest town in Malaysia on this coast, and if this wind holds we could make it in 19 or 20 hours. Maybe about sundown tomorrow."

"Aye, aye, skipper." They gathered together their duffle

bags, the fruit, bread, and beer they had bought at the Rattaphum market, the last village they had passed through. Hank picked up wet weather gear out of the closet. Under an attap shed at the edge of the beach they righted the skiff Hank used to get out to the sloop and dragged it through the sand down to the water. They shoved off, Zablonsky manning the oars, and came up under the transom of *Black Tern,* tying the skiff to a cleat on her starboard quarter.

An hour later they were well out to sea, the low-lying coast only a dim line. The limestone mountains forming the spine of the Isthmus of Kra shimmered like a blue haze in the distance. The two men sat silent much of the time, Hank at the tiller with his eye on the compass, trying to hold to a heading of 136 degrees, and Zablonsky glancing at the speed gauge now and then and saying, "She's doing 5.8 knots."

The morning passed slowly. They changed places at the tiller after a couple of hours. "Hold her on 136, Sergei. According to the chart that ought to put us just off Kota Bahru."

"You've been down to this place before?"

"Never. Never have seen the town or the harbor. That's the reason I didn't want to try a night landing."

At noontime, they ate bananas and scarlet rambutans, washed down with beer. The long afternoon passed even more slowly than the morning. The sea around them surged and slapped at the sloop's bow as she bore on under the steady wind, heeled well over to starboard. No other boats were to be seen all the way out to the horizon, and only an occasional seabird came by, moving swiftly down wind on the strong breeze.

Zablonsky became restless. "I say, Bladesly, you don't happen to have any whiskey on board?"

"Down in the cabin, that first cupboard on the starboard side."

"Good chap." In a moment the Russian emerged with a bottle of Bell's 12 and a big grin. "First class accommodations on this ship." He took a strong swig out of the bottle, then another. He held the bottle toward Hank. "Have a pop?"

"No thanks." Zablonsky took another long drink. "Take it easy on the whiskey, Sergei."

The Russian took the bottle away from his mouth and held it in his fist. He scowled and shook his head. "No one tells Zablonsky how much to drink." He started to put the bottle to his mouth again, but Hank reached up and grabbed it away.

"I told you to knock off the goddam whiskey."

Zablonsky, his face a glowering red, moved toward Hank his fists clenched. "Listen to me, you fucker. I drink when I want to and as much as I want to."

"Not on this boat you don't. I want you sober enough to take the boat later, tonight. We've got a long night to get through."

"Give me the goddam bottle!" Zablonsky reached for it but Hank swung it away. "Who the hell do you think you are telling me not to drink? I'm a bloody Russian KGB general. I can drink any six lily-livered Americans under the table." He reached again. "I want that goddam bottle."

Hank got to his feet, releasing the tiller and letting *Black Tern* wheel in a long arc to port up into the wind. He stood with feet braced and fists at his waist. "Now get this, Zablonsky, you arrogant Russian son of a bitch. I'm doing my godamndest to get you to safety. You can fight me, if you want, for that stupid bottle of whiskey, and you might even beat me. But unless you kill me — and remember I'm your best guarantee of safe passage — I'll kill you the first chance I get and throw your body into the sea."

Zablonsky sneered. "A lot of good a dead KGB officer would do you, my friend."

"Don't kid yourself. You don't mean a fucking thing to me

personally. Recruiting you has got me all the glory I'm ever going to get out of you. Dead or alive doesn't matter now. I'm just trying to carry out my end of the bargain."

Zablonsky contined to glare for a long moment. Then he stepped back and sat down. "I see." His eyes narrowed and then he nodded. "I see," he said again, and then after another moment, "We'll save the whiskey for later. Let's get back on course."

Hank pulled the mainsheet in as he moved the tiller to port, and the big sail filled and swelled and soon the sloop was back at speed. For the next hour neither man spoke a word, and an hour later they were watching the sun set over the dim shore, sliding at last below the ragged mountains on the western horizon.

In the gathering dusk the wind freshened and soon brought along a drenching shower. Zablonsky took the tiller while Hank broke out rain gear. He sat then watching the heavy raindrops bounce off the foredeck and run in streams off the starboard gunwale. For the first time since Zablonsky's signal for escape he had a chance to reflect. He wondered for the first time whether his plan was the right one. His intention was to get the Russian out of the immediate reach of the KGB. He knew they would have Don Muang Airport covered, as well as the rail and bus routes in all directions out of Bangkok. By driving the Mercedes down to Songkhla he had thwarted that move. The purpose of sailing down to Kota Bahru, the nearest town across the Thai border, was to avoid the inevitable border watch the KGB would establish at Betong. Once in Malaysia, Hank and his charge could proceed by public transport to Singapore where he hoped somehow to get Zablonsky on an airplane headed toward the United States. It still seemed like a good plan. Only the growing darkness and the heavy rain had played on his mounting anxiety and stomach-wrenching tension to put it in doubt.

After the passing squall, the wind dropped to a whisper

and the sea flattened out. Hank waited for a breeze to rise from another direction but the air remained calm and slowly the clouds cleared. Time to start the engine. He dropped down the four steps into the cabin, pulled up a floorboard, and opened the fuel valves for the Gray diesel engine. A glance at the fuel gauge told him they could run for four to five hours. After that . . .

The engine started after a moderate amount of cranking and ran smoothly, pushing them toward Kota Bahru at a steady 5 knots. Overhead moist yellow stars hung low in the black sky. Hank located the Southern Cross, seemingly a half-hearted effort at forming a cross, and pointed it out to Zablonsky. "Misshapen affair, isn't it?" he said. "Doesn't compare with Charles' Wain. Now that *looks* like a cart."

"In the States we call it 'The Big Dipper'."

"Dipper? Oh, I see, the other way up."

After a while Hank noticed Zablonsky's head dropping until his chin was on his chest. "Sergei. Go down in the cabin and stretch out. I'll call you to take over about midnight."

Alone in the cockpit, with the sounds about him of the smoothly running diesel and the wash and sizzle of the sea along *Black Tern's* sides and at her boiling stern, Hank mused aimlessly. Off to the west he could see low on the horizon the twinkling lights of a small town which a glance at the chart told him was probably Sai Buri, a Thai town slightly over halfway between Songkhla and Kota Bahru. The town lights somehow brought Hanson to mind, and he wondered dispassionately how Winton Jackson was faring with *The Courier* and what the two women in his life in Maine, Margaret and Anne, were doing at that moment. But it all seemed infinitely remote and of only passing interest. Once again, he had exchanged one side of the planet for the other, and all aspects of his life had changed accordingly.

Shortly after midnight he and Zablonsky changed places, and Hank fell quickly into deep sleep on the bunk. He awoke suddenly some three hours later when the throbbing of the engine abruptly cut off. In the cockpit he found the Russian pushing repeatedly on the starter button, *"Start,* you bastard, start!"

"It's no use, Sergei. We're out of fuel. We'll have to go back to sailing."

"Sail? We're becalmed."

Becalmed they certainly were, and the jib and mainsail of the sloop slopped around back and forth in response to little puffs and vagrant eddies and swirls of air. It was hopeless but there was nothing to do but wait for a breeze to rise. Zablonsky muttered something in Russian and went back down into the cabin to the bunk. After about an hour, Hank heard a low growling noise ahead in the night. It grew louder and louder, sounding more and more like a freight train bearing down on the sloop. He peered searchingly into the blackness but could see no lights such as would mark an oncoming ship. In another few minutes he could see what it was, a foaming rush of water heading straight at him. Before he could react the onrushing wind struck *Black Tern* like a heavy hand and lay the sloop over on her gunwale. Hank slacked the jibsheet and let the mainsheet run, fighting the tiller to pull the bow up into the wind. The sloop lay over on her starboard side, struggling like a downed horse to regain her feet, but the howling wind thrashed at her mast and rigging and her exposed port flank and held her pinned.

Zablonsky emerged from the cabin, wild-eyed. "What the hell's going on, Bladesly? Threw me out of the damned bunk."

"Line squall. Get your weight up to windward and hang on!"

Slowly, ever so slowly, the bow of the beleaguered boat came up into the wind and she pulled her starboard rail free of the foaming seas. Hank trimmed the sails and put her on a beating tack with a heading of 180 degrees, a course that would eventually pile them up on the eastern coast of Thailand unless he came about. The shallow and notoriously stormy South China Sea quickly mounted big, foaming breakers under the driving gale. *Black Tern* shoved her nose into one green sea after another, and the foaming, boiling water rushed down the foredeck, sprayed high into the air as it hit the mast and the forward edge of the cabin housing, and slopped in big glops into the cockpit. Hank was soon drenched and shivering as the wind drove into his wet clothes but for the better part of an hour his hands were too full with holding the head of the struggling sloop up to allow him to put on wet weather gear.

He had swung *Black Tern* through a change in tack during one brief lessening of the squall and was heading out away from the shore when disaster struck. Suddenly there was a loud crack aloft and the mainsail came slamming down into the cockpit and over the port rail. Scrambling around trying to free himself from the clinging, sodden sail and holding the tiller steady, Hank could only imagine what had happened. Either the halyard had parted or the block on the mast had let go. The important thing now was to get the sail under control and in the boat if possible.

Zablonsky emerged from under the canvas spluttering and muttering in Russian. "See if you can get the sail into the boat, Sergei. I'll try to keep her steady with the jib until this wind lets up."

Without a word the big Russian began to haul the heavy sail over the rail with his powerful arms and hands. Hank pulled the boom midship and cleated it down. With astonishing speed Zablonsky got the mainsail aboard and stuffed and crammed it into the cockpit out of the reach of the wind. "We can get the sail off the boom when the wind gives us a chance to breathe."

Which it did in another half hour. Slowly it moderated to a steady southerly breeze, and shortly later a golden sun lifted out of the eastern horizon. As the greyness of the dawn sky gradually modulated to clear blue it was obvious that a blistering hot day on the sea lay ahead of them and their crippled boat. Again, it was hopeless but nothing to do but wait.

In another hour as the temperature climbed in the sluggish boat, Hank spotted a dim speck on the sea off in the direction of Kota Bahru and then another and another. A half dozen boats heading out to sea. Probably it was the fishing fleet starting out on the day's work. He turned the tiller over to Zablonsky and made his way up the foredeck to the bow stay. As one boat neared he began to shout and wave his arms but the boat crew ignored him and the vessel passed several hundred yards off to port. He tried again with another and another, and at last one fishing boat swung over and hove to some fifty yards away. "We need a tow."

"Hai?"

"Tow. We need a tow."

The Malay fishing skipper shook his head. "No Ingliss."

Hank resorted to pantomime. He pointed to the mainsail in the cockpit and made falling, fluttering motions. Then he made up and down piston motions with his fists while shaking his head and turning his right hand like a propeller and stopping it suddenly.

The Malay fisherman, his face creased from years in the sun and almost black, nodded his head. "Aha!"

Hank reached down for a line and made a gesture of handing it to the boatman. The Malay shook his head, pointed to his nets and indicated he was on his way to the fishing grounds.

Hank held up his hand. "Wait! Wait!" He ran to the cockpit and pulled his wallet out of the duffle bag. He stood at the rail and waved a half dozen U.S. bills in his hand. "Kota Bahru," he said gesturing. "Kota Bahru." The fisherman turned to his two crew members, small lithe young Malays, and conferred. In a moment he turned back nodding and grinning. Shortly later he had *Black Tern* under tow and headed for Kota Bahru.

As Malaysian Airways Flight 138 lifted off the Kuala Lumpur runway bound for Singapore, Hank sat beside Sergei Zablonsky watching the ground fall away. It was the last leg of their journey together, and nearing the end of the third day. After docking and securing *Black Tern* at Kota Bahru they had boarded a ramshackle bus for Ipoh and had traveled half a day in the company of Malay rubber tappers and farmers, some of them carrying crates of ducks and chickens to market and one farmer carrying a trussed goat which rode 15 miles bawling piteously while suspended on the back of the bus. Then from Ipoh another bus, this one in somewhat better trim, to Kuala Lumpur. During the two-hour wait at the KL airport, where Hank kept a taut, anxious watch for pursuers, he had managed to telephone Collins Champion, the new CIA man in Singapore, and told him to meet him with a car at Palam in Singapore.

The Malaysian Airways Convair flew over rubber groves and a tin dredger squatting in its pond, and then lifted through a layer of cloud with a slight bump. White and grey fleece hid the ground below from view. Zablonsky turned from the window and said conversationally to Hank, "I suppose you know they'll be there when we arrive."

"Who will be there?"

"KGB security. They'll have a watch posted."

"In Singapore? Why would they be watching Singapore?"

"It's obvious. They'll know by now that you and I are together, and your KGB file links you to Singapore. Oh, they'll probably have watches set up at Rangoon and Saigon as well, but their number one bet will be on Singapore. That's where I'd look, and as I told you, I trained most of these guys."

Hank sat silently, pondering. After several minutes, the Russian said, "What do you plan to do?"

"I'm not sure. But Singapore is my beat. I'll come up with something."

Forty minutes later the Convair let down gently onto the runway and taxied up to the gate. Hank and Zablonsky walked down the long corridor toward the immigration and customs area, most of their fellow passengers branching off under a sign reading "Singapore and Malaysian Passports" while they with a handful of others followed the lane designated "Foreign Passports." They had just finished having their passports stamped by the Singapore Immigration officer and were moving toward the customs inspector when Zablonsky said, "There they are!"

"Where?"

"Those three over against the far wall."

Hank then spotted them outside the customs barrier, standing close together and making a futile effort to appear casual. He took the KGB general's arm and pulled him over to a place where a wall hid them from view from the three Russians. "Stay here. They can't come inside the customs area and now they can't see you to shoot you."

"They don't intend to shoot me. They want me alive. They want to grab me and ship me back to Moscow where they'll stand me in a tub of water and fasten 240 volt electrodes to the end of my penis."

"Stay here. I'll work something out." He left Zablonsky and found a Singapore Police officer standing alongside a customs inspector. He approached the bland-faced Chinese and showed him his diplomatic passport and his CIA identification. He gestured toward Zablonsky. "That man there is my prisoner. Has the Special Branch detail arrived to guard him until I can get him on an airplane for the United States?"

The officer looked around for the fictitious Special Branch detail. "No, sir. Not to my knowledge."

"Well, I wonder where they can be?" Hank looked out across the customs barrier and saw the three Russians in huddled conversation. Nearer the gate he also saw Collins Champion. "Excuse me, officer, but one of my associates from the Embassy has arrived to meet us. Could I ask him to come into the customs area to stay with the prisoner while I locate the Special Branch people?"

The Chinese police officer looked to the customs official who nodded. "No objection." The official went to the gate and brought Champion to Hank.

In a few sentences Hank explained the situation to Champion who said, "I was wondering who those three goons were." On his way out, after introducing Zablonsky to Champion, Hank said to the Chinese officer, "Keep an eye on him for me, please. I don't want anything to happen to him."

"Right, sir. Will do."

Hank walked quickly past the three KGB security men who stared first at him and then back toward the customs area. Outside the airport he found the Agency car with the station's veteran driver, Talib, standing beside it. "Government House," said Hank. "Quick as you can."

Almost before the car had stopped at the curb Hank was out the door and up the steps. In the Prime Minister's outer office he found Peter Yee's young Chinese assistant at his desk. "Mr. Bladesly."

"I must see the Prime Minister at once. It's an emergency."

"Afraid that's impossible, sir. He has a foreign visitor."

But at that moment the door to Yee Hock Tho's office opened and he escorted a tiny Burmese gentleman out. His eyes flickered when he saw Hank but after a prolonged series of bows and ceremonious handshakes the Burmese left and Peter Yee turned to Hank. A broad smile creased his broad pock-marked face. "Henry, what a surprise! I thought you were in Bangkok."

"I am. I was. But just now I've got a problem."

Behind the closed door of Peter Yee's office Hank quickly sketched out the situation with Sergei Zablonsky. "I need your help in getting him safely on an airplane for the United States."

"But Henry, think of what you are asking! You want me to involve Singapore in something that will incense the Soviet Union. I can't risk that, much as I'd like to help."

"Peter, I'm not asking you to do anything overt. Just give me the services of your best Special Branch man, and we'll slip that KGB officer out of here without a trace."

"It's a terrible risk."

"Peter, I've never asked you for anything before. This I badly need and you can easily do it."

Peter Yee stared at Hank reflectively for a moment and then walked to his desk and pushed a buzzer. "Tell Chin Wat Lee to come in," he told the young assistant.

Within a minute the Special Branch officer was standing in the doorway saluting his Prime Minister. "Take Mr. Bladesly to your office and give him the help he needs."

"Yes, sir."

"Good luck, Henry," said Yee Hock Tho. "And no slips."

On the way back to Palam in the unmarked Special Branch sedan Hank outlined to Chin his plan for evacuating the Russian to Clark Air Force Base in Manila. "Sounds right, Mr. Bladesly. I'll have a Special Branch medic come to the Changi base after we move the Russian gentleman there."

Inside the customs area once more Hank introduced Zablonsky to Chin Wat Lee. "The KGB guys have disappeared, and Major Chin will escort you safely to a place where you can stay until we get the evac airplane here."

It was an hour later on his way out to Changi Air Base behind Talib in the station car once more that Hank thought to himself, "Well, at last my agent of influence, Yee Hock

Tho, has delivered some influence." Not world-shaking to be sure but at this moment essential. After taking Chin Wat Lee to Zablonsky he had gone back to the Embassy and through a series of FLASH precedence messages had got the arrangement made for moving his KGB prize to Manila and from there straight into Washington.

A young Special Branch officer greeted him at the door of the car as they pulled up at the Changi Air Base Headquarters. "Mr. Bladesly? This way, please." He led the way through a series of heavy doors until he arrived at a barred door marked "Officer's Brig." He unlocked the door to a spacious cell. Zablonsky got to his feet, flushed. "Bladesly, for God's sake! Is this your idea of a joke? Locking me up in a goddammed cell?'

"You're safe, aren't you Sergei? Safe. That was the idea."

"Safe, yes, but what a shitty way to treat a KGB general!"

"Even rank has to bow its head occasionally in the interests of safety." He pulled a bottle out of the duffle bag he was carrying. "I brought along some of your favorite medicine to soothe your ruffled spirit."

"Bell's 12." Zablonsky's frown faded. "You know, Bladesly, every now and then you almost attain a Russian standard of courtesy."

"Thanks. Your evac plane arrives in about an hour. Let's have a drink or two until then."

They sat down at the table, talking first about what Zablonsky could expect when he arrived in Washington and then about their flight to safety from Bangkok. "You know, Bladesly, I was just about to think you were a pretty good sailor and then you broke the goddammed sail." He took a deep swig of his third drink, wearing his supercilious, sardonic smile.

"To hell with you, Sergei. I never did think you were much of a sailor. And I still think you're an arrogant Russian son of a bitch."

Zablonsky guffawed and raised his glass to Hank. "Here's to you, you Number One Yankee shit!"

There was a tap at the cell door. "The medical evacuation airplane has arrived, sir, and here is Dr. Nair to treat the patient."

"Patient? Who's the patient?" asked Zablonsky.

"You are," said Hank. "This is a medical evacuation. You've got to go out of here on a stretcher. Dr. Nair is going to give you an injection that will knock you out for about an hour."

"What?"

"You'll wake up in an hour with a clear head," said the Indian doctor. "That is" — and he gestured toward the bottle of scotch — "unless you've imbibed too much of that."

Zablonsky looked at Hank in wonderment. "You know, Bladesly, you deceptive bastard, I underrated you. This is an operation almost worthy of the KGB. A KGB colonel, perhaps. Certainly not a general." He bared his arm. "Shoot away, doctor," After the shot he lay down on the stretcher that had been brought in and when he felt himself getting drowsy he turned to Hank and said simply, "Thanks, old son. See you in Washington."

Hank followed as they wheeled the stretcher to an ambulance outside the door. Very shortly the uniformed attendants loaded it onto the white U.S. Air Force medical evacuation plane, and Hank watched as the aircraft taxied out to the runway and then ran swiftly along until it lifted off toward Manila. His bagged KGB trophy was on its way to CIA Headquarters.

Postlude

His head propped up against the headboard, Hank held his bare feet together at the heels and angled them out in a V. Through the V he could sight down the length of his naked torso and out across the dazzling white Songkhla beach to *Black Tern* lying serenely on a sheet of sun spangles glinting and sparkling on the cerulean sea. Through the nearby archway to the living room came the diamond-edged sound of Bill Evans' piano, stepping with delicate grace through the melody of "Never Let Me Go", moving slowly with the tenderness of a young girl walking through a meadow carpeted with spring wildflowers. It was Sunday noon of a joyous weekend and Hank sighed with deep contentment.

"Tell me, darling," said Mai Tin, "do you ever wish you had stayed in Maine, running your newspaper, instead of coming out here to do spying?"

Trying to hear the meaning of the words through the enchanting sound of Mai Tin's voice, Hank said, "Do you want an honest answer or one I might give to a lovely nude woman whose head is on my chest and whose finger is tracing circles around my navel?"

She slapped him on the belly. "Honest, of course. You and I are always honest with each other."

"Honest. Well, let me consider." Bill Evans, having laid out the melody of "Never Let Me Go" was now weaving arabesques of dazzling complexity and beauty around, through, and within the melodic lines. Hank, caught, listened for a moment and then said "I believe the honest answer must be 'yes'."

Mai Tin was silent for a minute or two. "Does that mean you are not happy now?"

He bent his head and kissed her fragrant, fine-spun hair. "I've never been happier in my life."

"Then how can you...?"

"Don't you think you can be entirely happy with what you've got and still wish you had something else too?"

During the ensuing silence from Mai Tin, Hank could hear Bill Evans moving into the third chorus of variations on "Never Let Me Go." Through the sliding window opening onto the beach and the sea a soft breeze stirred and *Black Tern,* out at her mooring, swung slowly about to display her port flank. "Well?"

"I'm thinking, trying to apply it to myself but I can't. If I wanted something else it would diminish my happiness with what I have. So how can you...?"

"Maybe *want* something else is too strong. Imagine *having* something else is better."

"Yes?"

"You'll forgive me if I have some trouble thinking while that lovely nude woman continues to trace circles around my navel."

She pulled her hand away quickly and rested it as a fist on his chest. "Sorry." He gently took her hand and put it back.

"What I mean, my love, is that one part of me wishes I could have lived a life more like my Uncle Jim's. I think it might have been wonderful to live to old age in a small New England town. Quiet streets lined with white houses with green shutters. To be deeply anchored in the life of the community, running the local newspaper, helping out the neighbors with their problems, going to high school football games and school plays and chaperoning school dances. Raking leaves in the autumn, shoveling snow in the winter, planting a garden in the spring. Marrying a local girl and raising kids."

"I'm afraid, darling, that to me that sounds like a story in a woman's magazine."

"To the other part of me, it does too."

Bill Evans had wrung out all the beauty he could find in "Never Let Me Go" and was now turning equally tender attention to "I Fall in Love Too Easily."

"But," said Mai Tin. "you had all that. Or you *could* have. Then why?"

"Why?" He stalled for a moment, thinking of Anne on the other side of the earth, asleep in midnight Maine, possibly asleep beside her Bruce. "A wise woman pointed out to me something I should have realized without help. I could not somehow" — this needed to be delicately worded for Mai Tin — "commit myself to that world, for whatever reason."

With her quick mind and subtle insight Mai Tin caught the point immediately. "Ah, yes. I understand. Just as you are not fully committed now — to me."

"But I —"

"Never mind. I'm very happy with what I've got. What you give me." She traced a stinging circle around his navel with her fingernail. He flinched and slapped her hand softly.

"At least," said Mai Tin after a long, deep yawn, "what you are doing now is more important than running that small town newspaper."

"I'm not a bit sure of that." Hank pondered as he watched tiny, gold-edged wavelets lap onto the sandy shore. "My

Uncle Jim, another wise person, once said, 'The world is real everywhere.' He felt that once you accepted that you could find satisfaction in your life doing what was right before you." Hank gently tweaked Mai Tin's left ear lobe. "What Uncle Jim did helped dozens of other lives."

They lay quietly for a time. Hank watched as a sea gull landed on the spreader on *Black Tern's* mast and stretched and spread his wings. "You know," he said, "Robert Frost once wrote a poem called 'The Road Not Taken' and it tells about two roads branching off and the man takes one and says something like he was sorry he could not take both, being just one traveler. Maybe that says it for me. I would like to have taken *both* roads. Maybe I should have had two lifetimes."

Mai Tin reached up and kissed his unshaven chin. "I have two lifetimes now. All at once. Here with you when we are together and my quite separate life as a Chinese matron in Singapore."

With his free right hand he reached down and pulled her satin-skinned body close to his. "Maybe that's what I should learn, my sweet. Teach me."